Anonymous

The Recollections and Reflections of J. R. Planche

Vol. II

Anatiposi

Anonymous

The Recollections and Reflections of J. R. Planche

Vol. II

Reprint of the original, first published in 1872.

1st Edition 2023 | ISBN: 978-3-38213-363-4

Anatiposi Verlag is an imprint of Outlook Verlagsgesellschaft mbH.

Verlag (Publisher): Outlook Verlag GmbH, Zeilweg 44, 60439 Frankfurt, Deutschland
Vertretungsberechtigt (Authorized to represent): E. Roepke, Zeilweg 44, 60439 Frankfurt, Deutschland
Druck (Print): Books on Demand GmbH, In de Tarpen 42, 22848 Norderstedt, Deutschland

RECOLLECTIONS AND REFLECTIONS.

THE RECOLLECTIONS AND REFLECTIONS

OF

J. R. PLANCHÉ,

(SOMERSET HERALD).

A Professional Autobiography.

"I ran it through, even from my boyish days,
To the very moment that he bade me tell it."
OTHELLO, Act i., Scene 3.

IN TWO VOLUMES.

VOL. II.

LONDON:
TINSLEY BROTHERS, 18, CATHERINE STREET, STRAND.
1872.

LONDON
BRADBURY, EVANS, AND CO., PRINTERS, WHITEFRIARS.

CONTENTS.

CHAPTER I.

CHAPTER II.

CHAPTER III.

CHAPTER IV.

CHAPTER V.

CHAPTER VI.

CHAPTER VII.

CHAPTER VIII.

CHAPTER IX.

CHAPTER X.

CHAPTER XV.

CHAPTER XVI.

CHAPTER XVII.

RECOLLECTIONS AND REFLECTIONS.

CHAPTER I.

During the Christmas week, 1837, I had been again despatched to Paris, by Bunn, to hear and report on Scribe and Auber's opera "Le Domino Noir." I took up my residence with my old friend, T. J. Thackeray, in the Faubourg St. Honoré, and Mr. and Mrs. Charles Gore having removed from the Bois de Boulogne, where I had visited them on a former occasion, to the Place Vendôme, they were more accessible, and kindly invited me constantly to dinner. Those who remember Mrs. Gore need not be told what pleasant evenings they were. Her account to me of her life at that period is worth recording. She was writing novels, plays, articles for magazines—almost every description of literature was flowing from her indefatigable pen. "When, and how do you manage it?" I asked her. "I receive, as you know," she replied, "a few friends at dinner at five o'clock nearly every evening. They leave me at ten or eleven, when I retire to my own room and write till seven or eight in the morning. I then go to bed till noon, when I breakfast, after which I drive out, shop, pay visits, and return at four to dress for dinner, and as soon as my friends have departed, go to work again all night as before."

On the 1st of January, 1838, I was sauntering on the boulevard without an overcoat, the sun shining gloriously, the air as balmy as in the mildest of Mays. All the world was abroad, laden with presents of every description, the customary tributes of the "Jour de l'An," to relatives, friends, and lovers. Two or three days afterwards Paris was enveloped in a dense fog of as rich a pea-soup colour as ever was seen in London in the month of November. "This forebodes a sharp frost," observed my host, and he was not a false prophet, for in about a week began what was called "Murphy's Winter," an individual of that name having published an almanack wherein he had luckily hazarded a prediction, the fulfilment of which put a large sum of money in his pocket, which I was told he afterwards lost, speculating in corn. My business, however, was with music and not meteorology. I heard "Le Domino," was enchanted by Mdlle. Cinti Damoureau, but felt it would do nothing at Drury

Lane, given as it must have been there. I wrote to Bunn my ideas on the subject, in which he coincided. "The view you take of 'Le Domino Noir,'" he replied, "is a very judicious one. It will evidently never do to risk it as a first piece as 'Auber's last opera.'"

It was, in fact, an "opéra comique," and presented none of the opportunities for grand spectacle which distinguished those Bunn delighted to transport from the Rue Lepelletier. My visit to Paris was, therefore, fruitless, as far as the theatre was concerned; but I had the gratification of being introduced to Lord Lyndhurst, and dining with him, by invitation, at Versailles, where his lordship, at that time out of office, was quietly residing with Lady Lyndhurst and his family. After dinner I played a game of chess with Miss Copley, Lord Lyndhurst's sister, which he watched with great interest, rubbing his hands with delight and embracing her most affectionately when she checkmated me. At the same time I made the acquaintance of Mons. Allou, Vice-President of the Society of Antiquaries of France, and author of several works on military antiquities, who introduced me to the Duke d'Istrie, the possessor of a very choice collection of ancient arms and armour, which he kindly exhibited to me himself—containing, amongst other objects of interest, a shield, said to have belonged to

Mathias Corvinus, King of Hungary. It was certainly of his time, *circa* 1450.

On the 28th of June I was present at Her Majesty's coronation, in Westminster Abbey, the Duke of Sutherland having kindly sent me one of his own tickets for a seat in that portion of the south transept appropriated to the families and friends of peers.

I had previously published a little work entitled "Regal Records," dedicated to the Duchess, who was then Mistress of the Robes, containing a description of the ceremonies at the coronations of the Queens Regnant of England, and had been fortunate enough to discover in the British Museum some MSS. which enabled me to correct several errors in, and add considerable information to previous accounts of those of Queen Mary (Tudor) and Queen Anne. Especially in that of the former, disproving a malicious story trumped up by the ambassadors of the Emperor, respecting Princess Elizabeth, who, according to their account, bore the crown and complained to the Duke de Noailles, the French ambassador, of its weight, adding, that she was weary of carrying it, to which he was said to have replied, "It will seem lighter, shortly, when upon your head." No such thing could possibly have occurred, as the princess never carried the crown at all—it was borne by the Duke of

Norfolk—and none of the ambassadors were in the procession!

In the early part of this year, 1838, Madame Vestris had entered into an engagement with Mr. Price to visit the United States, in company with Charles Mathews, and an extension of the licences of the Olympic and Adelphi Theatres having been granted by the Lord Chamberlain to their respective lessees, I wrote a sort of "Revue" for the former, to be produced on Easter Monday (April 16th), entitled the "Drama's Levee; or, a Peep at the Past," which concluded with a valedictory speech by Madame Vestris, and was the second piece of that class which had ever been seen on the English stage, "Success," at the Adelphi, in 1825, having been the first.

As Madame Vestris contemplated being absent from England during the whole of the ensuing Olympic season, she paid me the compliment of placing the theatre in my charge; but, before her departure, determined on passing a few days at Calais, where Madame Bartolozzi, her mother, was then residing. Mathews and I accompanied her, and took up our quarters at Dessein's, and a very pleasant week we passed there. I was desirous of visiting a small village called Tournehem, in order to ascertain if any portion remained of the old castle, which had belonged to Anthony of Burgundy, whose portrait I had identified for the Duchess-Countess of Sutherland, and it was agreed that we should *pic-nic* there.

To Tournehem accordingly we went, paying a visit, *en route*, to the famous Field of the Cloth of Gold, where "those two suns of men met in the Vale of Ardres;" and, to my great delight, I found the principal part of the castle still in existence; but, alas! it was doomed. A posse of workmen were busy with pick and spade, demolishing the walls and filling up the fosse. I was in time, however, to sketch the most interesting remains, and discovered, over a miller's door in the village, a long stone slab which had been removed from some part of the castle, and whereon were sculptured, in fine relief, the arms and badges of its chivalrous founder. Another day, Mathews, who is an excellent draughtsman, accompanied me on a sketching excursion along the coast. I had just completed the opera I was engaged to write for Mendelssohn, the scene of which was laid in Calais and its neighbourhood—and I availed myself of this opportunity to acquire some personal knowledge of the locality, which might furnish some useful hints for the scenery. Fort Nieulay was one of my points; and while rambling over the ramparts we were startled by a stentorian shout of "Faut pas marcher sur le talus!" which pro-

ceeded from a stout man tightly buttoned-up in a green coat, almost strangled with a black stock, and "each particular hair" on his head standing on end, "like quills upon the fretful porcupine." His appearance was amusingly recalled to me by a few pen-and-ink scratches on the back of a letter from Charles Mathews some time afterwards, and of which I venture to insert a fac-simile, for the sake of the portrait, at the imminent peril of incurring an indignant protest from my facetious friend, but whose abilities as a draughtsman are too well known to suffer any disparagement from this breach of confidence. We descended meekly; and having—with this peremptory gentleman's permission—sketched the most picturesque portions of the walls, proceeded to Sangatte, in hopes of discovering some relics of its ancient importance; as, in the fourteenth century it was a sea-port of consequence, and boasted a castle in which Queen Philippa resided during the siege of Calais by Edward III. Alas! its fate has been worse than that of Sandwich, its rival in those days on the opposite coast. The harbours of both have been choked up by the sand from which each derives its name: Sangatte being merely a corruption of the English appellation Sandgate. The quaint little Kentish town still exists: while every vestige of Sangatte, castle and all, has disappeared, and a long straight row of modern brick cottages on the flat, sandy shore was all that presented itself to our disappointed eyes.

A joke immediately occurred to Mathews. We first made a slight but faithful sketch of the row of huts with their appendant pig-styes in all their simple ugliness, and then, drawing on our imagination, we pictured Sangatte as we had hoped to have found it after our success at Tournehem: the majestic ruins of a castle crowning a cliff overhanging a mediæval town with crenelated walls, at the angles of which still crumbled watch-towers, and one large gate in good preservation with machiocolated battlements, portcullis, and drawbridge. With these dishonest views we returned to Calais; raved of our interesting excursion, which we declared threw the trip to Tournehem quite into the shade: were loud in our regrets that the ladies had not accompanied us; and, to prove the loss they had had, displayed our romantic drawings, made —as we could truly assert—"upon the spot;" and which were duly admired and commented upon by our unsuspicious victims. It is needless to add that when the play was played out, and the sketches from nature produced, the books were flung at our heads, and no end of righteous indignation manifested at our base designs.

Mr. and Mrs. Charles Mathews, having entered into the bonds of Hymen, at Kensington, sailed for the New World, and left me to open the Olympic Theatre at the commencement of October, which I did with a pleasant comedy by Charles Dance, entitled "Sons and Systems." The American engagement, however, not turning out advantageous, the Mathewses returned to England before Christmas, to my great surprise, but to my infinite relief; for, good—not to say great—as was our company, including Farren, who had replaced Liston, and Mrs. Nesbit, who had been engaged at a heavy salary to supply, if possible, the place of Madame Vestris, and the favourable reception of the various dramas produced, particularly Oxenford's charming little comedy, "The Idol's Birthday," and Mr. Smith's drama, "The Court of Old Fritz," in which Farren admirably sustained the characters of Frederick the Great and Voltaire—nothing could compensate the public for the absence of their bright particular star, who, to the great delight of her faithful worshippers, made her reappearance on the 2nd of January, 1839, as Fatima, in the fairy extravaganza of "Blue Beard," the production of the Christmas piece having been postponed for a week with that object. "Blue Beard" was a great success. No longer "a very magnificent three-tailed Bashaw," as in Colman's well-known and well-worn spectacle, he appeared with equal magnificence in the mediæval costume, the scene of the piece being laid, according to the original legend, in Brittany, during the 15th century, and was run through, not only "his wedding clothes," but the season.

"Faint Heart never won Fair Lady," one of my most fortunate *transformations* from the French—the original is a long, spun-out three-act piece—and "The Garrick Fever," also of Gallic origin, but fitted to an English subject, respecting which a similar story is told, completed my contributions to the Olympic while under the management of Madame Vestris, as she continued to be called in the profession, and must ever be distinguished, for, at the end of the season, a negotiation was opened with her, by the proprietors of Covent Garden, which resulted in Charles Mathews becoming the lessee of that still national theatre, vice Mr. Macready, resigned, and the transference to it of the whole of the Olympic company.

CHAPTER II.

My poor friend, Haynes Bayly, whose health had been failing for some time past, died at Cheltenham on the 22nd of April, 1839, leaving his widow and two little girls, the eldest a cripple, in sadly straitened circumstances. Mrs. Bayly wrote to ask me if I thought the music-publishers would raise a subscription for her. I replied that it was possible a small sum might be collected from them and private friends; but that if she would allow me to get up a public representation at one of the great theatres, avowedly for "the benefit of the widow and children of the late Thomas Haynes Bayly," I was inclined to hope for much better results than could be expected from personal solicitation. She shrunk at first from the publicity of such an appeal, but at length consented; and, with the ready and zealous co-operation of Charles Dance and the majority of my brother-dramatists, a most attractive bill of fare was speedily advertised; Bunn giving us the use of

Drury Lane, and the *élite* of the dramatic and musical professions their gratuitous services.

In this good work I was greatly assisted by a most kind-hearted but singular man, with whom I had been long intimate, not only in consequence of his being a constant frequenter of the green rooms at all the principal theatres, but from the circumstance of one of my brothers-in-law being a principal clerk in his department, which was a branch of the Audit Office. This was the Hon. Edmund Byng. He not only collected for me a good round sum in subscriptions, but gave a dinner to the Duchess of Bedford and some half-dozen other ladies of high rank, in order to secure their personal attendance at the theatre, and thereby that of a large proportion of their acquaintance. Mr. Lockhart, Theodore Hook, Captain Marryat, and other private friends also exerted themselves most laudably. Miss Burdett Coutts, with her usual large-heartedness, on my application for her private box, sent me £20 in order to retain it for herself. A characteristic note of Hook is worth recording :—

FULHAM, Tuesday.

I send you a bit more for our poor widow, and hope to do more to-morrow. I will, and I can. One of my friends, whose taste is theatrical, but whose disposition is *thrifty*, would like four tickets for the performance as a set-off for his *mite.* I suppose he may or *must* have them; if so, perhaps you would put them under cover to me, directed hither per post. I have often heard of the golden *mean.* I now know what it is.

Yours very truly,
THEODORE E. HOOK.

We had a brilliant and overflowing house, and cleared between four and five hundred pounds. But most useful and important to her as was such a sum at the moment, it was, as Mrs. Charles Gore wrote to me, "little enough for a widow and two children," * as a provision for the future, and with the greatest economy would soon be exhausted.

By Mrs. Bayly's desire it was placed in the hands of Lord Nugent and myself as trustees, to be drawn upon by her as circumstances might require; but now comes the most gratifying part of the story.

Mrs. Bayly possessed in her own right a small estate in Ireland, which was in the hands of what is called in that country "a middleman," and from whom she not only received no remittances, but continual demands for money for repairs and every imaginable purpose. Of this Lord Nugent and I knew nothing; but it

* "I wrote," she added, in a postscript, "to two fine ladies, begging them to patronise the representation, but most likely without success, for during the London season, and especially in such very hot weather *nobody cares for his fellow-creatures.*"

occurred to Mrs. Bayly that if she could contrive to repay this gentleman, into whose debt she was daily getting to an extent which threatened the absorption of the whole property, she could go and live in Ireland in a house of her own, and on her own land, comfortably. Most providentially the proceeds of the benefit enabled her to do this, and fifteen years afterwards I had the pleasure of escorting her to Her Majesty's drawing-room to present her youngest daughter. The substantial "benefit" which thus resulted to my old friend's wife and family is an event I look back upon with the greatest gratification. Charles Kemble used to tell a far different story about some poor foreigner, dancer or pantomimist in the country, who, after many annual attempts to clear his expenses, came forward one evening with a face beaming with pleasure and gratitude, and addressed the audience in these words: —"Dear Public! moche oblige. Ver good benefice—only lose half-a-crown—I come again!"

I have incidentally mentioned Mr. Edmund Byng, and his kind exertions in behalf of Mrs. Haynes Bayly. As my intimacy with this gentleman extended over very many years to the day of his death, I will take this opportunity of expressing my regard for one whom I ever found foremost in the cause of charity and kindness of every description.

I do this the more eagerly because he was, from infirmity of temper and other peculiarities—I may say eccentricities—extremely unpopular in many circles; even, unfortunately, with his own family. Amongst his numerous praiseworthy actions was the interest he took in cheering the last years of the veteran, Thomas Dibdin. An annual dinner was established by Mr. Byng at Evans's Hotel, Covent Garden, the tickets one guinea each; and the guests through his personal influence rarely fell short of a hundred. Half the money went to pay for the dinner; but it was a good fifty pounds per annum to the old man, and procured him many comforts he might otherwise have stood sorely in need of. The day fixed for the dinner was the 21st of March, the anniversary of the birthday of "the last of the three Dibdins," and the author, as it has been asserted, of 800 dramatic pieces. The first took place in 1837. He died in 1841, at the age of seventy.

I had the pleasure of acting as Mr. Byng's lieutenant on these occasions, and the gratification of receiving from the veteran dramatist the following proof of his appreciation of my earnest, however humble, exertions in the good cause:—

DEAR SIR,

If words could express genuine thanks, you should have a specimen of more than common eloquence from a pen that can only plainly acknowledge your repeated and persevering kindness exhibited on the birthday anniversaries of,

Dear Sir,

Your truly obliged Servant,

THOMAS DIBDIN.

King Street,
March 24, 1839.
R. Planché, Esq.

Mr. Byng's own dinners were things to remember. Lord Blessington, by no means a bad judge, used to say, "Byng, I often go out to dinner; but when I desire to *dine* I come to you." They were first-rate old English dinners. No soups; no *kickshaws;* large dishes of magnificent fish; a haunch of four-year-old Southdown; a pheasant pie; a coursed hare; or other equally excellent edibles, according to the season, and nothing *out* of it. No *forced* asparagus; no *house* lamb; and in the centre of the table stood always a large wooden bowl, as white as milk, filled with the finest potatoes perfectly boiled in their "*jackets.*" He kept an Irish kitchen-maid expressly for that purpose; and palled must have been the palates, and morbid the appetites, of those who could not enjoy such fare as was always to be found in Clarges Street. As to the company, it was as good as the dinner. By no means *select* in one sense of the word, as his guests were rarely selected. The first eight or ten men he met with as he walked down to his club or found there, peers, poets, players, painters, soldiers, sailors, doctors of law, medicine, or divinity—"the three black graces," as James Smith called them; for Mr. Byng's acquaintance was most miscellaneous: any friends or agreeable persons whom gentlemen could not object to meet, were verbally invited for the next or an early day, "to dine and go to the play," for such was the usual programme. Here I met the Duke of Gordon, the late Marquis of Hertford, Lord Milford, Lord Methuen, Sir John Conroy, the Hobhouses, and many other men of note or "about town;" and passed many a pleasant evening, adjourning altogether to a theatre or its green-room, and occasionally winding up with a supper at Evans's. Latterly Mr. Byng's eyesight became seriously affected, and his natural irritability increased with his years. I visited him to the last—one of the few who did so of "those his former bounty fed"—and shall ever cherish a grateful recollection of his many kindnesses. À propos of dinners, Mr. Luttrell once said to me, "Sir, the man who says he does not like a good dinner is either a fool or a liar."

At this period I was in constant correspondence with Mrs. Charles Gore, of whose lively letters I have a pile, but they are too full of private business and personal allusions to justify their publication, most amusing as they are. I select two as specimens of her style, the second containing the announcement of an event which she knew would be interesting to me :—

DEAR MR. PLANCHÉ,

Will you tell me (like an honest man as you are, though author and dramatist), if you had a five-act tragedy ready for representation, what would you do with it? I have one completed—original, historical, English—containing a fine part for Macready, and some striking scenic effects which Bunn could bring out; and am afraid of sending it to either, lest their hands should be full, and my play be postponed till the fatal rehearsal of the pantomimes.

I have no doubt that an old stager like Macready is encrusted with poets and tragedies as an old ship is with barnacles; and as to our friend Bunn, I think he would set his face against five acts, though they were the acts of the Apostles. I am sure you will advise me wisely and kindly, and, being on the spot, you have probably some insight into their engagements. Do me the favour to answer my troublesome inquiry by the post, to relieve the suspense of

Your much obliged,

C. F. GORE.

Place Vendôme,
Paris.

16TH MAY, 1839.

DEAR MR. PLANCHÉ,

Many thanks for your letter. If I did not know that dramatic authors are the most crazy of God's creatures (inasmuch as they indite plays while England abounds in bad roads, wanting stones to be broken upon them), I should be annoyed to find that my friend Madame —— had sent a five-act tragedy to the Olympic instead of the *one-act farce* she proposed. She is a clever woman, sister of our fashionable Madame D——, and daughter-in-law of Sir S—— S——, but without the least notion of the fitness of things. It seems that the Adelphi has been using her ill, and I cannot succeed in persuading her that all authors are ill used by all managers, and that "sufferance is the badge of all our tribe." Do not use yourself so ill, however, as to read her melodrama, which is clearly not for your market. . . . The dramatic world seems to be thriving in everything but its finances. All your theatres bankrupt, or thereanent, and yet good plays constantly produced. Here, on the contrary, they fill nightly in every quarter of the town, and have only very moderate pieces inimitably well acted. I have not yet seen Madame Rachel, but hear she is going down in public favour.

You will be amused to hear that the little person you have hitherto seen in a bib and tuckers, as Miss Gore, is metamorphosed into one of the reigning belles of Paris; presented, introduced, adored, and all the rest of it. I never saw so successful a début.* We have had a long and very gay season, lasting from November till now; but Lady Granville's ball next week, on the Queen's birthday, will, I conclude, put us chaperons out of our pain. It is to be a splendid affair; no ladies admitted except in white with pink flowers, in order to give a uniform appearance. We have had a *revolutionette,* scarcely worth mentioning. There was a regiment bivouacked in the Place Vendôme, and a friend of ours, with whom you once dined here, had his hand shot off.

* The young lady here mentioned is now Lady Edward Thynne.

It is expected that the attempt will be renewed by the "Société des Droits d'Homme" a month or two hence.

Pray give my compliments to Mrs. Planché. Is there any use in sending her the new pieces, or has she given up the theatre?*

Ever yours,
Truly obliged,
C. F. G.

It was in this year, before the close of the Olympic, I received the last written communication from my kind friend James Smith.† It contained these lines:—

THE ALPHABET TO MADAME VESTRIS.

Though not with lace bedizened o'er
From James's and from Howell's,
Ah! don't despise us twenty-four
Poor consonants and vowels.

Though critics may your powers discuss,
Your charms applauding men see,
Remember you from four of us
Derive your X L N C.‡

I handed them to Madame, who requested me to acknowledge their receipt for her, which I did thus:—

* Mrs. Planché had amused herself by translating and adapting several French dramas. "The Sledge Driver," "A Handsome Husband," "The Welsh Girl," "A Pleasant Neighbour," and "Hasty Conclusions," had considerable success, and still keep the stage.

† He died 24th December.

‡ The same idea is to be found in one of his jeux d'esprit, entitled "Alphabetical Rivers."

MADAME VESTRIS'S ANSWER TO THE ALPHABET.

Dear friends, although no more a dunce
  Than many of my betters,
I'm puzzled to reply at once
  To four-and-twenty letters!

Perhaps you'll think that may not be
  So hard a thing to do,
For what is difficult to me
  Is A B C to you.

However, pray dismiss your fears,
  Nor fancy you have lost me,
Though many, many, bitter tears
  Your first acquaintance cost me.

Believe me, till existence ends
  Whatever ills beset you,
My oldest literary friends,
  I never can forget you.

CHAPTER III.

Covent Garden Theatre opened for the season 1839—40, under the management of Madame Vestris, with, for the first time within the memory of that generation, Shakspeare's comedy of "Love's Labour Lost;" and as "Superintendent of the Decorative Department," I had the pleasure of continuing my reform of the costume of the national drama which I had commenced at this theatre, with the additional advantage of the great taste and unbounded liberality of the manageress, whose heart was thoroughly in the cause, and spared neither time, trouble, nor money in promotion of it. The return to those boards of some of the old favourites—Madame Vestris, Farren, Keeley, &c.—naturally recalls to memory those who had retired from them full of years and full of honours — Charles Young, Liston, and Charles Kemble.

Young made his farewell bow to the public, 30th May, 1832. His son, the Rev. Julian Young, has recently published a memoir of him, and I shall, therefore, limit mine to a few characteristic anecdotes, hitherto unrecorded. One of the noblest tragedians on the stage, and a most perfect gentleman in private society, Young was an irrepressible *farceur*, constantly playing with imperturbable gravity the most whimsical pranks in public. He undertook to drive Charles Mathews (*fils*) to Cassiobury on a visit to the Earl of Essex. Having passed through a turnpike and paid the toll, he pulled up at the next gate he came to, and, addressing himself most politely to a woman who issued from the toll-house, inquired if Mr. ——, the toll-taker, whose name he saw on a board above the door, happened to be in the way. The woman answered that he was not in the house, but she would send for him, if the gentleman wished to see him particularly. "Well, I'm sorry to trouble you, madam, but I certainly should like to have a few minutes' conversation with him," rejoined Young. Upon which the woman called to a little boy, "Tommy! run and tell your father a gentleman wants to speak to him." Away ran Tommy, down a straight, long path in the grounds of a nursery and seedsman, the entrance to which was close to the turnpike,—Young sitting bolt upright in the tilbury, solemn and silent, to the astonishment of Mathews, who asked him what on earth he wanted with the man. "I want to consult him on a matter of business," was the reply. After some five or six minutes, the boy, who had entered a building at the extreme end of the path, re-appeared, followed by a man putting on a jacket as he walked, and in due time both of them stood beside the tilbury. The man touched his hat to Young. "You wished to see me, sir?" "Are you Mr. ——?" "Yes, sir." "The Mr. —— who is entrusted to take the toll at this gate?" "Yes, sir." "Then you are precisely the person who can give me the information I require. You see, Mr. ——, I paid sixpence at the gate at ——, and the man who took it gave me this little bit of paper" (producing a ticket from his waistcoat-pocket), "and assured me that if I showed it to the proper authorities at this gate I should be allowed to drive through without payment." "Why, of course," said the man, staring with amazement at Young. "That ticket clears this gate." "Then you do not require me to pay anything here?" "No! Why, any fool—— " "My dear Mr. ——, I'm so much obliged to you. I should have been so sorry to have done anything wrong, and therefore wished to have your opinion on the subject. A thousand thanks. Good morning, Mr. —— " And on drove Young, followed, as the reader may easily imagine, by a volley of imprecations and epithets of anything but a flattering description, so long as he was within hearing.

One of his chief delights was to abuse Meadows for residing at so great a distance from the theatre. As soon as he caught sight of him, wherever it might be, he would shout, "Meadows! where do you live?" "N^o. —, Barnsbury Terrace, Islington," was the invariable answer, which as invariably brought down upon the respondent a torrent of whimsical invective, such as Young alone could extemporise, and uttered with a volubility and a vehemence as startling as humorous. One day, leisurely riding his well-known white cob up Regent Street, he espied Meadows walking in the same direction, considerably ahead of him. Fearing he might escape him, Young exerted all his magnificent power of voice in putting the usual question, "Meadows! where do you live?" Meadows turned at the sound of his name, and, to the utter discomfiture of his persecutor, bawled in reply, "N^o. —, Belgrave Square," rapidly disappearing round the corner of Jermyn Street, before a most emphatic impeachment of his veracity rolled like thunder over the heads of the amazed but amused pedestrians from Waterloo Place to Piccadilly.

Young was a special favourite with the late Lord Essex, and they were so much together, and on such familiar terms, that Poole being asked what Englishmen he had seen in Paris, said, "Only Lord Young and Mr. Essex." The last time Young called on me at Brompton he left his card, inscribed, "'Tis I, my lord—the early village cock." The last time I called on him was at Brighton, a few months before he died. He gave me a miserable account of himself, and wound up by saying, "I am seventy-nine, and seventy-nine is telling its tale." I never saw him again.

As long as I can remember, the peculiar style of joking of which I have related an example has been popular in the dramatic profession, and, strange to say, some of the most humorous and audacious pranks have been perpetrated by actors who would never have been suspected of such a propensity. Such as Egerton, a dull, heavy man in society; and Liston, who was an extremely shy man. Munden never saw me in the street, that he did not get astride his great cotton umbrella, and ride up to me like a boy on a stick. Wallack and Tom Cooke would gravely meet, remove with stolid countenances *each other's* hat, bow ceremoniously, replace it, and pass on without exchanging a word, to the astonishment of the beholders. Meadows continually would seat himself on the curb-stone opposite my house after we became neighbours, in

Michael's Grove, Brompton, with his hat in his hand, like a beggar, utterly regardless of passing strangers, and remain in that attitude till I or some of my family caught sight of him, and threw him a halfpenny, or threatened him with the police. The peculiarity of these absurdities was that they were never premeditated, but were the offspring of mere "gaieté de cœur" —prompted by the whim of the moment. Unlike the elaborately planned hoaxes of Theodore Hook and other "mad wags," at one time so much the folly of the day, or the later mischievous and dangerous *escapades*, the removal of signs, the wrenching off of knockers and bell-handles, and other more reprehensible outrages in which young men of rank and fashion were weak enough to find amusement.

Liston had taken his formal farewell of the public after the close of the Olympic in 1837 by a benefit at the Lyceum Theatre. The extreme depression under which that great comic actor occasionally laboured has often been recorded; and there was also, no doubt, a strong romantic and sentimental side to his character; but his love of fun was great, and his humour, on and off the stage, irresistible. Like Young and others, his contemporaries, he delighted, as I have already premised, in practical joking in the public streets. Walking one day through Leicester Square with Mr. Miller, the theatrical bookseller of Bow Street, Liston happened to mention casually that he was going to have tripe for dinner, a dish of which he was particularly fond. Miller, who hated it, said, "Tripe! Beastly stuff! How can you eat it?" That was enough for Liston. He stopped suddenly in the crowded thoroughfare in front of Leicester House, and holding Miller by the arm, exclaimed, in a loud voice, "What, sir! So you mean to assert that you don't like tripe?" "Hush!" muttered Miller, "don't talk so loud; people are staring at us." "I ask you, sir," continued Liston, in still louder tones, "do you not like tripe?" "For Heaven's sake, hold your tongue!" cried Miller; "you'll have a crowd round us." And naturally people began to stop and wonder what was the matter. This was exactly what Liston wanted, and again he shouted, "Do you mean to say you don't like tripe?" Miller, making a desperate effort, broke from him, and hurried in consternation through Cranbourne Alley, followed by Liston, bawling after him, "There he goes!—that's the man who doesn't like tripe!" to the immense amusement of the numerous passengers, many of whom recognised the popular comedian, till the horrified bookseller took to his heels and ran, as if for his life, up Long Acre into Bow Street, pursued to his very doorstep by a pack of young ragamuffins, who took up the cry, "There he goes!—the man that don't like tripe!"

Our intimacy, which commenced with the production of "Charles XII.," continued throughout his life, the latter days of which were very deplorable. His sole occupation was sitting all day long at the window of his residence in St. George's Row, Hyde Park Corner (the house has just been pulled down), with his watch in his hand, timing the omnibuses, and expressing the greatest distress and displeasure when one of them appeared to him to be late. It became a sort of monomania. His spirits had completely forsaken him. He never smiled or entered into conversation, and eventually sank into a lethargy from which he awoke no more in this world. I attended his funeral by invitation, walking with Charles Kemble, who was much affected by the loss of his old friend and fellow-comedian.

Mr. Kemble had been appointed Examiner of Plays, on the decease of Mr. Colman, and had in consequence taken his leave of the stage during Mr. Osbaldiston's management of Covent Garden Theatre, December 23rd, 1836, though he afterwards played some of his principal characters, by the express desire of her Majesty, for a few nights, during the occupancy of that theatre by Mr. and Mrs. Charles Mathews. On his retirement, the members of the Garrick invited him to a dinner at the Albion Hotel, Lord Francis Egerton (afterwards Earl of Ellesmere) in the chair. His lordship made a most eloquent and brilliant speech in proposing the toast of the evening. He spoke of the Kembles as "that illustrious family," and declared that, all Conservative as he was, he had been so excited by the oratorical power of Charles Kemble in the character of Antony, that at the close of his speech to the citizens over the body of Cæsar, he had frequently felt he could have rushed into the streets with the most democratic of mobs, and "sacked the houses of the senators." He was indeed an Antony that might have "raised the stones of Rome to rise and mutiny." The following song, written by John Hamilton Reynolds, and set to music by Balfe, was sung by the latter after the toast:—

1.

Farewell! our good wishes go with him to-day!
Rich in fame—rich in name—he has play'd out the play.
We now who surround him would fain make amends
For past years of enjoyment. We hail him as friends:
Though the sock and the buskin for aye be removed,
Still he serves in the cause of the Drama he loved.
Our chief, nobly born, genius crown'd, our zeal shares:
His coronet's hid by the laurel he wears.*
Well! wealthy we have been, though fortune may frown,
And they cannot but say that we have had the crown.

* Lord Francis Egerton was, as is well known, distinguished for his literary abilities.

2.

Shall we never again see his spirit infuse
Life—life in the young gallant forms of the muse?
Through the lovers and heroes of Shakspere he ran—
All the soul of the soldier—the heart of the man!
Shall we never in Cyprus his revels retrace?
See him stroll into Angiers with indolent grace?
Or greet him in bonnet at fair Dunsinane?
Or meet him in moon-lit Verona again?
　　Well! wealthy we have been, though fortune may frown,
　　And they cannot but say that we have had the crown.

3.

Let the curtain come down—let the scene pass away—
There's an Autumn, though Summer has squander'd its day:
We may sit by the fire, though we can't by the lamp,
And re-people the banquet—re-soldier the camp.
Oh! nothing can rob us of memory's gold;
And though he quits the gorgeous, and we may grow old,
With our Shakspere in hand, and bright forms in our brain,
We may dream up our Siddons and Kembles again.
　　Well! wealthy we have been, though fortune may frown,
　　And they cannot but say that we have had the crown.

Only those who have had the good fortune to witness those performances can appreciate the happy allusions in the second verse to the characters of Cassio, Falconbridge, Macduff, and Romeo, in which during my time I have never seen his equal.

Charles Kemble had been amongst the first to recognise the dawning genius of Macready, and had remarked to John Kemble, "That young man will be a great actor one of these days." "Con quello viso

Charles?" was the doubtful answer of that "noblest Roman of them all," who, pardonably enough, considered classical features indispensable to the effective representation of classical characters. Mr. Kemble became, in his later years, exceedingly deaf, but still continued to enjoy society, and contribute his full share to "the feast of reason and the flow of soul."

I will conclude this chapter with my recollections of two other celebrities, with whom my position at Covent Garden Theatre brought me into intimate relations—Sheridan Knowles and Leigh Hunt. The former had already won his spurs in the dramatic world by the production of "The Hunchback;" and during the management of Madam Vestris three of his plays were produced, viz., "Love," "John of Procida," and "Old Maids," all of which I had the pleasure of putting on the stage, I believe to his satisfaction. Of all the eccentric individuals I ever encountered, Sheridan Knowles was, I think, the greatest. Judge, gentle reader, if the following anecdotes may not justify my assertion. Walking one day with a brother-dramatist, Mr. Bayle Bernard, in Regent's Quadrant, Knowles was accosted by a gentleman in these terms:—"You're a pretty fellow, Knowles! After fixing your own day and hour to dine with us, you never make your appearance, and from that time to this not a word have we heard from you!" "I couldn't help it, upon my honour," replied Knowles; "and I've been so busy ever since I haven't had a moment to write or call. How are you all at home?" "Oh, quite well, thank you; but come now, will you name another day, and keep your word?" "I will—sure I will." "Well, what day? Shall we say Thursday next?" "Thursday? Yes, by all means—Thursday be it." "At six?" "At six. I'll be there punctually. My love to 'em all." "Thank ye. Remember, now. Six next Thursday." "All right, my dear fellow; I'll be with you." The friend departed; and Knowles, relinking his arm with that of Bayle Bernard, said, "Who's that chap?" not having the least idea of the name or residence of the man he had promised to dine with on the following Thursday, or the interesting "family at home," to whom he had sent his love. Upon one occasion when he was acting in the country he received an anxious letter from Mrs. Knowles, informing him that the money—£200, which he had promised to send up on a certain day, had never reached her. Knowles immediately wrote a furious letter to Sir Francis Freeling, at that time at the head of the Post-office, of which, of course, I cannot give the precise words, but beginning "Sir," and informing him that on such a day, at such an hour, he himself put a letter into the post-office at such a place, containing the sum of £200 in bank-notes, and that it had never been delivered to Mrs. Knowles; that it was a most unpardonable piece of negligence, if not worse, of the post-office authorities, and that he demanded an immediate inquiry into the matter, the delivery of the money to his wife, and an apology for the anxiety and trouble its detention had occasioned them. By return of post he received a most courteous letter from Sir Francis, beginning "Dear sir," as, although they were personal strangers to each other, he had received so much pleasure from Mr. Knowles' works, that he looked upon him as a valued friend, and continuing to say that he (Knowles) was perfectly correct in stating that on such a day and at such an hour he had posted a letter at —— containing bank-notes to the amount of £200, but that, unfortunately, he had omitted not only his signature inside, but *the address outside*, having actually sealed up the notes in an envelope containing only the words, "I send you the money," and posted it without a direction! The consequence was that it was opened at the chief office in London, and detained till some inquiry was made about it. Sir Francis concluded by assuring him that long before he would receive his answer the money would be placed in Mrs. Knowles' hands by a special messenger. Knowles wrote back, "My dear sir, you are right, and I was wrong. God bless you! I'll call upon you when I come to town."

One day also in the country he said to Abbot, with whom he had been acting there, "My dear fellow, I'm off to-morrow. Can I take any letters for you?" "You're very kind," answered Abbot; "but where are you going to?" "*I haven't made up my mind.*"

Seeing O. Smith, the popular melodramatic actor on the opposite side of the Strand, Knowles rushed across the road, seized him by the hand, and inquired eagerly after his health. Smith, who only knew him by sight, said, "I think, Mr. Knowles, you are mistaken; I am O. Smith." "My dear fellow," cried Knowles, "I beg you ten thousand pardons—I took you for your *namesake*, T. P. Cooke!"

An opera was produced at Covent Garden during my engagement, the story of which turned upon the love of a young count for a gipsy girl, whom he subsequently deserts for a lady of rank and fortune; and in the second act there was a fête in the gardens of the château in honour of the bride elect. Mr. Binge, who played the count, was seated in an arbour near to one of the wings witnessing a ballet. Knowles who had been in front during the previous part of the opera, came behind the scenes; and, advancing as near as he could to Binge without being in sight of the audience, called to him in a loud whisper, "Binge!" Binge looked over his shoulder. "Well, what is it?" "Tell me. Do you marry the poor gipsy after all?" "Yes," answered Binge, impatiently, stretching his arm out behind him, and making signs with it for Knowles to keep back. Knowles caught his hand, pressed it fervently, and exclaimed "God bless you! You are a good fellow!" This I saw and heard myself, as I was standing at the wing during the time.

The production of "The Legend of Florence" brought me into personal communication with Leigh Hunt, which ripened into the most intimate friendship, terminating only with his death. Of all my literary acquaintances, dear Leigh Hunt was, I think, the most delightful, as assuredly he was the most affectionate. Living within a short walk of us, his disengaged evenings were usually passed in Brompton Crescent, and most charming evenings he made them by the brightness, the originality, and loving-kindliness of his nature. Suffering severely from the res angusti domus, there was no repining, no bitterness, no censoriousness in his conversation. He bore his own privations with cheerful resignation, and unaffectedly rejoiced in the better fortune of others. He was greatly delighted with the success of his play, and began another, the scenes of which he brought to us as he wrote, and read as only he could read. He had the wildest ideas of dramatic effect, and calculated in the most utopian spirit upon the intelligence of the British public. As I often told him, if he read them himself, the magic of his voice, the marvellous intonation and variety of expression in his delivery, would probably enchain and enchant a general audience as it did us; but the hope of being so interpreted was not to be entertained for a moment. As an example of the playfulness of his fancy, take the following:—I was on my way to the theatre one morning with Charles Mathews in his carriage. We had not spoken for some minutes, when, as we were passing a wholesale stationer's at the west end of the Strand, Mathews, in his whimsical way, suddenly said to me, "Planché, which would you rather be? Roake or Varty?" such being the names painted over the shop-windows. I laughed at the absurdity of the question, and declined hazarding an opinion, as I had not the advantage of knowing either of the persons mentioned. On my return home in the evening, for I usually dined at the theatre, I found Hunt at tea with my family, and told him the ridiculous question that had been put to me. "Now, do you know," he said, "I consider that anything but a ridiculous question. I should say it was an exceedingly serious one, and which might have very alarming—nay, fatal consequences under certain mental or physical conditions. You might have become impressed by the notion that it was absolutely necessary for you to come to some decision on the question, and so absorbed in its consideration that you could think of nothing else. All business, public or private, would be neglected. Perpetual pondering on one problem, which daily became more difficult of solution, would result in monomania. Your health undermined, your brain overwrought, in the last moments of fleeting existence, only a few seconds left you in which to make your selection, you might rashly utter "Roake!" then, suddenly repenting, gasp out "Var," and die before you could say "ty.'"

He had a most amusing habit of coining words. Having paid my poor invalid wife, what she considered a great compliment, she said, "Oh, Mr. Hunt, you make me really begin to fear that you are—pardon me the epithet—a humbug." "Good gracious!" he exclaimed, "that a man who has been imprisoned for speaking the truth should be accused of *humbugeism!*"—the softening of the *g* adding elegance to the novelty of the expression. He had familiar names—*noms d'amitié*—for us all, made to rhyme according to an Oriental custom. My two daughters, Kate and Matilda, were, of course, "Katty and Matty." My wife's name, Elizabeth, instead of Betty, became "Batty." Her sister, Fanny, was transmuted to "Fatty," which she indignantly objected to as personal. "And what is papa's name to be?" asked one of my girls. "Papa's? oh, James must obviously be "Jatty," and so we remained to the end of the chapter.

Ex. gra.—A note to Mrs. Planché, who had written to congratulate him on the success of his play.

CHELSEA, *Feb.* 13, 1840.

DEAR BATTY,

(For as you have consented to accept the name, I shall continue to rhyme you and yours together after the social Oriental fashion), many thanks for your most kind letter, which I should have answered immediately, but that I have received so many letters I did not know which to answer first: so you must forgive my seeming inattention (most attentive in heart and memory), by reason of the happy delirium into which you have thus conspired with others to throw me. I got news of you from time to time—of the recovery of Matty, and the happy non-necessity for recovery of Katty, though I do not hear such good news of yourself and your ultra-womanly nerves; which may heaven bless and strengthen. Meantime, I am enabled to congratulate *you* upon the success of your husband's "Masque," in which he has made all the prominent parts of English history leap with such brief force and sufficiency out of the canvas, and give us victorious knocks on the head—a happy thought and capitally well seconded by the scene-painter and machinist. There is a dance in it one could dance for ever, and a haymaking village scene, with an embowered church spire fit to live and die in, especially for honey-moons.

Your obliged and sincere friend,

LEIGH HUNT.

The Masque alluded to in the above letter was "The Fortunate Isles," produced Wednesday, 12th February, 1840, in honour of Her Majesty's marriage; the original music composed by my old friend and collaborateur, Henry Bishop. On the Queen's return to London, Covent Garden Theatre was honoured by a Royal command, and Her Majesty, accompanied by Prince Albert, paid it a state visit on the Friday following.

A day or two before this event I received a few lines from Thackeray, of which, with the amusing pen-and-ink sketch that surmounted them, I exhibit a fac-simile. His request was granted by Charles Mathews, on condition of his receiving a similar drawing, which was duly sent, and Mr. and Mrs. Thackeray were amongst the closely packed throng of privileged persons who enjoyed the wonderful sight the house presented, viewed from the stage as the curtain rose to the first bars of the National Anthem on that memorable evening.

CHAPTER IV.

Independently of my superintendence of the painting-room and the wardrobe, I was requested by the management to be reader, or as Kenney more appropriately called it *weeder*, to the establishment. That is to peruse all the dramas sent in by *strangers* to the theatre, and select those I might deem worthy of consideration by the management. It is by no means an agreeable position, as it frequently involves you in a long unsatisfactory correspondence, and endangers your being accused of every species of literary dishonesty under the sun. Nothing but my personal regard for the new lessee, could have induced me to accept the office, and I consider it one of the whitest feathers in my cap, that I passed through the fire without singeing. During my three months' experience at the Olympic the previous season, I had arrived at the melancholy conclusion that the supply of *good* dramatic commodity was by no means equal to the demand. At Covent Garden, I waded in one season, through nearly two hundred plays and farces, without finding one I could conscientiously recommend to Madame Vestris. With the authors of three or four which had considerable literary merit, I entered into correspondence, but without a satisfactory result. One remarkable example occurred in the case of a three-act drama entitled "Richelieu," purporting to be the composition of a cadet at Woolwich, and which I felt convinced, notwithstanding the smartness of much of the dialogue and knowledge of dramatic effect displayed in its composition, could not hold its ground upon the stage, even if it escaped the *veto* of the Licenser. The curious confirmation of my opinion will appear in a later chapter. An exceedingly poetical but utterly unactable play by Mr. Atherstone, and a farce or two by a lady writing under the name of "Bellone," were the meagre grains of wheat in the bushels of chaff forwarded by untried authors to the new management of Covent Garden. One gentleman sent in three five-act comedies on the subject of the noble game of cricket. That they were bowled out pretty rapidly need scarcely be added. I afterwards learned that the writer was a clergyman, not quite in his right mind.

A Harlequinade being unavoidable at Christmas time at Covent Garden, the Fairy Piece, which had become an institution under Madame Vestris' *régime*, was postponed to Easter, and Charles Dance and I having dissolved partnership, in consequence of his taking a partner for life, I was left to provide for the emergency as best I might. It proved eventually, however, a fortunate circumstance for me, as the great success of "The Sleeping Beauty," "Beauty and the Beast," and "The White Cat," notoriously all my own, dissipated the idea, which I discovered had been entertained, not only in England but in America, that the fun was all Dance's, and merely the stage carpentry mine. To such an extent had this notion been propagated in the United States, that even many of my dramas, in which Dance had not the slightest share, were advertised as his only; but as, however beneficial to the American manager, not one complimentary dollar found its way into the pockets of either of us, the empty honour was not worth scrambling for, had I even been aware of the fact.

The extremely absurd laws which at that period trammelled the minor theatres not affecting the patent houses, the vague title of burletta was no longer necessary to describe the particular style of drama I had originated in England. "The Sleeping Beauty" was therefore announced as an extravaganza —distinguishing the whimsical treatment of a poetical subject from the broad caricature of a tragedy or serious opera, which was correctly described as a burlesque. I was rather nervous before the curtain rose,* as it was a first experiment on so large a stage, and the responsibility was entirely on my own shoulders, but the hearty roar from all parts of the house at an early line in the first scene,

"We stop the press to say—we've no more news,"

relieved me of all anxiety.

"The Sleeping Beauty" brought crowded houses to the end of the season, and the theatre re-opened with it the following one.

On the evening of Wednesday, May 6th, 1840, I was present at a very large and brilliant gathering at Gore House. Amongst the company were the Marquis of Normanby and several other noblemen, and, memorably, Edwin Landseer. During the previous week there had been a serious disturbance at the Opera, known as "The Tamburini Row," and it naturally formed the chief subject of conversation in a party, nearly every one of whom had been present. Lord Normanby, Count D'Orsay, and Landseer were specially excited; there was some difference of opinion, but no quarrelling, and the great animal painter was in high spirits and exceedingly amusing till the small hours of the morning, when we

* Easter Monday, April 20, 1840.

all gaily separated, little dreaming of the horrible deed perhaps at that very moment perpetrating, the murder of Lord William Russell by his valet Courvoisier. Lord William was one of Landseer's most intimate friends; and the shock caused by the suddenness of the intelligence conveyed to him by the morning papers brought on a serious attack of illness, under which he laboured for a considerable period.

Three months afterwards, August 2nd, 1840, I had been dining at Notting Hill, and was walking home to Brompton between ten and eleven. On arriving opposite Gore House, I thought I would avail myself of my pleasant privilege, and "drop in" for half an hour. There had been a small dinner party, and only four gentlemen were remaining. Two of them I knew, Lord Nugent and the Hon. Frederick Byng (familiarly called "Poodle"); the other two were strangers to me; but the youngest immediately engaged my attention. It was the fashion in that day to wear black satin kerchiefs for evening dress; and that of the gentleman in question was fastened by a large spread eagle in diamonds clutching a thunderbolt of rubies. There was but one man in England at that period who, without the impeachment of coxcombry, could have sported so magnificent a jewel; and, though I had never to my knowledge seen him before, I felt convinced that he could be no other than Prince Louis Napoleon. Such was the fact; and his companion was Count Montholon. There was a general conversation on indifferent subjects for some twenty minutes, during which the Prince spoke but little, and then took his departure with the Count. Shortly afterwards Lord Nugent, Mr. Byng, and I, said, "Good-night," and walked townward together. As we went along one of my companions said to the other, "What could Louis Napoleon mean by asking us to dine with him this day twelve-months at the Tuileries?" Four days afterwards the question was answered. The news arrived of the abortive landing at Boulogne and the captivity of the Prince, who had fallen into the trap so astutely laid for him. After his escape from Ham, the Prince, as is well known, returned to England, and continued to be a welcome guest at Gore House. "Time's whirlgig" upset the throne of the Citizen King, who landed at Newhaven as "a party of the name of Smith;"—and, "Hey, presto, pass!" Louis Napoleon was once more in France—and, this time, "President of the Republic." While the sun shone for him, a cloud came over his friends at Gore House. D'Orsay, "the glass of fashion and the mould of form," took refuge, in his turn, in Paris, and was soon followed by Lady Blessington. I heard by accident of her intended departure, called, and sat with her two hours alone on the day before she left. It is a great gratification to me that I had the opportunity of paying the last attention in my power to one who, whatever may have been her errors, was uniformly kind to me, and under whose roof I have passed so many enjoyable hours in the society of the most distinguished "men of the time," foreign as well as English. Naturally enough both Count D'Orsay and Lady Blessington calculated that the President would rejoice in his power to repay the hospitality and kindness he had received from them in his exile; but, unfortunately, they did not make sufficient allowance for the extremely delicate position in which he was placed. For D'Orsay he did what he could, and would doubtless have neglected no opportunity of serving him, compatible with his responsible situation. But what could he do for Lady Blessington? Receive her at the Tuileries? Impossible! and yet that was the thorn that rankled in her breast. Driving one day in the Champs Elysées, she was overtaken by the President on horseback. After the first salutations and the exchange of a few sentences, the Prince, unfortunately, asked, "Comptez-vous rester long-temps ici?" "Et vous?"

was the bitter retort, by which "more Hibernice," she answered a question by a question. Her Irish blood was roused, and, like a true Celt, reason was disregarded. Certainly, whatever sins the Emperor has to answer for, ingratitude to old friends is not of the number. At a moment when his "star" is clouded, and he is again an exile amongst us, I cannot deny myself the pleasure of recording an anecdote, the truth of which was recently vouched for to me by a son and daughter-in-law of the great artist who is the subject of it. On the occasion of the visit of Her Majesty and the Prince Consort to Paris, strict orders were issued respecting the admission of strangers to the Park of St. Cloud during the promenade of the Imperial and Royal party. Amongst the select few admitted was the late most popular vocalist, Signor Lablache. His remarkable person immediately caught the eye of the Emperor, who is said to have exclaimed, "There is Lablache! I only know him by sight. I should like to speak to him." And the Queen and Prince Albert being well acquainted with him, one of the gentlemen in attendance was sent for him. After presentation, the Emperor said, "You have a son, I believe, in my army?" "I have, sire?" "What is his rank?" "He is a sous-lieutenant in the —— Regiment, sire." The Emperor of the French turned to the Queen of

England, and said, "*Would not your Majesty like to make Lablache's son a captain?*"—and a captain, of course, he became. Not having been present, I can only "say the tale as 'twas said to me;" but it is highly characteristic of the Emperor's taste and tact, and I have every reason to believe it substantially true for the reason I have already given.

À propos of Lablache, it was after dinner at Gore House that I witnessed his extraordinary representation of a thunderstorm simply by facial expression. The gloom that gradually overspread his countenance appeared to deepen into actual darkness, and the terrific frown indicated the angry louring of the tempest. The lightning commenced by winks of the eyes, and twitchings of the muscles of the face, succeeded by rapid sidelong movements of the mouth which wonderfully recalled to you the forked flashes that seem to rend the sky, the notion of thunder being conveyed by the shaking of his head. By degrees the lightning became less vivid, the frown relaxed, the gloom departed, and a broad smile illuminating his expansive face assured you that the sun had broken through the clouds and the storm was over. He told me the idea occurred to him in the Champs Elysées, where one day, in company with Signor de Begnis, he witnessed a distant thunderstorm above the Arc de Triomphe.

CHAPTER V.

In September, 1840, while superintending the production of Knowles' "John of Procida," I met with an accident, which I only mention for the sake of a characteristic anecdote in connection with it. In passing from the stage into the pit over some planks that had been placed for the purpose of our going to and fro to see the effect of the scenery, one of them slipped, and, falling on the back of a pit seat, I broke a rib, and was consequently confined to my house for about a fortnight. On my first visit to the theatre afterwards, I crawled out to get some luncheon at the Garrick, and, returning to the theatre at a very slow pace, I met under the piazza one of the reporters of the "Morning Herald," with whom I was slightly acquainted. He stopped me, and remarked upon the alteration in my appearance, and the difficulty I seemed to have in walking. I explained to him the cause, upon which he exclaimed, "God bless me! How sorry I am I never heard of it!" I was both touched and surprised by the evident interest he took in the matter, considering we knew so little of each other, and was about to express my appreciation of his sympathy, when, before I could speak, he added, "It would have made such a capital paragraph!"

During the time I was compelled by my accident to sit quietly at home in my arm-chair I occupied myself with the revision of another of our glorious old English comedies, Beaumont and Fletcher's "Spanish Curate," which was produced on the 13th of October, 1840, with a most effective cast, Farren and Keeley especially distinguishing themselves as the cunning curate and his worthy clerk. A third important revival was Shakespere's "Midsummer Night's Dream" on a scale of great splendour, and for the first time with the overture, wedding march, and other music by Mendelssohn. When this revival was first suggested, Bartley said, "If Planché can devise a striking effect for the last scene, the play will run for sixty nights." I pointed out that Shakespere had suggested it himself, in the words of Oberon to his attendant fairies—

> "Through the house give glimmering light,
> * * * * * *
> Every elf and fairy sprite
> Hop as light as bird from brier,
> And this ditty after me
> Sing, and dance it trippingly."

It was accordingly arranged with Grieve, the scenic artist, who is at this day still adding to his great reputation, that the back of the stage should be so constructed that at the command of Oberon it should be filled with fairies, bearing twinkling coloured lights, "flitting through the house," and forming groups and dancing, as indicated in the text, carrying out implicitly the directions of the author, and not sacrilegiously attempting to gild his refined gold. The result was most successful, and verified Bartley's prediction.

The season of 1840–41 was distinguished by the production of the best original five-act comedy of modern English manners produced within my recollection. "London Assurance" took the town by storm, and is at this present moment, thirty-one years after its first production, nightly attracting crowds to a metropolitan theatre, whose hearty enjoyment of its wit, characters, and situations is a triumphant answer to the assertion so often repeated that the public now-a-days object to five acts. Give the public that which is good, and the number of acts will not affect its verdict.

The last season of Madame Vestris's management of Covent Garden in 1841–42 is memorable for the *début* of Miss Adelaide Kemble (now Mrs. Sartoris) in the opera of "Norma," my English version of which, made in 1837 for Madame Schrœder Devrient, I had the pleasure of revising on this interesting occasion. Miss Kemble's performance of the heroine was admitted on all hands to be worthy of ranking with the greatest of the many triumphs achieved by her gifted family in other branches of the dramatic profession.

On the 12th May, 1842, Her Majesty gave her first *Bal Costumé* at Buckingham Palace, and I had the honour of being consulted by their Royal Highnesses the Duchess, Prince George, and Princess Augusta of Cambridge respecting the dresses which were to be worn on that occasion, not only by their Royal Highnesses, but by all the ladies and gentlemen composing what was termed "the Duchess of Cambridge's quadrille." The Queen had expressed her desire that the costume should be historical and strictly accurate. Her Majesty selected that of Queen Philippa; the Prince Consort wore the robes of Edward III.; and all their household, as well as the great officers of state, were attired in the habits, civil or military, of that reign. The rest of the company were at liberty to select the attire of any other age or country, with the above *proviso.* National dresses were allowed; but not what are called fancy or emblematical costume. Authorities, therefore, had to be furnished beyond the reach of the tailors and dress-makers who were employed in the masquerade ware-houses of that day, or in the wardrobes of the theatres. No play of the reign of Edward III. had been produced by Madame Vestris or by Mr. Macready, who had then become the lessee of Drury Lane. I had recently published my "History of British Costume," and was engaged at that moment in editing a new edition of Strutt's "Dress and Habits of the People of England," and his "Regal Antiquities," and had consequently accumulated considerable material particularly useful on this occasion.

I need scarcely say with what pride and pleasure I placed my humble services at the disposal of those members of the Royal Family who flattered me by their request, and have ever since most graciously evinced their recollection of them. They were also readily given to such of the nobility as were personally known to me; but it was positively astonishing how many persons, to whom I really could not remember having ever been presented, did me the honour of recollecting what I presume I must entirely have for-gotten. To these add a number of ladies and gentlemen who freely construed the French maxim, "Les amis de nos amis sont nos amis," and a few who, considering their official position justified their self-introduction, frankly and politely solicited my assistance, and the reader may imagine my occupation during the four or five weeks previous to the great event—for I trust I was courteous to all, and in only one instance declined paying any attention to an application beyond acknowledging its reception and presuming it must have been addressed to me under some mistake—which I hope for the writer's sake it was, though no admission or apology ever reached me. I must mention one incident, in the hope that my readers may think it as amusing as I did at the time. A nobleman, an utter stranger to me, except, of course, by name, in whose family a courtly office was hereditary,—sent me a very polite note of eight pages, closely filled with questions of every description respecting the duties and costume of the holder of that office and his attendants in the reign of Edward III., and the bearer informed my servant that his orders were to *wait for an answer!* I was so tickled with the idea of any one supposing so many abstruse archæological questions could be replied to off-hand, that, having by accident the principal authorities before me at that very moment, I sent word down that he might wait, and immediately went to work, and in the course of about an hour wrote as many pages as were contained in his lordship's letter, answering minutely every question *seriatim*, and despatched them to him by his own messenger. I presume they reached his hands; but I never heard they did, and only supposed he must have thought it so easy a thing for me to do, that it was not worth "thank ye." This was, however, I am bound to say, a solitary instance of obliviousness; for, after all, perhaps, he may have thought he had said it: and I made many agreeable acquaintances and some very kind friends by the pleasant service I was enabled to render them—for costume was my hobby, and I enjoyed such an opportunity of riding it.

One of my most troublesome pupils was the Earl of Cardigan. He had decided on representing the Chevalier Bayard, and had ordered a complete suit of mail to be made for him by a theatrical tailor, whose only notion of mail was silver spangles. I pointed out to his lordship that, in the first place, mail would be incorrect. That there were several fine suits of plate-armour of the time of Bayard in existence, which could be hired or purchased; and that his *costumier* would turn him out more like a "sprite" in a pantomime, than a *preux chevalier* of the sixteenth century. He was very obstinate, and stuck to his spangled pantaloons; and on my hinting something about the criticism he might expect from the Press and the public, growled out,—

"Why, what 'll they say if I do wear 'em?"

"That you are Bayard *sans peur*, but certainly not *sans reproche*."

He gave a gruff "Heugh!" but I heard no more of the pantaloons.

The ball—which I was enabled, by the kindness of Lord Delawarr, at that time Lord Chamberlain, to witness,—was a magnificent sight and a great success.

Madame Vestris's management of Covent Garden terminated with this, her third season (1841—2). The heavy expenses entailed on her by the addition of chorus, extra band, and other necessities of an opera company, after she had completed all her engagements for comedy and tragedy (Miss Kemble's appearance having been decided on at the last moment), could only be met by continuous receipts of as much money as the house could hold; and, after the run of "Norma" and the Christmas pantomime, they fell considerably below that average. A new opera, "Elena Uberti," proved a dead failure; and though a vigorous rally took place at Easter, from the consecutive successes of "The White Cat," the opera of "The Marriage of Figaro," for the first time completely rendered in English, and the masque of "Comus," with additional scenic effects and music, introduced from Dryden and Purcell's opera, "King Arthur," there was a deficit of some £600 in the payment of the rent of as many thousands; and, with the usual liberality and good policy of the proprietors of theatres in general, Madame Vestris, who had raised Covent Garden once more to the rank it had held in the days of the Kembles, and paid her heavy rent to the shilling during two brilliant seasons, was denied the opportunity of recouping herself from losses caused by a most exceptional circumstance, and coolly bowed out of the building. A singular instance occurred of the way in which that "wonderful woman" jumped, with true feminine felicity, at conclusions for which she could not herself account, and which to others appeared preposterous. I dined with her and Mathews nearly every day, in their room in the theatre, George Bartley, the acting manager, making occasionally a fourth. One day when I was alone with them, and long before any calculation could be fairly made of the ultimate result of the season, Madame Vestris said, abruptly, after a short silence, "Charles! we shall not have this theatre next year." "What do you mean?" he and I exclaimed simultaneously. "Simply what I say." "But what reason," inquired Mathews, "can you possibly have for thinking so?" "No particular reason; but you'll see." "Have you heard any rumour to that effect?" I asked. "No; but we shall not have the theatre." "But who on earth will have it, then?" we said, laughing at the idea; for we could imagine no possible competitor likely to pay so high a rent. "Charles Kemble," was her answer. "He will think that his daughter's talent and popularity will be quite sufficient, and we shall be turned out of the theatre. But," she continued, seeing us still incredulous, "three things may happen: Miss Kemble may be ill; Miss Kemble may not get another opera like 'Norma;' and Miss Kemble may marry." Every one of these predictions was fulfilled. The rent not being fully paid up according to the conditions of her lease, it was declared forfeited; and Mr. Charles Kemble took the theatre himself upon his own shoulders. Just before the season commenced, Miss Kemble *was* taken ill, and the opening of the theatre had to be postponed in consequence. The opera prepared for her did not prove attractive; and very shortly afterwards she became the wife of Mr. Edward John Sartoris, now M.P. for Caermarthenshire. The theatre closed prematurely, and after an abortive attempt of Henry Wallack, and a brief and desperate struggle of Bunn, ceased to be a temple of the national drama.

CHAPTER VI.

On the 24th of August that year I lost my ever-kind friend, Theodore Hook. His two last notes to me are without date, but I well remember the circumstances under which they were written. I had a general invitation from him for Sundays, which I rarely availed myself of, as we generally had a friend or two to dinner ourselves on that only day in the week professional persons—medical men excepted—can count upon with security, and a few of our pleasant neighbours would occasionally drop in in the evening; but I heard that Hook had been ill, and wrote him word that I would run down to see him on the afternoon of the following Sunday. I received this reply:—

FULHAM
(Blowing a gale of wind).

Don't come here next Sunday, for I shan't be at home. Do come Sunday week; and if my house stands through the gale of wind which is now shaking it, I shall be delighted. Come at *one*, and (I don't mean a rhyme) have lunch*eon*.

Yours truly,

T. E. H.

I went, of course, and found him pretty nearly himself again—full of fun and anecdote,—but I remarked with regret that he ate nothing, but drank tumbler after tumbler of claret. His most intimate and attached friend, Mr. Broderip, the magistrate—"the Beak," as Hook always introduced him—who was present, told me that solid food rarely passed his lips, and that he feared the digestive organs were fatally impaired. On being pressed to eat a portion at least of a cutlet, he merely shook his head, and said, "À propos of cutlets, I once called upon an old lady, who pressed me so urgently to stay and dine with her that, as I had no engagement, I could not refuse. On sitting down, the servant uncovered a dish which contained two mutton chops, and my old friend said, "Mr. Hook, you see your dinner." "Thank you, ma'am," said I; "but *where's yours?*"

Having written to him from St. Leonard's-on-Sea, on some private matters which had annoyed me, he wound up his reply in these words:—

I have been *very* ill, and am, as you may perceive, scarcely able to hold my pen. I wish *I* was at St. Leonard'son-Sea to enjoy the fresh breezes, and then I would tell you *personally,* as I now write you, that I am vexed at what you communicated, and that I am truly yours,

THEODORE E. HOOK.
(Hand shaky.)

Mr. and Mrs. Charles Mathews had accepted the offer of an engagement from Mr. Macready for the following season at Drury Lane, and I wrote for them the two-act comedy, "The Follies of a Night," in which they appeared, 5th of October, 1842. Some disagreement arising between them and Mr. Macready, they left Drury Lane abruptly, and transferred their services to Mr. Benjamin Webster at the Haymarket; and there I had the gratification of restoring another fine old comedy to the modern stage—Congreve's "Way of the World." I shall never forget the astonishment of Macready at the announcement. "My G—d!—why, they're going to do the 'Way of the World!'" "Yes; I have arranged it for them." "You!—why, what in heaven's name have you done with Mrs. Malfort?" "Made a man of her." And such was the fact. By simply changing "Mrs." into "Mr." I converted a most objectionable woman—the character which had been a stumbling-block to the revival of the play—into a treacherous male friend, without omitting or altering an important line in the part; as the phrases which would not have been tolerated in these days from the lips of a female, became perfectly inoffensive when uttered by an unprincipled man of the world, and the plot was in no wise interfered with by the transformation. The comedy, strongly cast, went off brilliantly,* and formed another sample of the wealth of that rich mine of dramatic ore which has only to be properly worked by managers, to improve their fortunes as well as the taste of the public. While employed on this work I received the following characteristic letter from Richard Peake:—

HALDERTON COTTAGE, QUEEN'S ELM,
November 3, 1842.

MY DEAR PLANCHÉ,—

There was much good sense in your remark when we were parting on Tuesday. I allude to the conjunction of *head-pieces* to produce an effective drama; and it is one of the things we may very safely borrow from our neighbours, the French.

As I think that you have a good opinion of my humour in a certain line, your humour may coalesce with mine: I acknowledge your superiority in tact and taste, and I cannot see any reason why we should not join forces, by way of experiment, in a two-act piece.

The subject of the drama, and the theatre, for after-discussion. *One* may lead to many. I am the more inclined

* 17th December, 1842.

to this, as associations are forming in our neighbourhood by *younger* writers than ourselves, and the result has been prosperous.

The "Clandestine Marriage" is, in my opinion, the *second* best comedy in the English language.

The *two* heads show their power in that play. If we cannot aspire to the fame of a Garrick or a Coleman, a drama created on our joint experience would, I apprehend, be certainly successful.

The rivalry of the two theatres, with the Haymarket as a reserve, would ensure acceptance.

Our friend Charles Dance has now more profitable views than dramatic authorship. You and I, alas! have not.

What say you to a conjunction?

IF. . . is a conjunction.

BUT. . . . . is another.

I am,

Dear Planché,

Yours very truly,

R. B. PEAKE.

J. R. PLANCHÉ, Esq.

The subject of the conversation to which he alluded in the above letter is one which is worthy of consideration, perhaps even more now than it was then; but English dramatists do not appear to appreciate the great advantages of collaboration, notwithstanding the evidence which the French stage has for so many years furnished, and is still giving them examples of. There can be no doubt that Scribe, one of the most prolific and popular of French dramatists, was perfectly competent to write a comedy, a drama, a vaudeville, or the libretto of an opera, whether comic or serious, without assistance, as long as he could hold a pen; but, notwithstanding his great and versatile power of composition, we find his name constantly in conjunction with one or more of less celebrity. Latterly, I have heard, he did little more than give the benefit of his experience and advice—but how valuable was that gift!—to the young vaudevillistes who sought him, and were proud to share the honour of his name in exchange for a moiety of the profits, which they might never have reaped unassisted by his judgment. He, in his turn, was frequently much indebted to others. I believe it is not generally known that the great duo in the fourth act of "The Huguenots" was not written by Scribe, but added, at the request of Meyerbeer, by another hand—if I recollect rightly, by Mons. Halevy. Of its immense importance to the Opera no one who ever heard it can raise a question.

Nothing, however, came of Peake's proposition, as he did not follow it up by any suggestion of a subject, and I speedily found myself with so much work upon my hands, that I could not have availed myself of it, had he done so.

Having promised Mr. Macready to write the Easter piece for him, I felt bound to decline an invitation from Mr. Webster to write one for the Haymarket, notwithstanding the advantage I should derive from Madame Vestris being then at the latter theatre. I did not consider that her quarrel with Mr. Macready justified me in breaking my word to him; and, although he very handsomely offered to release me from my promise, in consequence of the lady's defection, I assured him of my intention to fulfil it to the best of my ability, if it were agreeable to him that I should do so. He eagerly and warmly thanked me, and the following Easter saw the production of "Fortunio," one of the most popular of my extravaganzas, and the first unassociated with the name of Madame Vestris. Much as I regretted being deprived of her services, I could not but rejoice that it gave an opportunity to a charming young actress and vocalist to "come to the front" in this class of entertainment, a position she holds to this day: I need scarcely mention the name of Priscilla Horton, now Mrs. German Reed.

At the close of the season, the proprietors of Drury Lane treated Macready with their usual shorsightedness, and he gave up the theatre, most unfortunately for all who retained any respect for the national drama, the character of which, both on the stage and *behind the scenes*, he had strenuously striven to keep up to the highest standard. The world was again before me where to choose. The Mathews's being at the Haymarket, I naturally turned my thoughts in that direction, and after writing for them the comedy of "Whose your Friend?" entered into an engagement with Mr. Webster to write for the Haymarket only, specially producing an extravaganza at Christmas and Easter, for three years and a half, the half including the Christmas of 1843 and the Easter of 1844. Singularly enough, I was again deprived of the talent and popularity of Madame Vestris, untoward circumstances suddenly compelling her and her husband to leave England before Christmas; and again I found an admirable substitute in Miss P. Horton, who continued to sustain the principal character in my fairy Christmas pieces at this theatre during the rest of my engagement, Madame Vestris and Charles Mathews, one or both, acting after their return only in the Easter pieces, which, for variety's sake, partook, with one exception, more of the character of a *revue*.

The Christmas pieces during this period were—"The Fair One with the Golden Locks," 1843; "Graciosa and Percinet," 1844; "The Bee and the Orange Tree," 1845; and "The Invisible Prince," 1846. The exception above alluded to was the classical extravaganza of "The Golden Fleece," produced Easter Monday, March 24th, 1845, suggested by the performance of "Antigone" at Drury Lane Theatre. The "Medea" of Madame Vestris and the "Chorus" of Charles Mathews were simply perfect. Respecting the Revues, I beg to be allowed to say a few words. Previous to my production of "Success; or, a Hit if you like it," at the Adelphi in 1825, no such entertainment was known to the English stage. Its favourable reception induced me to make a second attempt to naturalise it thirteen years afterwards, when Madame Vestris took her farewell at the Olympic, on her departure for America; but in the latter instance it was specially a *pièce d'occasion*, and the majority of the allusions necessarily personal. In its successor at the Haymarket the scope was wider, and in reviewing the popular productions at other houses and the various exhibitions and entertainments which had attracted public attention during the current season, I found opportunities for expressing my humble opinion on theatrical affairs in general, which, however open to correction, were as honestly entertained as, I trust, they were inoffensively promulgated.

"The Drama at Home," the first of these, at the Haymarket, produced on Easter Monday, 1844, comprised in its cast Charles Mathews, James Bland, Miss P. Horton, and Mrs. Glover! I confess, it was with some timidity I saw that noble actress enter the green room in obedience to a call for the reading of the "new burlesque!" But great was my pride and gratification to observe that she enjoyed every line of it, and received the part assigned to her without the slightest hesitation. How she acted it, those who remember her alone can imagine. It was worth writing, indeed, for such an interpreter. The monopoly of the legitimate drama by the great houses, and the limitation of the seasons of the minors, had been recently abolished, and free trade in theatricals was established by law throughout the metropolis. This important fact was thus commented upon. The Drama, about to emigrate, was stopped by Portia, in her "Doctor of Laws" attire:—

Portia. Tarry a little!
Drama. Portia!
Portia. Even so.
Drama. "Come you from Padua, from Bellario?"
Portia. No, Ma'am—from Westminster—why should you roam?
Drama. Because they've ceased to care for me at home.
Portia. Then you've not heard the news—the Drama's free!
Drama. Free!
Portia. To go where she will—
Drama. It cannot be
Except to exile; therefore in despair
"To foreign climates my old trunk I bear."
Portia. I say you're free to act where'er you please,
No longer pinioned by the patentees.
Need our immortal Shakespere mute remain
Fixed on the portico of Drury Lane;

Or the nine Muses mourn the Drama's fall
Without relief on Covent Garden's wall?
Sheridan now at Islington may shine,
Marylebone echo "Marlowe's mighty line;"
Otway may raise the waters Lambeth yields,
And Farquhar sparkle in St. George's Fields;
Whycherley, flutter a Whitechapel pit,
And Congreve wake all "Westminster to *wit*."
* * * * * * *

Drama. O joyful day!—Then I may flourish still!
Punch. *May*—well, that's something. Let us hope you *will*.
A stage may rise for you now law will let it,
And Punch sincerely "*wishes you may get it.*"

The doubt implied by Punch has been painfully illustrated. A recent writer in the "Quarterly Review," commenting on this subject, says:—"Of what avail was it to multiply theatres and give them the right to perform the higher drama, unless you could also provide actors to keep pace with their demands? These are a commodity not to be turned out in any quantity to order. No amount of demand will produce a corresponding supply. Natural gifts and training must go to their production, and the only real training-school is a theatre of good actors, working together with a pride in their art, and under a system of intelligent discipline. But the change of system made the existence of such a school impossible: for how could such actors of ability and experience as then existed be kept together when they were being continually bribed away, by offers of increased salary and higher rank, to the host of competitive theatres which soon afterwards sprang into existence? Companies became of necessity broken up; actors, who by time and practice might have been tutored into excellence, were ruined by being lifted into positions far beyond their powers; every player became a law to himself; the traditions of the art were lost, the discipline which distinguished the old theatres was broken down, and the performance of a comedy of character or of a poetical play, as these used to be represented, became, as the elders of the craft had foretold, simply impossible."*

These are sad truths. I quote them because I am desirous to show that writers of much more weight than I, feel as acutely the present position of our national stage and acknowledge the results of the shortsighted legislation which abolished the privileges of the patent theatres, to have been what the great actors predicted, and I ventured to hint, thirty years ago. I say shortsighted, because, in amending laws no longer suited to the age, not the slightest prevision was exercised by the reformers, who simply yielded to the outcry justly raised against the absurd, incongruous, and partial regulations that oppressed and degraded

* Quarterly Review for January, 1872, p. 13.

the profession, without providing for the security of its best interests and the encouragement of its noblest aspirations.

The present generation of play-goers can scarcely imagine the vexatious and anomalous state of affairs that existed in the theatrical world when I first became a member of it. The Theatres Royal Drury Lane and Covent Garden enjoyed, by their patents, the exclusive privilege of being open *all the year round*, if their lessees so willed it, for the performance of any species of dramatic entertainment. "Tragedy, comedy, history, pastoral," &c., as old Polonius had it, "for the law of writ and the liberty" (to act it) "they were the only men." The little theatre in the Haymarket had a *limited licence*, as a summer theatre, for the performance of what is called the regular drama. With these exceptions, no theatre within the bills of mortality was safe from the common informer, did its company venture to enact any drama in which there was not a certain quantity of vocal or instrumental music. The Lyceum, a new establishment, was specially licensed for the performance of English opera and musical dramas, and the Adelphi and Olympic Theatres had the Lord Chamberlain's licence for the performance of *burlettas* only, by which description, after much controversy both in and out of court, we were desired to understand dramas containing not less than five pieces of vocal music in each act, and which were also, with one or two exceptions, not to be found in the *repertoire* of the patent houses. All beside the above-named six theatres were positively out of the pale of the law. There was no Act of Parliament which empowered the magistrates to license a building for *dramatic* performances. Astley's, the Surrey, the Victoria, Sadler's Wells, &c., had, in common with Vauxhall, a licence "for music and dancing" *only*, by which was originally meant public concerts and balls; gradually permitted to extend to ballets and pantomimes and equestrian performances: but no one had a legal right to open his mouth on a stage unaccompanied by music; and the next step was to evade the law by the tinkling of a piano in the orchestra throughout the interdicted performances. There is perhaps no greater folly than permitting laws to exist which changes of times and circumstances have rendered so absurd that justice is obliged to wink at the breach of them. It being considered hard that the inhabitants of St. George's Fields, Lambeth, Islington, Marylebone, &c., should be compelled to make a positive journey in order to enjoy the rational amusement of the theatre, the proprietors of the public places of "entertainment for man and horse" in those vicinities were suffered to violate the law nightly with impunity; and the unwillingness of magistrates to convict, when occasionally compelled to notice the offence, became at last so notorious that the holders of the royal patents, who were most interested in suppressing the innovators, finding nothing but odium was to be gained by their opposition, after two or three ineffectual struggles, gave up the cause in despair, and regular dramas were soon acted as boldly and almost as well at the minors as at the majors. Still the law was not repealed. It existed and could be put in force at any moment; nay, what was more ridiculous, though the entire disregard of it was tolerated at the Surrey or in Tottenham Street, had "Macbeth" or "The School for Scandal" been acted at the Adelphi or the Olympic Theatres, legally licensed for the performance of some description, at least, of the drama, the Lord Chamberlain would have pounced upon the audacious manager or lessees, and shut up his doors *instanter*. Notwithstanding this even, the Strand Theatre, which had been added to the number of dramatic establishments, was kept open for nearly two years in defiance of his lordship's authority, and the only way at last discovered was the petty one of common information against the poor actors.

Lent arrived, and the theatres in the parish of St. Paul, Covent Garden, were rigorously restricted from the performance of a moral or poetical play on Wednesdays or Fridays during that period; but a theatre that happened to be on the other side of Oxford Street or of Waterloo Bridge was unaffected by this prohibition, and though the manager of the Adelphi might not dream of playing the whole of one of the spectacular "burlettas," which were at that period so popular there, no objection was made to his exhibiting tableaux from them, and adding any tomfoolery which was *not* dramatic, by way of keeping holy the said Wednesdays and Fridays. The performers at Drury Lane and Covent Garden lost two nights' salary every week, but then they could go to Greenwich or Richmond, and act what they pleased there. Lent was only a sacred season within the circle described by the wand of the Lord Chamberlain. Passion Week itself was unknown in the theatres two or three miles from St. James's Palace. Such was England during the first quarter of the nineteenth century! At length the injustice became intolerable, and the regulations supremely ridiculous; but, in conceding what reason demanded, no precautions were taken against the almost inevitable misuse of the liberty accorded. The gates were recklessly thrown open, and the glorious drama of England, free to roam wherever she would, has never since found a permanent resting-place for the soles of her feet. A stage has not yet risen for her, and her true lovers are still "sincerely wishing she may get it."

CHAPTER VII.

It was at the commencement of my engagement at the Haymarket that Mr. Webster publicly offered a prize of £500 for the best five-act comedy. A committee, comprising Charles Kemble, Charles Young, and several competent and disinterested critics, was formed, and within the period prescribed over one hundred comedies were sent in, but two of which were even actable, and the best of these two proved to be by my old friend Mrs. Charles Gore, who had already been successful as a dramatist; and, consequently, the complaints of neglected genius and managerial favouritism were triumphantly refuted, as not a single hitherto "mute inglorious" Sheridan or Colman was discovered by the experiment, which, as I was not a member of the committee, I am at liberty to assert was most fairly made by all concerned, and the only persons to be pitied were the judges, who conscientiously waded through the mass of extraordinary compositions which the writers had complacently considered comedies.

In the preface to her play, which I did not see till long after publication, Mrs. Gore stated that a gentleman connected with the management, who was acquainted with her handwriting, recognised it in the MS., and divulged the secret. She was under an error which, for her own sake, should be corrected, as had such been the case, the decision might have been influenced by the information. Mr. Farren and I were the only two persons connected with the management to whom her writing was familiar, and I never set eyes on the MS. till I had to get up the comedy, nor, I have every reason to believe, did Mr. Farren, if he saw it, recognise the hand or reveal the authorship; for I happened to enter the theatre by the box-office just as the committee had broken up, and hearing that the prize was awarded, I asked one of the members whom I met in the lobby, but whose name I cannot at this moment remember, who was the fortunate candidate, and his answer was, "Webster tells us it is Mrs. Gore." The declaration only being made by him when summoned to receive the final opinion of the committee. It is but justice to all parties to state that their opinion was unanimous, and uninfluenced by any personal feeling or suspicion even of the authorship of the comedy.

The season of 1844-45—for the Haymarket, no longer restricted to four summer months, now competed with its larger, but no longer more favoured, rivals—saw the production of "Graciosa and Percinet" at Christmas, and of "The Golden Fleece," the latter an undeniable burlesque, suggested by the performance of "Antigone," after the Greek manner, on a raised stage, and with a chorus, which, with Mendelssohn's music and Miss Vandenhoff's declamation, had made some sensation at Covent Garden.

The personation of Medea by Madame Vestris, and of the Chorus by Mathews, can never be forgotten by those who witnessed it; and they were admirably seconded by Bland and Miss Horton. The piece remains in the *répertoire* of my friend Charles, and the present Mrs. Mathews has adopted the part of Medea with considerable success.

In 1846, at Easter, I hazarded a step in advance, and adapted "The Birds of Aristophanes" to the modern English stage. It was a "succès d'estime," I am proud to say, with many whose opinion I value highly, but not "d'argent," as far as the treasury was concerned. My object was misunderstood, and consequently not appreciated. As I have elsewhere stated, they were greatly mistaken who imagined I had no higher object in view than the amusement of holiday audiences. I was impressed with the idea that I was opening a new stage-door by which the poet and the satirist could enter the theatre without the shackles imposed upon them by the laws of the regular drama. I fancied what might have been effected by the authors of "Don Juan" and "The Twopenny Post-Bag," of "Rejected Addresses," of "The Ingoldsby Legends," of "Whims and Oddities;" and my ambition was to lay the foundation for an Aristophanic drama, which the greatest minds would not consider it derogatory to contribute to. Though disappointed, I could not help being amused, and in some degree flattered. A popular foreign artiste pronounced the piece to be "too d——d clever." One critic in a daily paper, who insisted on comparing it with "The Golden Fleece," was shocked at the introduction of Jupiter, and remarked that his language was "far too earnest and too literal; it was no longer burlesque,—it was no less than the voice of offended Heaven." The critic meant this for condemnation; I received it as the highest compliment. It was exactly what I had been working up to. I never contemplated burlesque. The fable was over, the allegory ended, the moral to be drawn (and I have never written those absurdities without one), however trite, was of the most serious character. I could not too earnestly point out (the sole aim of the piece)

> "What dire confusion in the world 'twould breed
> If fools *could* follow whither knaves *would* lead;"

and it is the feebleness, and not the strength or gravity, that I regret of the language in which the concluding exhortation is couched,—

> "On wings *forbidden* seek no idle Fame,
> Let men BE men, and WORTHY OF THE NAME!"

It is related of Charles II. that, being present at a meeting of the Royal Society, he gravely requested to know the reason, Why the insertion of a fish of three pounds weight into a bucket of water made no difference in the weight of the bucket? A vast quantity of learning and ingenuity was immediately put in requisition to account for the phenomenon; at length one gentleman observed that, before they endeavoured to ascertain the reason, they should establish the fact, and that, with submission to his Majesty, he believed that the insertion of the fish *would* make a difference in the weight of the bucket. "You are quite right," said Charles; "it would." Had the dissentient critic of my "Birds," before he discussed the merits of the piece *as a burlesque*, ascertained that it was *not a burlesque*, his verdict might have been more favourable. It had never been advertised or officially entitled "a burlesque." It was described in the bills as a "Dramatic Experiment," and was undertaken with the object already stated, and with a view of ascertaining how far the theatrical public would be willing to receive a higher class of entertainment than the fairy extravaganza I had already established in England, or the Revue, which I was endeavouring to establish. Although, from the probable disappointment of the lovers of mere absurdity, and the natural mystification of a few good-humoured holiday spectators, the immediate consequences were by no means what I contemplated, I do not abandon hope. The success of "The Palace of Truth," and still more that of "Pygmalion," upon those very boards, has proved that there is a public who can enjoy good writing and good acting, unassisted by magnificent scenery and undegraded by "break-downs."

The season 1846-47 was signalised by the return to the stage of that charming woman and actress, Mrs. Nisbett, then Lady Boothby, and for the second time a widow but slenderly provided for. During her brief sojourn in Derbyshire she had endeared herself to all classes, particularly the poor, in the neighbourhood or Ashbourne, by whom her memory was cherished long after her leaving it, as I can avouch from personal experience when visiting in that locality in 1851.

Her engagement suggested the idea to me of reviving "The Taming of the Shrew," not in the miserable, mutilated form in which it is acted under the title of "Katherine and Petruchio," but in its integrity, with the Induction, in which I felt satisfied that excellent actor Strickland would, as Christopher Sly, produce a great effect. It also occurred to me to try the experiment of producing the piece with only two scenes—1. The outside of the little ale-house on a heath, from which the drunken tinker is ejected by the hostess, and where he is found asleep in front of the door by the nobleman and his huntsmen; and, 2. The nobleman's bedchamber, in which the strolling players should act the comedy, as they would have done in Shakespere's own time under similar circumstances—viz., without scenery, and merely affixing written placards to the wall of the apartment to inform the audience that the action is passing "in a public place in Padua,"—"a room in Baptista's house,"—"a public road," &c.

Mr. Webster, to whom of course I proposed this arrangement, sanctioned it without hesitation. I prepared the comedy for representation, gave the necessary instructions for painting the two scenes, and made the designs for the dresses. One difficulty was to be surmounted. How was the play to be finished. Schlegel says that the part "in which the tinker, in his new state, again drinks himself out of his senses, and is transformed in his sleep into his former condition, from some accident or other, is lost." Mr. Charles Knight observes upon this: "We doubt whether it was ever produced, and whether Shakespere did not exhibit his usual judgment in letting the curtain drop upon honest Christopher, when his wish was accomplished, at the close of the comedy, which he had expressed very early in its progress—

"'Tis a very excellent piece of work, Madame Lady—would 't were done."

Had Shakespere brought him again on the scene in all the richness of his first exhibition, perhaps the patience of the audience would never have allowed them to sit through the lessons of 'the taming school.' We have had farces enough *founded* upon the legend of Christopher Sly, but no one has ever ventured to *continue* him. I was the last person who would have been guilty of such presumption, but after studying the play carefully, I hit upon the following expedient:—Sly was seated in a great chair in the first entrance,

O. P., to witness the performance of the comedy. At the end of each act no drop scene came down, but music was played while the servants brought the bewildered tinker wine and refreshments, which he partook of freely. During the fifth act he appeared to fall gradually into a heavy drunken stupor, and when the last line of the play was spoken, the actors made their usual bow, and the nobleman, advancing and making a sign to his domestics, they lifted Sly out of his chair, and as they bore him to the door, the curtain descended slowly upon the picture. Not a word was uttered, and the termination, which Schlegel supposes to have been lost, was *indicated* by the simple movement of the *dramatis personæ*, without any attempt to *continue* the subject.

The revival was eminently successful, incontestably proving that a good play, well acted, will carry the audience along with it, unassisted by scenery; and in this case also, remember, it was a comedy in *five* acts, without the curtain once falling during its performance.

No such Katherine as Mrs. Nisbett had been seen since Mrs. Charles Kemble had acted it in the pride of her youth and beauty. Strickland justified all my expectations. As powerful and unctuous as Munden, without the exaggeration of which that glorious old comedian was occasionally guilty. Buckstone was perfectly at home in Grumio, and Webster, although the part was not in his line, acted Petruchio like an artist, as he acts everything.

Of the "Induction," which had been for so many years neglected, that intelligent critic, Charles Knight, says: "We scarcely know how to speak without appearing hyperbolical in our praise. It is to us one of the most precious gems in Shakespere's casket. If we apply ourselves to compare it carefully with the earlier Induction upon which Shakespere formed it, and with the best of the dramatic poetry of his contemporaries, we shall in some degree obtain a conception not only of the qualities in which he equalled and excelled the highest things of other men, and in which he could be measured with them, but of those wonderful endowments in which he differed from all other men, and to which no standard of comparison can be applied." My restoration of this "gem" is one of the events in my theatrical career on which I look back with the greatest pride and gratification.

While this revival was in preparation, I received a letter from Mr. Webster, who was fulfilling a provincial engagement, in which he requested me to obtain from Mrs. Nisbett a list of the plays and farces she might be advertised for. I print her characteristic reply to my requisition :—

"SATURDAY.

"MY DEAR MR. PLANCHÉ—

"Strange as it may apppear, I have no favourite character, and have not for such a length of time acted in farces, that I have no list to name. All the *old comedies*, with *suitable parts*, I am *ready* in, or should be with a little notice: therefore you and Mr. Webster had better select, and let me know as soon as you can. If, upon further reflection, I think of any more, I will write again.

"Wives as they were, Maids as they are."
"A Match in the Dark."
"The Wedding Day."

"But you and Mr. Webster are the most able to decide on any pieces you think best, with a part in my line. I have but to obey, but I *shan't*, unless I like, notwithstanding *Katherine's sermon*.

"Believe me,
"My dear Mr. Planché,
"Ever sincerely yours,
"L. C. NISBETT."

"The Grange,
North End."

We were sitting in the Green Room one evening during the performance, chatting and laughing, she having a book in her hand which she had to take on the stage with her in the next scene, when Brindal, a useful member of the company, but not particularly remarkable for wit or humour, came to the door, and, leaning against it, in a sentimental manner, drawled out,—

> "If to her share some female errors fall,
> Look in her face——"

He paused. She raised her beautiful eyes to him, and consciously smiled—*her* smile—in anticipation of the well-known complimentary termination of the couplet, when, with a deep sigh, he gravely added—

> "——And you *believe* them all!"

The rapid change of that radiant countenance—first to blank surprise and then to fury, as, suiting the action to the look, she hurled the volume in her hand at the culprit's head—was one of the most amusing sights imaginable. Concentrating the verbal expression of her indignation in the word, "Wretch!" she burst into one of her glorious laughs, too infectious to be resisted even by the contrite offender, who certainly was never, to my knowledge, guilty of anything so good either before or after.

This season, which was the last of my engagement with Mr. Webster, also witnessed the *début* on those boards of Miss Reynolds, whose abilities as a vocalist, as well as an actress, contributed mainly to the great success of my fairy extravaganza, the "Invisible Prince," at Christmas, and of "The New Planet," another *Revue*, at Easter, which was received with considerable favour: the cast of the latter comprising, for the first time, Buckstone, in one of my pieces of this description, in addition to my constant supporters, James Bland, Miss P. Horton, and the pretty and popular Miss Julia Bennett.

Many other circumstances occurred during these last three or four years, which I shall have to record in my next chapter; but I thought it was better not to break the thread of my theatrical recollections in the middle of a particular epoch. The dissensions unfortunately occurring, almost constantly, between Mr. and Mrs. Charles Mathews and Mr. Webster rendered my official position in the Haymarket Theatre occasionally very uncomfortable; but I can safely assert I never suffered any feelings for my old friends to affect my loyalty to my employer, and I have the satisfaction of believing that, in spite of the industrious efforts of some of those mischief-making creatures, by whom a manager seems fated to be surrounded, Mr. Webster is thoroughly convinced of that fact.

CHAPTER VIII.

To revert then to the close of 1843. A movement took place at that period in the literary world, the consequences of which were of an importance not yet even to be fully estimated, but unfortunately disgraced by a quarrel exceeding in virulence and bitterness any recorded by Mr. Disraeli, senior—a gentleman whose acquaintance, I must not omit to say, I had the pleasure of making at the house of my valued friend Mr. Douce, and from whom I received many kind and encouraging encomiums. The lethargy into which the Society of Antiquaries had fallen, the dreariness of its meetings, the want of interest in the communications, and the reluctance of the council to listen to any suggestions for its improvement, induced three or four of the more actively-minded fellows to set on foot a project for forming an association such as existed in France, which, having correspondents in all parts of the country, should receive the earliest intelligence of any discoveries, and the opinions of local antiquaries, and once a year hold a congress in some principal city or other place distinguished for archæological interest. The original promoters of this scheme were Mr. Thomas Wright, who, as corresponding member of the French Society of Antiquaries, was conversant with the mode of proceeding on the continent, Mr. Charles Roach Smith, the enthusiastic Roman and Anglo-Saxon antiquary, and Dr. Bromet. Mr. T. J. Pettigrew, fellow of the Royal Society, and one of the most eminent students of Egyptian antiquities, Albert Way, Crofton Croker, and other gentlemen readily consented to share in their deliberations; and it was finally decided upon that they should commence an active canvass amongst their friends and acquaintances—ladies as well as gentlemen—and obtain the names of as many as possible, who, whether antiquaries or not, were willing to forward the object of the association.

As no subscription was demanded, and no liability was incurred, the adhesions multiplied exceedingly, and early in 1844 amounted to thousands. A committee was formed by the original projectors. A small fund was obtained from voluntary donations, to meet the expenses of advertising, circulars, &c., and Mr. Pettigrew undertook the unsalaried office of treasurer, Messrs. Way and Smith consented to be honorary secretaries, and Lord Albert Conyngham accepted the presidency of "The British Archæological Association," the title assumed by this new peripatetic and, as far as members went, *un*-limited company. I need hardly say that I was a hearty and active supporter of the movement. My constant attendance at the evening meetings of the Society of Antiquaries had cruelly dissipated the illusion I was under previous to my election. I felt humiliated by the conviction that the ridicule and contempt which had been so plentifully heaped upon professed antiquaries were not so undeserved as I had imagined. The owl-like solemnity of the scanty conclave ordinarily assembled on the appointed Thursdays at Somerset House, the ponderosity or triviality of the papers—an account of the prices of eggs and butter in the reign of Queen Elizabeth, copied by one of the clerks at the British Museum, or something equally unfitted for reading on such occasions—wearied and disgusted the few fellows and their friends who came perhaps miles, in hopes of "hearing something to their advantage," and it was with an obvious feeling of relief that at the close of the proceedings we hurried to the adjoining apartments of the Royal Society, where, by general invitation, we partook of tea and coffee, and enjoyed the conversation of many of the most distinguished of our scientific countrymen. There were great men, learned men, witty men, on the roll of the Society of Antiquaries. The members of the Royal Family were *de règle* fellows without ballot. I was present with Theodore Hook when H.R.H. the Prince Consort was admitted; but was it to be expected that they would attend such meetings, or take any interest in so *fainéant* a society. Was it surprising that men who, like myself, deeply felt the injury that these Drs. Dry-as-dust were doing to a branch of literature as interesting as it is important, should be eager to redeem it in the eyes of the world from the contempt into which it was daily falling, and endeavour to show the people of England the true value of critical archæology. This, however, was done in no hostile spirit to the parent society. Our committee proposed that they should be considered merely a peripatetic branch of it—corresponding members, not fellows—and that all the important papers contributed should, if approved by the council, be published in the society's own transactions. But the proposal was coolly declined, and the association started unshackled and independent.

Canterbury was fixed on as the city in which we should hold our first congress, and there we accordingly assembled in goodly numbers, September 9th, 1844. The prognostications of a ludicrous failure indulged in by some of the old twaddlers were not verified: a most agreeable and interesting week was passed by some two or three hundred ladies and gentlemen, and the congress was unanimously declared a success. This success, however, was unfortunately the cause in a great part of the deplorable dissensions which speedily divided the association. While it was dubious, no one cared to hold unpaid offices, or accept responsible positions; but the congress at Canterbury had altered matters amazingly. It was seen that the officers and leading men in such an association would be received with consideration by the nobility and gentry of the county in which the congress was held; that there were opportunities for nobodies to become somebodies, at least for a week; and duties which had been undertaken purely for the love of science became enviable when they were discovered to be passports into society, and tickets for turtle-soup. The commercial element also was stimulated into unwholesome activity. The admirable lectures of Professor Willis, the interesting researches of Mr. Stapleton, the investigations of Messrs. Wright and Roach Smith into the conditions of our Anglo-Saxon forefathers, were too valuable material for an enterprising publisher to permit to appear in a sort of amateur journal, and vanity, envy, and self-interest combined to create a commotion little imagined, I suspect, by the instigators, and which resulted in the "split" that took place in the following February, 1845.

It is not my intention to fan into fresh flames a controversy which has burnt itself nearly out, and ought never to have been kindled: a breath might do it, for

"Still in its ashes live its wonted fires,"

but it could not be altogether dismissed from my "Recollections." I would it could. Not that I regret the part I took in it. I remained in the ranks of the old association because I considered it then, as I do still, to have had right and justice on its side, and for that reason only. I should rejoice in seeing an amalgamation of the two societies; but perpaps for the interests of archæology we are better apart. One sad reminiscence of the quarrel is, the belief that it accelerated the death of the Rev. Thomas Harris Barham (Tom Ingoldsby), who, suffering seriously from bronchitis, travelled to town from Norfolk in the most inclement weather to give us the support of his vote and influence. He was one of our warmest friends. Expostulating with one of the chief fomenters of the discord, the latter, by way of excuse, said, "Oh, we of the —— always hang together!" "Ah!" retorted Barham, "that's only metaphorically—I should like to *see* two or three of you hanging separately."

At the general meeting regularly called by the treasurer, on the requisition of 160 members, the officers who had resigned were unanimously re-elected. Lord Albert Conyngham again accepted the presidency. A new committee was formed, and rules adopted for a more systematic conduct of the society, which it was resolved should be no longer subject to the personal interests or prejudices of irresponsible and non-subscribing members. That the general body should consist of associates, correspondents, and honorary foreign members. The associates, being approved of and elected by the council, to pay one guinea per annum, or ten guineas as a life subscription, for which they should be entitled to receive a copy of a quarterly journal to be published by the association, to attend all meetings, vote on the election of officers and council, and admit one visitor to each of the public evening meetings.

Thus regularly organized and constituted, we held our second congress, in 1845, at Winchester, as originally determined, and in the four following years at Gloucester, Warwick, Worcester, and Chester, under our noble and zealous president, whose intimate friendship I had the gratification of enjoying to the day of his lamented death.

To several of these pleasant and instructive gatherings I shall allude in due course. The sneers at them, in which some writers in the public journals occasionally indulge, do not detract from their enjoyment, or abate their utility, and are best answered by the published proceedings of the association, and those of the numerous and excellent provincial societies to which it has given birth, the spirit of critical inquiry it has evoked, and the interest in the preservation and illustration of our national antiquities which it has stimulated and disseminated.

I mentioned, in the fourth chapter of this volume (p. 42), a correspondence I had been led into respecting a drama sent into Covent Garden while I was reader there, the author of which described himself as a "Cadet at Woolwich." On the 8th of March, 1844, I received the following letter:—

"DEAR SIR,—

"Have you altogether forgotten a certain *Cadet of Woolwich*, who wrote a comedy which you once honoured with your praise? If so, perhaps the accompanying pamphlet may recall to you that passage in 'Auld Lang Syne.' I know that misfortunes are no great recommendations to the memories of our friends, but I will not believe that mine can have any effect in diminishing the kindness which I am sure you once entertained for me.

"If you should happen to have leisure and inclination to inform me that you have received the copy of this unhappy comedy, which I have directed to be forwarded to you, be so kind as to direct simply to 'The Author of Richelieu, care of Mr. Colburn,' for I am, by necessity, still anonymous, even to my publisher; but if I possessed a name as glorious in literature as my ambition dreamed once to make its shadow I should be proud to subscribe it, as you formerly permitted me, in the list of your friends.

"J. R. Planché, Esq."

I acknowledged the receipt of this letter and of the copy of the play, which the examiner had refused to license, as I had predicted, and hinted to the writer that I had some suspicions respecting the identity of my correspondent with any "Cadet at Woolwich," an intimation which produced the following reply:—

"21st March, 1844.

"My dear Sir,—

"I am singularly obliged by your acknowledgment of my poor Richelieu's arrival, in all senses, but even in a literal one! Your flattering distinction between my *genus* and "genius," to use *your* word, cannot but reconcile me to the fact that you know it exists; but tell it not in Gath, nor in Ashkelon! I am not anxious that any one who hears I am a *lady* in *private* should win a reputation for courage by abusing me as a *gentleman* in *public*. Not that the experiment would answer, for I am far more afraid of having too hot a champion than of wanting one. This is one of the reasons of my anonym. I, therefore, throw myself on your *chivalry* not to countenance such a statement.

"I believe I have all your letters still in 'high preservation,' but at a distance from me at present, and I do not care that any one should rummage among my papers: I believe your impressions are substantially correct, but I do not remember anything about a reconstruction of the plot. You wished, indeed, to compress it into two acts, which, I suppose, would have squeezed out a good deal; but I think that, on my objecting so, you assured me to the contrary. Our correspondence extended over some time, and, on returning the piece, you emphatically declared that it was not *declined*—that you had no power to decline an *actable* drama—for that epithet, then new to me, remains distinctly on my memory. For what reason, though *not* declined, the play was *not* accepted at Covent Garden, puzzles me *now*, doubtless because I cannot recollect the reasons assigned. I am *sure* that you never mentioned a word about the licenser to me, because, until the precise moment when he put his extinguisher on me, I had no idea that such a dignitary existed. As to the probability of the 'examiner' of that period (if it was *five* years ago?) crushing it, will you allow me to differ from you? Was not 'Charley' Kemble the licenser then? And would he who had been acting Shakespere all his life, whose daughter wrote Francis I., who took his farewell of the stage as Don Felix—a jovial and good-hearted man withal—have pretended to find any harm in such a piece as 'Richelieu?'

"Your question relating to the 'impossible' scene may be readily answered so as to acquit Mr. Webster of any intention to do an impossibility, which, indeed, would be rather difficult on the English stage. The piece was at *first* printed from a copy made at the theatre, in the vain hope of removing the Right Hon. objections, *everything* being omitted which could by *possibility* be construed into offence. Musing over this, it occurred to me that the licenser might pretend I had left out some of the grounds of his justification. I therefore directed the restoration of all that I imagined had been submitted to his magnifying glass. One or two of these additions are made in wrong places, in the confusion, but, as I did not see the piece till it was published, I had no opportunity of rectifying errors. But these two scenes 'walk upon each other' so singularly, from the omission of one which ought to have intervened, which perhaps you may remember in the original, 'at the Lys d'Or,' and which I intended should be inserted, but that part was printed from the wrong copy. I shall alter this and several other errors in a second edition, which is very likely to be called for. Among other matters, I have been made to commit the crime of *lèse-majesté* by leaving out the 'Mr.' to *Mr. Farren's* name, which looks, I think, too familiar in print, although, to be sure, one never says 'Mr. Garrick,' or 'Mr. Kean,' &c. Strange as it may appear, the chief point on which I troubled myself was, that *the licenser* should have no reason to complain. And, doubtless, if he thought he had, he would have favoured the public with his opinion, as he must have friends among the Tory writers, and no one who reads a newspaper can pretend to be ignorant that 'Richelieu' is published.

"You will forgive the vanity of an author if I assure you that I do not think my play would have experienced any fate from which I should thank the 'examiner' for a deliverance. When one considers what modern audiences receive with satisfaction—or, at least, endure—I own I should not have felt much terror in submitting my 'Richelieu' to their judgment. Since its publication, I have received such extraordinary and enthusiastic commendations from people who differ, in intellect, rank, and opinions, as much as any audience in the world, that, although I hesitate to differ from your experience, I cannot admit your doubt as a truism. What pleases me above all is, that *women*—women of the *highest talents* and *station*—are lavish in praise of my Queen, so she cannot be so *very unladylike!*

"As to Mr. Webster's opinion of the play, he proved it principally by the frank and cordial manner in which he behaved towards it. He is a generous man, and, as a French lady once told me, 'He *merits* to look like Napoleon!' I never knew he thought so very highly of it until two or three days ago, when, for the first time, I saw an article in the *Observer* of January 14th, which was sent to me to prove a point which I disputed, namely, that there was any authority to state that 'Richelieu' was written by the author of a novel which appeared some months ago. Neither did I know that Mr. Webster had alluded to it in his 'valedictory address,' last year, being in a part where I could not procure the London newspapers easily. But you are mistaken in thinking I could not have borne the condemnation of the *public* better than that of the 'examiner.' It is the galling slavery of having to submit to a despotism that makes my heart beat thickly at the remembrance. Are you a dramatic author, and do you not feel this?

"As to what I *ought* to do, 'far beyond Richelieu,' I am much indebted to your kind opinion; but how am I to do it? They have clipped my wings just as I spread them. I might as well be an oak in a desert, showering my acorns on the winds.

"You will think I have given you an abundance of 'I,' but I am really anxious to stand well in *your* opinion. A faithful and a sincere friend—a literary one, too—is indeed a treasure. It is impossible to displease me by telling the truth, so long as I discern—as in the present instance— that my adviser is animated by the desire to let me know it, and not simply to give me pain. I am wax to kindness, marble to severity—which, indeed, is most people's case.

"Remember you have brought this avalanche of a letter on yourself, but, at the same time, that it comes from one who is, my dear Sir,

"Faithfully and obligedly yours,

"THE AUTHOR of 'RICHELIEU.'

"J. R. Planche, Esq."

"P.S.—Pray do not imagine I have *delayed* answering you."

I had kept no copy of my letters, and could not, therefore, disprove the "lady's" (if she was a lady, for there is still some doubt of the fact) decided assertion. I only know that such was my conviction upon reading the play, and that I am still under the impression that I communicated it to the author. Whether or not could have been settled by a reference to my letters, which, it appears from the above, had been preserved; but I heard no more from my mysterious correspondent, whose motive for remaining unknown has never, to my knowledge, transpired. The refusal of the examiner to license the piece caused an excitement in literary and dramatic circles, and the author was said to be a mathematical instrument maker, a bookseller, and a bookseller's daughter, which latter might be the fact. Some thirty years have elapsed since the "Cadet at Woolwich" sent *Richelieu* to Covent Garden, and the mystification is at this time not worth unravelling. It is only as affecting the still vexed question of the censorship, and the power vested in the Lord Chamberlain, which has cropped up again recently in relation to the Christmas pantomimes, that the above circumstances appeared to me worth recording, because, as well as my recollection serves me, the case was a peculiar one. The piece was undoubtedly actable, in the theatrical sense of the word; that is, it was constructed with sufficient knowledge of the requirements of the modern stage. The succession of scenery and conduct of the incidents presenting no obstacle to its representation. I had therefore, as I stated, no power to decline it on that ground, which was the only one which would have justified my returning any drama to its author without consulting Madame Vestris.

In this case there was sufficient cleverness about the piece to make one regret there should be anything in the tone of it which would render its success problematical, and call in question, not only the judgment, but the good taste of the management. It was thought that the drama had scarcely strength enough in it for three acts in so large a theatre as Covent Garden, and that its compression into two might be effected by the excision of much that tended to jeopardise its favourable reception. It was therefore returned to the author with these suggestions, and not definitively rejected, and would probably have been accepted had the alterations been made. No doubt there would have been great difficulty in disinfecting the play of the objectionable atmosphere which pervaded it, and evidently impressed the examiner as unfavourably as it did me. It was not this or that sentence or expression, nor the impossible scene the author alludes to, whatever that may have been, for I have forgotten it, and have not the play to refer to. Anything so tangible could have been dealt with, and the licenser would have simply directed its omission. It was the general tone of the work which jarred upon the sense, as undefinable as the objection of the school-boy who did "not like Doctor Fell," although "The reason why, he could not tell," and possibly for the same reason the licenser did not favour the public with his opinions. And here, then, arises the question as to the limit of the discretionary power of the Lord Chamberlain. That it has been extended, whether legally or not, there can be no doubt. The office was first created for political purposes only. The play might be as licentious in its language, as immoral in its tendency, as profane almost in its ejaculations as the author had the bad taste to make it: provided always there was, as Puff says, "no treason against Queen Elizabeth," nothing subversive of "the peace of our Lord the King," or distasteful to the Government for the time being, no objection to its representation was made by the licenser; any other demerit was no affair of his. Such was, I believe, the practice up to the time of the decease of the first holder of the office I can remember, Mr. Larpent. His successor, my old friend George Colman, was certainly, either in pursuance of instructions or of his own mere motion, the inaugurator of a more rigid system of supervision, and became a "censor morum" in the general acceptation of the phrase, drawing on himself continual expostulations from managers and authors, animadversions in the public journals, and jests in abundance. The old story of his son, on observing the accidental obliteration of the last syllable in the word Schiedam on the label of a bottle of that liquor, which his father placed on the table, saying, "So you've been at your old work, I see, cutting out the *damns*," is no doubt familiar to many of my readers; and I have already alluded more than once to his scrupulous excision of any passage or expression which might be misconstrued by the audience, or offend the religious feelings of persons of any denomination; but Charles Kemble had succeeded him, as my correspondent truly observes, at the time I first perused the play, and his son John must have been in the actual exercise of the office, as his father's deputy, when the prohibition was issued, so that my misgivings could not have arisen from any consciousness of the personal feeling or prejudices of the examiner, but from my own sense of the effect the play was likely to produce on any competent judge entrusted with that delicate duty. The result was as I had predicted, and a fresh outcry arose against the Lord Chamberlain and his officer.* Since that period there have been other interferences with theatrical managements unconnected with literary delinquencies. Accidents and offences of one description or another, the neglect of proper precautions against fire, the indelicacy of the dresses of the ladies of the ballet, have given rise to regulations and remonstrances more or less attended to, but demonstrating that his lordship's authority extends at present to matters never imagined to be within his cognizance and jurisdiction. The correspondence last Christmas respecting certain personal allusions to members of the Cabinet, which had been prohibited by the present examiner, brought the whole subject again before the public, and opinions were strongly expressed respecting the necessity of some definite understanding being come to of the power entrusted to the Lord Chamberlain, and the question again raised of the propriety of

* The examiner's sanction was obtained several years afterwards, and the play was performed with a very strong cast, at the Haymarket, in 1852, but made no favourable impression.

its entire abolition. It is a very important question, and should not be hastily decided; but decided it must be at no very distant date, for the present state of affairs is unsatisfactory to all parties, and no law is good and worthy of preservation the open violation or ingenious evasion of which is, for any reason, constantly permitted to pass unpunished, or frequently feigned to be unobserved.

The best interests of the drama are so vitally affected by this question—so much property is involved, and so many persons concerned in its settlement, that I trust I shall be pardoned for dwelling upon the inconsistencies of the present system, and pointing out the difficulties which attend its reformation.

It was the anomalous and ridiculous character of the regulations respecting theatres during the early portion of this century, and which I have already incidentally alluded to, that compelled the consideration of them by a committee of the House of Commons, destroyed the monopoly of the patent theatres, and "annihilated space and time," as concerned in the seasons of the Haymarket, Lyceum, and the minors generally. The history of the Strand Theatre abounds with the most ludicrous instances of defiance and evasion of the power of the Lord Chamberlain, who, being at last exasperated by the contempt into which his authority was brought, in 1835, forcibly closed the doors, caused the actors to be summoned and fined at Bow Street, and suddenly deprived eighty-six families of their means of subsistence.* And what was the consequence? So great was the feeling excited by this perfectly legal, however severe, act—defensible also on the ground of a long series of provocations of the most audacious and galling description—that the very next year his lordship was constrained to sanction the re-opening of the theatre, and, in 1841, the invidious distinctions were, by act of Parliament, abolished altogether. The whole of the metropolitan theatres being, by the new act, placed under the control of the Lord Chamberlain, but without any restriction as regarded the character of the performances or the duration ot the season, the necessity of obtaining his lordship's license for the performance of a new drama was extended accordingly. It was no longer requisite, in order to avoid prosecution, for a piano to be kept tinkling in the orchestra throughout the representation of a tragedy or comedy, nor compulsory that there should be at least five pieces of vocal music in each act of a drama produced at the Lyceum; but of every new

* Vide an excellent article in the *Era* Almanack for the present year. Amongst the expedients resorted to, one of the most amusing was the entrance-money being taken at a *window*, because it was declared "illegal to take money at the *doors*."

piece a manuscript was to be forwarded to the examiner of plays, and his directions as regarded any omissions or alterations implicitly complied with. Any additional songs or matter subsequently introduced were to undergo the same inspection, and were liable to a proportionate fee. Now, what has been the result of the new regulations? A copy of the new piece is duly sent to the licenser, and not performed till the official permission is received. But are the alterations and additions, however important, ever submitted to him? Are his directions as to the omissions which are to be made invariably attended to? Does he ever ascertain personally or by deputy that his request has not been complied with, or that some new matter which he would have objected to, has been introduced? And if he do ascertain, are any steps taken to compel the manager's obedience to the official mandate? It is notorious that such is not the case. I could give a volume of personal evidence to the contrary. Then what is the use of the law? What is the value of the regulation to the morality of the drama, or the preservation of the peace of our sovereign lady the Queen? Any profane expression or indecent situation, any coarse allusion or personal insult to those in authority over us, may be, and *has been*, foisted into a burlesque or a pantomime after its performance has been sanctioned by the licenser; and, in the recent instance of the Christmas harlequinades, it is well known that the examiner's directions to omit the common-place jokes upon certain members of the Cabinet, while they gave rise to considerable acrimonious correspondence in the daily journals, and some mild expostulations from the honourable and amiable gentleman who is the present occupant of that responsible and invidious office the examinership of plays, were never paid the slightest attention to, but continued to be uttered and to excite the roars and plaudits of the galleries to the last night of representation. Is such a state of things creditable to our legislation in the 19th century? There can be no escape from the horns of the dilemma; either the regulations are just and reasonable, and compliance with them should be strictly and invariably enforced, or they should be rescinded, either as no longer necessary, or incapable of being carried into effect. The latter opinion has been very strongly expressed by correspondents and in editorial articles, with reference to the last conflict between the managers and the official authorities; and the arguments in support of it were powerfully and eloquently urged, but, unfortunately, the most important, in my humble opinion, is founded on assumption, which I regret most deeply to contend is not founded on fact.

We are assured that the censorship of the drama is unnecessary, because the good taste and good feeling of the public is a sufficient guarantee for the preservation of decency and decorum on the stage, and that the preservation of the peace in the body of the theatre may be safely left to the police. I should be extremely happy if my experience enabled me to endorse this assertion. Is it not too lamentably notorious that in this immense metropolis an audience can be attracted by the lowest, most degrading, and indecent exhibition that the bad taste or cupidity of the *showman*, I will not honour him so much as to call him manager, may induce him to offer to the public. Admitted that in the most respectable theatres that gross profanity or obscenity would immediately arouse the indignation of the majority of the audience, is nothing *contra bonos mores* to be heard or seen at any of our dramatic establishments, even under the present lax and capricious surveillance? How long is it ago that a late admirable low comedian, at one of the most popular theatres in London, degraded his art and himself by the constant introduction of what is called *gag* of the most disgusting description in the sufficiently broad farces that were written expressly for him, but whose authors would have indignantly disclaimed their complicity in such violations of common decency, which were nevertheless roared at and applauded to the echo, night after night, by the majority of the audiences. The examiner of plays, had he been accused of negligence, would have answered that nothing of the sort was even insinuated in the copy of the piece forwarded for his inspection. But of what service is the supervision of the Lord Chamberlain if such an insult can be nightly offered to the decent portion of the visitors with impunity for the greater part of the season? I could multiply instances of such conduct were it necessary, but one so notorious as that to which I allude is sufficient to prove the utter inefficiency of the existing system, and, at the same time, shadow forth what might be the consequences were all control abolished, and the vulgar and the vicious unblushingly invited to revel in any abomination that could be presented to them which would not subject the purveyors of it to an indictment?

It is idle to talk of relying upon the good sense and good taste of a general audience for the repression ot indecency, even of the coarsest description, and, as it is more usually presented in a form calculated to attract the sensualist, and be tolerated, if not enjoyed, by the ordinary play-goer, the standard of morality is gradually and imperceptibly lowered, and the respectable and intellectual members of society do not take the trouble to abate the nuisance, but cease to visit the theatre. This is the case even at present to a more considerable extent than is generally imagined. What it would be were all surveillance abandoned I fear to think. But, leaving the question of morality, what might be expected from the expression of political feeling, if personal attacks upon members of the Government, or strictures upon their measures, were allowed to be made on the stage? In that case, there would be no feeling of propriety, no sense of shame to appeal to. The passions of men would be aroused, the applause of one party would be answered by the groans and hisses of the other, and the theatre become a bear garden. The nightly uproar at the Alhambra when the orchestra played alternately "The Marseillaise" and the "Wacht am Rhein" has scarcely ceased to ring in our ears, and, in lieu of being suppressed by any feeling for order in the public, it was encouraged by them, and the receipts of the establishment were largely augmented by this unseemly conflict between the hostile nationalities.

What, then, is to be done? Are the present imperfect, inoperative, and vexatious regulations—vexations, because while they are obeyed by some managers they are laughed to scorn by others, who know very well that the authorities consider it more discreet to wink at the violation than provoke the anger of the public, and the sarcasms of the press—are these regulations to remain a constant source of controversy and irritation, or is the desperate remedy to be resorted to of utterly effacing them from the books of the Lord Chamberlain's office, and pensioning off the Examiner of Plays?

At present there is a law that *can* be enforced in extreme cases. The objections to it are obvious enough; but, if it cannot be rendered more efficient and consistent, it may be better for us to "bear the ills we have than fly to others that we know not of." The results of our former attempts to improve the condition of our national drama by increased freedom of action have not been so satisfactory as to encourage a repetition of the experiment.

CHAPTER IX.

In connection with the Society of Antiquaries were, and still are, two convivial associations, "The Cock'd Hat Club" and "The Noviomagians," composed strictly of members who had previously obtained the privilege of appending to their names or other titles the letters F.S.A. The Noviomagians, or, as it was more particularly designated, "The Society of Noviomagus Redivivus," was not merely convivial, like the "Beef Steak" clubs of the Lyceum and Drury Lane, "The Eccentrics," "The Stupids," and several others then in existence. Momus was a divinity who divided the honours with Bacchus, and Fun the order of the night at all the Wednesday dinners of the society, held at Wood's Tavern, Portugal Street, Lincoln's Inn Fields. The minutes of the meetings were also printed "for the society only," as was expressly stated on the wrapper, with the additional notice, "No hawkers need apply." Upon particular evenings the officers of the society, consisting of a president (Crofton Croker), a vice-president, a treasurer, and a secretary, a lord chancellor, a high admiral, a father confessor, a physician, and a Chinese professor, received orders to attend in full costume, and the table certainly presented a most extraordinary sight to the visitor who for the first time had been honoured by an invitation. Croker generally made his appearance in the full-feathered and elaborately beaded costume of a North-American Indian chief, mocassins and all, the lord chancellor in gown and wig, and the rest in every imaginable and incongruous attire, conspicuous amongst which, in those days, were "the garb of old Gaul," and the *pink* and top-boots of the hunting field. The secretary took notes of all the jokes or pranks of the evening, and at the next meeting printed copies of these minutes, drawn up with much humour, were distributed amongst the members, and were the source of great amusement. Of this club I was elected a member shortly after my becoming a Fellow of the Society of Antiquaries, and at the commencement of "the session" 1844-5, I received one day a mysterious parcel, which, on opening, I found to contain an immense raw potato, imbedded in which was a large, old-fashioned, plated shoe-buckle, which had grown naturally around it, and accompanying it was a letter from the secretary, my old (then young) friend George Godwin, gravely informing me that he had been requested by the president at their recent meeting, which I had not attended, to submit this curious relic to me for examination, hoping that I would favour the society with my opinion respecting the date of the buckle. My reply, as follows, was read at the next meeting, 15th January, 1845:—

"MICHAEL'S GROVE LODGE, BROMPTON,
"*December 30th*, 1844.

"MY DEAR SIR,—

"I return you the very curious relic presented from Mr. Lawrence, of the Post Office, to the society at its first ordinary meeting for the present session, Wednesday, November 20th, 1844, and beg you will express to my brother Noviomagians how highly I estimate the honour they have done me in referring the subject to my consideration. In the absence of any precise information as to the locality in which the vegetable envelope, with its metallic enclosure, was *posted* at the time of its discovery, I can only, of course, speculate upon probabilities; and the first I shall, with all humility, submit to the society is, that the union was originally formed in Ireland, a country as notorious for combinations of the most extraordinary and *radical* description as it is pre-eminent for the culture and consumption of the Solanum Tuberosum. It is a singular coincidence that shoe-buckles and potatoes were cotemporaneously introduced into this kingdom, viz., towards the close of the 16th century. At least it is about that period we first read of the shoe-buckle, properly so called—Kemp, in his 'Nine Days' Wonder,' describing the host at Rockland, 'with his black shoes shining, and made straight with copper buckles of the best.' And potatoes are recorded to have been first imported from

America by Sir Walter Raleigh, in 1586, and first planted in Ireland at Youghal, in 1588.

"The coincidence becomes still stronger as we advance, and find, firstly, that buckles did not gain ground in British costume till about the year 1680, and that potatoes were still struggling for naturalisation at the same period, being only once mentioned in an Irish MS. on agricultural matters in 1676; and, secondly, that the wearing of shoe-buckles became general in the reign of Queen Anne, and the cultivation of potatoes in all parts of the British empire established before the termination of that of her immediate successor, George I.

"Having thus dismissed the historical portion of the subject, I will venture a few remarks upon the relics themselves, and, in the first place, beg most respectfully to differ in opinion with the learned Seneschal, who, in the "Momentous Minutes," is stated to have asserted that 'the buckle had a tongue of its own;' unless 'the noble' and erudite gentleman was speaking in the past tense, and meant it 'had had,' for decidedly there is a *lapsus linguæ* in the present specimen. In the words of Shakespere, I may say, 'Give it an understanding but no tongue;' and the understanding I give to it is, that the buckle belonged to James II., and was lost in the land of potatoes, at the time he so completely 'put his foot in it.'

"I am aware that this opinion may be combatted by many of the society, and that some visionary antiquaries may consider I have degraded the relic by assigning to it so recent a date. It would have been easy for me to have suggested, from the large size of the buckle, that it had fastened one of the brogues of

> 'That monstrous giant Fin Mac Hauyle,
> Whose carcass, buried in the meadows,
> Took up nine acres of potatoes,'

which would allow of one potato to each buckle at least; but my respect for truth will not permit me to give the reins to my imagination.

"As an old, but unworthy, Noviomagian, however, I request, before I close this letter, to call the attention of the society to two or three remarkable circumstances more or less connected with the subject under discussion. I cannot dismiss an impression that 'more is meant than meets the eye' (I do not allude to an eye in the potato) in this combination at the present juncture. I am not thinking of the repeal of the Union, nor how far the potato, having a *peel* of its own, might be independent of the buckle, or the buckle, having lost its *tongue*, make a point of remaining attached to the *pratie*: nor am I led by the latter peculiarity to do more than allude to the well-known Irish repast called 'potato and point;' but I cannot help thinking that the society ought to embrace the opportunity so singularly afforded to it, and make a point, in fact, of adding to the decoration and distinction of its members by founding the order of 'The Potato and Buckle.' The reasons for such a step are so many, and so obvious, that I feel I ought almost to apologise to the society for naming one of them! I surely need not recall to their recollection that their president is named Croker, and that potatoes were called '*crokers*' as early as 1640, from their having been first planted in Croker's field, at Youghal! Is it necessary to remind them that Edward III. gave his garter and *buckle* as a badge of union to the knights companions of the most noble order of which he was the founder? And can anything be more affectingly symbolical of the attachment of our president to the society than the lusus naturæ in question, in which the potato has evidently grown round the buckle, and wears it 'in it's heart's core, aye, in its heart of hearts,' as Hamlet did Horatio?

"That such a curiosity should have been discovered at such a moment is, I expect, pregnant with matter for the most serious consideration of the society. This buckle, like murder, 'though it hath no tongue,' appears to me 'to speak with most miraculous organ;' I shall therefore conclude with simply suggesting that, to complete the allusive character of the badge or order, its foundation should take place on the anniversary (if the date can be ascertained) of the evening previous to the elongation of Mr. Lawrence (the namesake of the presenter of the curiosity, vulgariter, 'the night before Lary was stretched.'

"I have the honour to be,

"My dear Sir,

"Your most obedient Servant,

"J. R. Planché."

"George Godwin, Esq., F.R.S., F.S.A.,
"Secretary to the Society of Naviomagians,
"&c., &c., &c."

The society, of which I ceased to be a member when I quitted the Antiquaries in 1852, still flourishes, and I had the pleasure of dining with it as a visitor some few months ago; but alas, how many of the dear old fellows who used to "set the table in a roar" have preceded me on the way "to dusty death!"

On the 6th of June, 1845, Her Majesty gave her second *bal costumé*, distinguished from the first as the *bal poudré*, the dresses being of the reign of George II., when hair-powder was in highest estimation. As nearly all our nobility and gentry possessed family portraits of the period, and some even had preserved the actual clothes worn by their great grandfathers or grandmothers, the number of applicants to me for advice or information was considerably reduced on this occasion. I was, nevertheless, sufficiently occupied during the few weeks previous to the event, as there were many questions of minute details respecting official and professional costume which could not be decided on simply pictorial authority.

Here are two letters, from my dear old friend Charles Mayne Young:—

"Dear Planché,—

"Here I come with one more application to all the 10,000 you have already respecting Her Majesty's ball in costume on ye 6th of June.

"I want a captain of the yeomen of the guards' dress in the years 1740 to 1760—I suppose there was no change between the periods—also a lady of the court.

"Now, will you help me? If you will, I shall thank you; if you won't, I cannot reproach you, for I fear, on such occasions, you must be annoyed to death with applications.

"Yours very truly,
"(In either case)
"C. M. Young."

"P.S.—If you say *aye*,
"When, how, and where shall we meet?

"121, Great Portland Street, Oxford Street,
"19th May, 1845."

"MY DEAR PLANCHÉ,—

"If I could help you through your troubles, most willingly would I do so. As it is, I cannot help adding to them. Lord Anglesey (to whom I read your letter by way of answer to his inquiries) said, 'Would he allow me to send my daughters?' meaning to *rummage*, as you called it, amongst the prints you may have left in Michael's Grove. I said (thinking I knew your nature well enough to do so) I was sure you would show them what you had; so pray expect a carriage some day with the Ladies Paget, and do what you can, reserving your anger, if you feel any, till you meet me and break my head in the highways.

"I, too, shall come sneaking with the Earl of Beverley, I dare say, ere long.

"To all other inquirers I shall limit myself to reading your letter.

"I am, dear *brother Pug*,

"Yours, with a sick headache,

"C. M. YOUNG."

"121, Great Portland Street,
"13th May, 1845."

Some explanation may be necessary of the affectionately familiar epithet of "dear brother Pug. It is simply this. I had been exceedingly amused, I might say interested, by watching at the Zoological Gardens the attentions of an old monkey to a poor little sick young one. How related I had not ascertained. But describing the scenes I had witnessed one day in Young's company, he was so tickled with my imitation of the little invalid, that he immediately commenced one of the elder monkey, and whenever we met, in public or private, for many years afterwards kept up the joke. Upon one occasion I was talking to Sloman, the carpenter, on the stage at Covent Garden at the time Sheridan Knowles was reading one of his plays ("Old Maids," I think) in the Green-room, when Young entered the theatre, and, seeing me, commenced his usual antics, to which, of course, I immediately responded. Sloman, who was a valuable old servant of the establishment, and on very familiar terms with everyone in the theatre, rushed into the Green-room and announced that Mr. Young and Mr. Planché were "playing at monkeys" on the stage. In a moment the room was deserted, the whole of the company, Mr. and Mrs. Charles Mathews at their head, poured out of it to witness the exhibition, to the extreme and very natural annoyance of poor Knowles, whose reading was thus unceremoniously interrupted. Another day, as I was strolling westward through Coventry Street, Piccadilly, I became aware that a hackney coach was intentionally keeping pace with me and attracting the attention of passing strangers. On turning my head to see what was the cause, I observed what appeared to be the face of a large baboon, occupying nearly all the glass of the coach window, the eyes fixed on me with the most intensely serious expression. Startled for the moment, I speedily recognised Young, and laughingly nodded to him, but not a muscle of his features relaxed, and the face remained at the window, with the awful eyes bent upon me, as long as our course was in the same direction. His letters to me, consequently, about this period frequently concluded with some allusion to this absurd practice of ours, as in the following note, without date.

"DEAR PLANCHÉ,—

"Is there? that is, do YOU know of any picture or engraving of a cavalier in the reign of Charles II. wherein said person wore his *own* hair *short*, and not a wig?

"I anticipate that you *do not;* but I fear I must ask you to say *aye or no*, and either will answer.

"Your loving, constant brother,

"THE OLD MONKEY!"

To many persons this may appear very silly, and unworthy of a great tragedian; but the charm of Young's character was the boyish spirit with which he entered into or appreciated any fun or frolic, harmless in its nature, and which made him as great a favourite in the profession as his noble acting did with the public, and his polished manners and intellectual acquirements in the highest circles of society.

Here is another specimen of his humour. The circumstances which gave rise to it have escaped my memory:—

"JUNE 26, 1846.

"SIR,—

"You are a gentleman! Go to, that is the fact! I did not recipiate your well-indited missive until the shades of evening had lowered on yesterday. Ergo, response could not well have been in any copious degree more matutinal or expeditional. Had it been otherwise, the affairs of life would have stepped in, 'twixt my wishes and my capabilities, to fulfil the amicitial ceremonial which your high breeding propounded.

"I am, Sir,
"With high considerations, too numerous
"to illustrate,
"Your faithful servant,
"COQ DU VILLAGE."

This signature, as well as that on the card I have mentioned at p. 26 of this volume, alluding to a well-known theatrical anecdote—that of an actor who, personating Ratcliffe in Richard III., in reply to the king's question, "Who's there?" had to answer—

"My Lord, 'tis I. The early village cock
Hath twice done salutation to the morn;"

but making a full stop at the end of the first line instead of continuing the sentence, astounded the monarch and amused the audience by announcing himself as the early bird *in propria personâ*.

The phraseology of the epistle reminds me of an extraordinary character, well known in theatrical and musical circles at that period—Tomkinson, the pianoforte maker. He was a wealthy man, and a liberal purchaser of pictures, having some pretensions to rank as a *connoisseur*. Extremely diminutive in person, the pomposity of his manner, the grandiloquence of his conversation, and the extravagance of his similes, formed the most amusing contrast to it imaginable. He was one of the delights of Young's existence. He would listen with the profoundest gravity to one of the little man's orations, and, at the end of it, snatch him up in his arms and carry him, struggling and kicking, round the room in the ecstasy of his admiration. A few flowers of rhetoric culled from the speeches of this remarkable individual will convince the reader that the eloquence was of no ordinary description, if it do not raise a reasonable doubt of the veracity of my report of it. Having bought a painting by one of the old masters—I forget the painter and the subject—he asked Mr. Mathews (the elder), who was fond of pictures, to call and see it. Ushering him, with much solemnity, into the room it had been hung in, and undrawing a green curtain by which it was covered, he silently quitted the room, leaving his visitor to contemplate the picture for some minutes.

On rejoining him and receiving his congratulations on having made so desirable an acquisition to his collection, Tomkinson said, "Sir! since ever you were born,—so long as you shall live,—never shall you see—such a picture as this!"

Calling one day on the Countess of Essex, she happened, in the course of conversation, to mention, casually, that she had not seen the new bridge at Southwark. "What!" exclaimed Tomkinson, with a start, "you have not seen Southwark Bridge! It is a marvellous work! To give you an idea of its magnificent proportions, you shall take St. Paul's Cathedral, you shall place it on the river, it shall float through the centre arch of Southwark Bridge, it shall never touch it! You shall take the monument, you shall lay it at full length across the river, it shall float through the centre arch of Southwark Bridge, it shall never touch it!" The language is absurd enough; but the emphasis with which it was delivered, the serious expression of his features, the apparently perfect unconsciousness of any exaggeration in his similes, it is impossible for words to describe, or to convey a notion of the effect upon his auditors. I don't remember that I ever saw him smile. I am satisfied I never heard him laugh; but the difficulty to avoid laughing at him has sometimes caused me considerable inconvenience.

As I find in my collection but one more letter from Young, I will conclude with it here my recollections of this delightful artist and man.

"11TH DECEMBER, 1846.

"DEAR PLANCHÉ,—

"'It is night, and I am alone!' I forget the rest, so I'll begin afresh.

"Why will people persist in annually tormenting me to tell them what I do not know, and thus force me (*malgré moi*) to torment you? Briefly, what is a *Nivernois* hat? and what is a Kevenhuller hat? Is not the latter to be seen on the Duke of Cumberland's pate in Cavendish Square? As to the former I've no idea, and most likely the notion I've expressed is a wrong one.

"Do write a hat, breeches, and pantaloon dictionary, and illustrate it with cuts, there's a good fellow!

"Dear Planché,

"Yours considerably,

"C. M. YOUNG."

"121, Great Portland Street."

His desire that I should "write a hat, breeches, and pantaloon dictionary," was so fully in accordance with one I had for some time entertained, that I determined to commence the task as soon as I had an opportunity. Twelve years had elapsed since the publication of my "History of the British Costume," the advantages of which to artists I had received so many gratifying proofs of. A new and improved edition was in contemplation; but useful as it was to a certain extent, it was not a dictionary the utility of which, "illustrated with cuts," would, I felt satisfied, be considerably greater to painter or sculptor than the little hand-book they had so flatteringly welcomed the appearance of. I was too much occupied at the moment to begin so compendious and important a work as it should necessarily be; but subsequently I did commence and continue it at intervals, and, could I have found a publisher, should by this time have completed it.

In the autumn of 1846 I was visited with the heaviest affliction I ever knew. On the 22nd of September my beloved wife, who had been seized with paralysis, which partially affected the brain, in 1843, but who had wonderfully improved, and given us hopes of entire restoration, succumbed to the attack of another fatal disorder. This is a subject that I could not dwell upon were it even desirable I should do so, but I hope I may be pardoned for inserting here a tribute to her memory from one who knew her well for many years, and which I can vouch for as sincere in feeling as it is true in description. It is extracted from the *Literary Gazette* of Saturday, October 3, 1846, and was written by its editor, William Jerdan.

"BIOGRAPHY.

"Mrs. Planché.

"With sincere sorrow we record the death of this amiable and accomplished lady, the wife of Mr. Planché, the popular dramatist, which sad event, endured with calm resignation, took place on Tuesday, the 22nd ult., when she had just completed her fiftieth year. She was born August the 8th, 1796, and married April 26th, 1821. In September, 1839, whilst in delicate health, the death of a beloved brother gave a shock to her system from which she never perfectly recovered, having, after a brief rally, been seized in November 1840, with the afflicting illness under which she languished for nearly six years, the last three aggravated by paralysis, which deprived her of the use of her left arm, and partially affected her speech and memory. During this long period, and particularly the first three years, her sufferings were of the most acute description, and her life constantly in danger, but her courage and cheerful nature kept up not only herself but all her family in the most trying moment of her affliction.

"Shortly after the opening of the Olympic Theatre by Madame Vestris, as an amusement during some leisure hours, she wrote the little drama called "The Welsh Girl," the plot being taken from "La Nouvelle Champenoise," and its success induced her to make some other dramatic attempts, among which, "A Handsome Husband" and "A Pleasant Neighbour" at the Olympic, and "The Sledge Driver" and "The Ransom" at the Haymarket, were exceedingly fortunate, and are still popular both in London and the provinces. Gifted with beauty, grace, and intelligence in no common degree, her character may be summed up in the one homely but expressive word, GOODNESS. Self never seemed to enter her thoughts. She appeared to live but for the welfare and happiness of others; and through the last miserable months of her existence her despondency was clearly caused by the consciousness that she should no longer be of service to her fellow-creatures.

"Knowing intimately her worth during a quarter of a century, we mingle a satisfaction with our deep regrets in paying this tribute to her memory. The excellence of her heart, and the sweetness of her temper, endeared her to all who ever enjoyed the pleasure of her society, in which the playfulness of a child and the modesty of the intelligent woman were equally delightful. She has left two daughters, one, if not both, of whom have already given public evidence that they are inheritors of her virtues and literary tastes and accomplishments."

Amongst the numerous letters of condolence I received on this occasion was one from Leigh Hunt, from which I cannot refrain publishing the following most characteristic extract:—

"We shall all see one another in another state—that's the great comfort; and there too we shall understand one another (if ever mistaken), and love and desire nothing but the extreme of good and reason to everybody. Nothing could persuade me to the contrary, setting even everything else aside, were it only for the two considerations, that the Maker of Love must be good, and that in infinite space there is room for everything."

CHAPTER X.

With the season 1846–7 my engagement expired at the Haymarket, and Charles Mathews, having become the lessee of the Lyceum Theatre, offered me the position which I had previously held at Covent Garden, viz., "superintendent of the decorative departments," with the understanding that I was expected to write the Christmas and Easter pieces, and any other dramas which were required, could I find time for it. The theatre, thoroughly and tastefully redecorated by Mr. William Bradwell, opened for the season, October 18th, 1847, with "The Pride of the Market," a piece in three acts, which I had adapted from the French; and at Christmas that year was produced "The Golden Branch," in which Miss Kathleen Fitzwilliam made her first appearance, and was most favourably received.

Drury Lane was at the same time let to Mons. Jullien, who having made a name and money by the "Promenade Concerts," in the conducting of which he had succeeded Eliason, was ambitious of becoming the manager of an English Opera House on a scale in accordance with the increased taste for and knowledge of music. An offer was made to me of a similar position at Drury Lane to that which I held at the Lyceum, and Mr. and Mrs. Charles Mathews having kindly permitted me to accept it, I entered into an engagement with Jullien which Alfred Forrester, better known as Alfred Crowquill, who was his acting-manager, was sanguine enough to believe would endure almost, if not quite, as long as I should—a belief which, with his facile "crowquill," he illustrated in pen-and-ink sketches of me "when I was engaging," and when my engagement should be finished. *Vide* facsimile—not of *me*, but of his fancy pictures. Unfortunately neither the verbal nor the pictorial prediction was to be fulfilled, notwithstanding the splendid start given to the enterprise by the success of the opera "Lucia de Lammermoor," in an English version of which Madame Dorus Gras made her first appearance on our stage as the heroine, and that now most popular tenor, Mr. Sims Reeves, took the town by surprise, as the hero, and ever since has held it triumphantly "against all (native) comers." Unfortunately Mons. Jullien was bound to produce a new opera by Balfe before Christmas, or forfeit £200; and in the midst of the run of "Lucia," which was averaging £400 nightly, and would have carried us gloriously up to the holidays, it was put aside for "The Maid of Honour," and the consequences were fatal. They had been fully foreseen by all but Jullien. Forrester and I had entreated him to pay the forfeit, if Balfe insisted upon it, and not to take "Lucia" out of the bills while its attraction was undiminished. What were £200 to the treasury, into which was pouring something like £2,400 per week, against the risk of a failure which might entail ruin? But no; he would not be advised. He would not even appeal to Balfe, who, in the face of the facts, might have consented to waive or reduce the penalty, and permit the postponement of his opera until novelty was required. To save £200 he sacrificed his whole property. "The Maid of Honour" did fail, and ruin followed. The salaries could not be paid. Jullien abandoned the helm to Mr. Frederick Gye, who had been his successful partner for some seasons in the promenade concerts. "Linda de Chamouni" was hastily produced, without Dorus Gras, and with a new tenor, who made no impression; and no funds being forthcoming to meet the expenses, the theatre closed, and Jullien became a bankrupt.

In the meanwhile the Lyceum was going gaily on, and the success of "The Golden Branch" at Christmas was fully equal to the most fortunate of its predecessors.

The beautiful scenery by Mr. William Beverley, an artist new to the public, and whose talent soon placed him at the head of his profession—challenged and received its well-merited share of approbation.

"Theseus and Ariadne," at Easter 1848; "The King of the Peacocks," at the following Christmas; and "The Seven Champions," at Easter, 1849, were in their turn illustrated and embellished by the same masterly painter. On the 26th of December in the latter year I produced "The Island of Jewels;" and the novel and yet exceedingly simple falling of the leaves of a palm tree which discovered six fairies supporting a coronet of jewels, produced such an effect as I scarcely remember having witnessed on any similar occasion up to that period. But, alas! "this effect defective came by cause." Year after year Mr. Beverley's powers were tasked to outdo his former out-doings. The *last* scene became the *first* in the estimation of the management. The most complicated machinery, the most costly materials, were annually put into requisition, until their bacon was so buttered that it was impossible to save it. As to me, I was positively painted out. Nothing was considered *brilliant* but the last scene. Dutch metal was in the ascendant. It was no longer even painting; it was upholstery. Mrs. Charles Mathews herself informed me that she had paid between £60 and £70 for gold tissue for the dresses of the supernumeraries alone, who were discovered in attitudes in the last scene of "Once upon a time there were Two Kings." I never saw the piece on the stage. I have no doubt it was very magnificent, and the effect may have justified the expenditure. All I have to say is, it was not the precise tissue of absurdity on which I had calculated for effect, and that with it I had nothing to do, my official connection with the theatre having ceased some time previously. The epidemic, however, spread in all directions, and attacked several other establishments and forms of entertainment with extreme violence. Where harlequinades were indispensable at Christmas, the ingenious method was hit upon of dovetailing extravaganza and pantomime. Instead of the two or three simple scenes which previously formed the opening of the pantomime, a long burlesque, the characters in which have nothing to do with those in the harlequinade, occupies an hour—sometimes much more—of the evening, and terminates with one of those elaborate and gorgeous displays which have acquired the name of "transformation scenes," are made the great feature of the evening; and, consequently, after which the best part of the audience quit the theatre, and what is by courtesy called the the "comic business" is run through by the pantomimists in three or four ordinary street or chamber scenes. The usual number of curiously dressed people stream in and out of exhibitions or cross the stage; the usual number of policemen are bonneted; the steps are buttered; the red-hot poker is exhibited; the real live pig let out of the basket; and then, *à propos des bottes*, a portion of the transformation scene is suddenly discovered, sufficiently shorn of its beams to escape recognition by the two or three score of persons who have courageously sat out the performance, and are too much occupied in putting on their coats and shawls to think of anything but their beds or their suppers. The "transformation scene" is, however, declared every year to be unparalleled. That is the object of attraction, and all the rest is "inexplicable dumb show and noise."

How different were the Christmas pantomimes of my younger days! A pretty story—a nursery tale—dramatically told, in which "the course of true love never did run smooth," formed the opening; the characters being a cross-grained old father, with a pretty daughter who had two suitors—one a poor young fellow, whom she preferred, the other a wealthy fop, whose pretensions were of course favoured by the father. There was also a body-servant of some sort in the old man's establishment. At the moment when the young lady was about to be forcibly married to the fop she despised, or on the point of eloping with the youth of her choice, the good fairy made her appearance, and, changing the refractory pair into Harlequin and Columbine, the old curmudgeon into Pantaloon, and the body-servant into Clown; the two latter, in company with the rejected "lover," as he was called, commenced the pursuit of the happy pair, and the "comic business" consisted of a dozen or more cleverly constructed scenes, in which all the tricks and changes had a *meaning*, and were introduced as contrivances to favour the escape of Harlequin and Columbine, when too closely followed by their enemies. There was as regular a plot as might be found in a melodrama. An interest in the chace, which increased the admiration of the ingenuity and the enjoyment of the fun of the tricks by which the runaways escaped capture, till the inevitable "dark scene" came—a cavern or a forest in which they were overtaken, seized, and the magic wand which had so uniformly aided them snatched from the grasp of the despairing Harlequin, and flourished in triumph by the Clown. Again at the critical moment the protecting fairy appeared, and, exacting the consent of the father to the marriage of the devoted couple, transported the whole party to what was really a grand last scene, which everybody did wait for. There was some congruity, some dramatic construction, in such pantomimes; and then the acting! For it was acting, and first-rate acting. Bologna, the Harlequin, was an excellent melodramatic performer. Barnes, the Pantaloon, was unsurpassable in the representation of imbecility; and Grimaldi!—There is no describing the richness of his humour, the expression of his countenance, the variety of his resources, and his skill in their employment. Those alone who can, like me, remember him as Kasrack, the slave of the magician, in Pocock's "Aladdin," and "The Black Pirate," a melodrama of that name at Sadler's Wells (of which theatre he was sometime manager), can conceive the power of his acting parts of character and depicting the passions.

I am digressing sadly. I have been insensibly led into the above retrospections by the singular and unexpected effect the gradual introduction of spectacle into extravaganza had upon a totally distinct species of entertainment, and could not resist commenting on the result. Have we improved or deteriorated? Do the triumphs of the painter compensate the play-goer for the absence of such acting as I have alluded to? It is not for me to answer the question.

In February, 1847, I received a note from Mr. Henry

Greville, paying me the compliment of requesting me to allow my name to be placed on the committee for the getting up of an amateur performance at the St. James's Theatre, for the benefit of the distressed peasantry of Scotland and Ireland; the other members being Lord Duncannon, now Earl of Bessborough; the Hon. Frederick Byng; Mr. Monckton Milnes (now Lord Houghton); Mr. Fullerton (brother-in-law of Lord Granville); Mr. Henry and his brother Charles Greville. The play fixed on was "The Hunchback," Mrs. Butler (Fanny Kemble) sustaining her original part of Juliet, and Mr. Vandenhoff that of Master Walter. The afterpiece was my little comedy of "Faint Heart never won fair Lady." The Duchess by Lady Boothby; the young King by her sister, Miss Jane Mordaunt; Ruy Gomez by Captain Henry (now General Sir Henry) De Bathe; and the Marquis de Santa Cruz by a gentleman (the son of a high legal functionary) who had frequently distinguished himself in amateur theatricals. The affair came off on the 13th of April. Every seat in the house was occupied by a most brilliant audience—Her Majesty personally patronising the performance, and remaining till the final fall of the curtain. The play went off admirably. I was of course anxious that my little drama, which had been so successful in public, should upon so special an occasion, and in such a presence, justify its selection. It is not necessary to be an author, I presume, to imagine my feelings on being accosted by the gentleman whom I have not named, as he entered the theatre rather late to get dressed for the part, thus:—"My dear Planché, I am very drunk!" Alas! there was no doubting the truth of the statement, and there was no remedy for the evil. He could stand on his legs, and he would act. Had he even declined; it was too late to replace him, and there was nothing left but to "grin and endure it." The audience politely did the same; indeed, they did more than grin, they laughed heartily, not at the piece, but the actor, who was personally well known to so many of the spectators, and whose infirmity was notorious (as I found too late) to nearly all.* Of course he scarcely knew a word of his part, and continually interpolated it with the observation, meant to be an aside, "It's all up with the Minister," which was naturally placed to the account of the author, the hilarity of the audience by no means compensating him for the utter destruction of the character. It was impossible to have a better Duchess than Lady Boothby; and Sir Henry De Bathe was, and still is, one of the best of our amateur actors;

* The poor fellow died a few years afterwards, a victim to his sad propensity.

but Lady Boothby was not very well, and exceedingly nervous, and the most accomplished actors in the world cannot give effect to their own parts where one principally concerned with them in the dialogue is thoroughly oblivious of his share in it. However, the piece was got through *somehow:* the audience were too well bred to hiss, and the curtain at length descended, and put me out of my misery. There was a great supper after the play, given by the Countess Dowager of Essex, at her house in Belgrave Square, and amongst the company was Lord Morpeth, who had been in attendance on Her Majesty all the evening. On my expressing to him my extreme regret that such an exhibition should have taken place, and my hope that Her Majesty did not think me guilty of the absurdities and vulgarities with which my dialogue had been interlarded, he said, "Oh, you authors are so particular! The Queen was very much amused." It was very good natured of the Queen to be so; but I confess I should have been much more gratified if Her Majesty's amusement had been derived from my drama; and as to authors being so particular, I felt sorely tempted to ask his lordship, who was an author of some reputation, how he would have liked it himself.

In the latter part of the year I was upon another

committee, formed for the carrying out of a project interesting to the nation at large, and particularly to the theatrical portion of the public, viz., the conservation of Shakespere's house at Stratford-upon-Avon. Upon this occasion I received the following characteristic epistle from John Hamilton Reynolds :—

"NEWPORT, ISLE OF WIGHT,
"*30th August*, 1847.

"MY DEAR PLANCHÉ,

"I am deeply interested, as must be every Englishman, whether he has a breeches-pocket or not, about the securing the dear old Shakesperian houses, and a magic circle of land around them, to the English nation. It is much to be regretted that this property, which 'bears a charmed life,' should be exposed to the contemptible puffing of a Robins (which I take, by-the-way, to be the 'ill wind that blows nobody good'); for if an American dollar could aggravate the percentage on the auction, the Piazza passion would be satisfied at 'the goods being bought for exportation.' The contest will be severe, and a good reserve price will probably be started against the national bidder. Money must be had. Now to my object in writing you. Put my name down as one of the committee, if proper; and as a committee-man I will try what I can do under the shades of Carisbrooke Castle. I want the appearance of authority to ask one or two for their guineas. *In* Carisbrooke Castle, as you know, Charles used to pass much of his time over Shakespere; so that the 'spirit walks abroad' in the noble shades here still.

"Charles's copy of Shakespere is at Windsor Castle, with many autograph annotations of George III. in it! Let me have one line from you. Time, as you know, is the gentleman we are walking against.

"I hope the Garrick men are mustering well. To all who remember me, remember me.

"Ever yours truly,

"J. HAMILTON REYNOLDS.

"J. R. Planché, Esq."

In 1848 I lost my good friend and learned master, Sir Samuel Meyrick. He had been our President at the Gloucester Congress of the British Archæological Association in 1846, and had from the first remained a staunch adherent to and supporter of our society. He had many great and sterling qualities: the most estimable was his love of truth in all things, and it was to this excellent virtue we are indebted for the valuable information which he has bequeathed to us on a subject of which the world of art throughout Europe was utterly ignorant previous to the publication of his "Critical Inquiry into Ancient Arms and Armour." It is remarkable that, nowithstanding all the researches that have been made since the publication of those valuable volumes, and the unworthy attempts to discredit his authority, which have emanated from men who were indebted to him for the rudiments of their science, that the principal facts which he established have never been controverted, and that a few errors in the translation of mediæval Latin and

Anglo-Norman French, affecting some minute details are all that his ungrateful detractors have been enabled, in four-and-twenty years, to pick out of the mass of information he had so industriously collected and so systematically arranged. His precision was equalled by his punctuality. During his brief visits to London all his movements were regulated by the clock, and no persuasion could induce him to stay anywhere five minutes beyond the time he had prearranged to remain. The two volumes of engravings in outline by Skelton of the principal suits and weapons in his collection, from drawings made to a scale by himself, present an astounding instance of his exactitude and determination, and of the singular good fortune which enabled him to carry out his intentions to the minutest particular. The plates representing the Grand Armoury, the Hastilude Chamber, and the Oriental Armoury, were designed by him, and engraved long before the completion of the building, and yet when it was completed, and the entire magnificent collection of armour had been brought down from Cadogan Place, London, and arranged in the rooms that had been specially constructed for its reception, every article, to a single dagger or gauntlet, occupied the exact position in which it appeared in the engraving, just as though the drawing had been carefully made after they had been placed there, instead of some years previous to the erection of the walls they hung upon. Such an instance of a man living to see the fulfilment of a lifelong desire, without changing an iota of his original plan, either from reconsideration or the force of circumstances, is, I should think, scarcely to be paralleled. Of the collection itself I shall have to say much hereafter.

CHAPTER XI.

I HAVE nothing particular to record during the years 1850 and 1851 which would be interesting to any but private friends. At Easter in the former year, I made another attempt to vary the style of Extravaganza by producing an adaptation of Garrick's "Cymon and Iphigenia" in irregular verse, with the original music of Dr. Arne, introducing Charles Mathews as April, to act as the "Chorus" in the Golden Fleece, explaining and commenting on the various incidents in the piece, and at Christmas came "King Charming: or, the Blue Bird of Paradise," of which the last lines were as open to the objection that they were not burlesque as those of "the Birds" aforesaid.

> "Ruin may fall on all else Earth above,
> But indestructible are Truth and Love!"

And I do not regret that upon every occasion I endeavoured to "point a moral," though my abilities might not enable me to "adorn a tale."

L 2

In the May of that year I had the pleasure of making the personal acquaintance of Eugène Scribe, the most charming as well as the most prolific of French Dramatic authors. I was introduced to him at the Garrick Club, with this observation, "Encore un qui vous a pillé." I replied, "Impossible de faire même du nouveau sans piller Mons. Scribe." I met him afterwards at Benedict's and elsewhere during his brief visit to London, and found his society as delightful as his dramas.

In 1851, a third Bal Costumé was given by Her Majesty, the period being that of the reign of Charles 2nd, 1660—1680, and my services were again in pretty general request, uncertainty respecting the Scotch dress of that date giving rise to many inquiries. I do not find anything, however, in my correspondence sufficiently curious or amusing to justify quotation.

During the two following years I continued to write for the Lyceum, though not exclusively, and "Once upon a time there were two Kings," founded on Madame D'Aulnoy's story, "La Princesse Carpillon," produced December 26, 1853, was the last extravaganza of mine at that house, and terminated my long theatrical connection with the management of Madame Vestris. The following season witnessed her final retirement from the stage, and she died on the 8th of

August, 1856, since which period no one has ever appeared possessing that peculiar combination of personal attractions and professional ability which, for so many years, made her the most popular actress and manager of her day.

In December 1852—both my daughters having married and settled in the country—I left London and went to reside with my younger daughter* and her husband, the Rev. H. S. Mackarness (brother of the present Bishop of Oxford), at Dymchurch, near Hythe; but in March 1854 I received an intimation from Sir Charles George Young, at that time Garter King of Arms, that a vacancy having occurred in the Herald's College, the Duke of Norfolk had kindly remembered that I had, some years previously, expressed a desire to become an officer of arms, and if I still entertained that idea, he should be most happy to give me the appointment. In the course of a few weeks I became Rouge Croix Pursuivant, and necessarily once more a resident in London.

I had all along, however, continued writing for the

* Authoress of "A Trap to Catch a Sunbeam," and many other popular tales and novels. My eldest daughter married in 1851, Mr. William Curteis Whelan, of Heronden Hall, Tenterden, Kent, only son and heir of Mr. William Whelan, formerly of the firm of Child & Co., Temple Bar, bankers. I have at the present moment to deplore the loss of both my sons-in-law.

stage, contributing a *pièce de circonstance* for the opening of the Haymarket, under the management of Mr. Buckstone, 28th March, 1853, entitled "Mr. Buckstone's Ascent of Mount Parnassus," a sort of travesty of Albert Smith's famous entertainment, "The Ascent of Mont Blanc," then in the height of its popularity. *A lever de rideau* for a similar introduction of Mr. Alfred Wigan as the new lessee of the Olympic Theatre, 17th of October following, called "The Camp at the Olympic," and my last fairy extravaganza for Madame Vestris as above mentioned.

In the "Ascent of Mount Parnassus," which was a species of *revue*, I introduced a scene representing the room at the Egyptian Hall fitted up for Smith's entertainment aforesaid, and in which the popular entertainer himself was personated by Mr. Caulfield, of the Haymarket company. I had previously asked and received Smith's permission to take this liberty with him, which was most good naturedly accorded by that genial artist, with whom I had been long on terms of intimacy, and who felt assured that he had nothing to fear from any use I should make of his name or his property.

He entered indeed into the fun of the thing with such spirit that he determined to act the scene himself some night without apprising Buckstone of his intention. Accordingly one evening, having privately intimated his intention to Mrs. Fitzwilliam, his own performance terminating at ten, affording him just time enough to reach the Haymarket before the scene was discovered, and no change being required in his dress, on the cue being given, Smith appeared "in his habit as he lived," to the astonishment and mystification of Buckstone—who alone had been carefully kept in ignorance of the matter—and the immense amusement of the whole company assembled at the wings to witness the effect. Smith was immediately recognised by the audience, who received him with repeated cheers, and in obedience to a unanimous call, he made his bow to them at the end of the scene, addressing a few pleasant words to them in explanation, and retired amidst hearty laughter and applause both before and behind the curtain. On publishing the piece I dedicated it to Smith in the following terms:—

MY DEAR SMITH,

Accept the dedication of this dramatic trifle, the idea of which was suggested by your deservedly popular entertainment. I have taken great liberties with you, but "whom can a man take liberties with if not with a friend?" And let me hope that in so doing, I have not forfeited the claim (which I assure you I value), to subscribe myself *yours*,

Most sincerely,

J. R. PLANCHÉ.

In this piece, as in many others, I took the opportunity of promulgating opinions which might be serviceable to the best interests of the drama. In reply to an observation of Fortune (Mrs. Fitzwilliam), the Spirit of Drury Lane replied—

> "Because of every other hope bereft,
> The Drama is to Fortune's mercy left,
> So much is she your slave, that e'en the weather
> Can ruin all the Theatres together.
> The State no temple to the Drama gives,
> She keeps a shop, and on chance custom lives
> From hand to mouth. What cares she for disgrace,
> While Basinghall Street stares her in the face?
> Will any manager, who's not a ninny,
> To walk the stage, give Roscius one poor guinea,
> When he can double his receipts by dealing,
> With a man-fly who walks upon the ceiling!"

"These be truths," reader, and were uttered nineteen years ago. Still the Drama is without a temple, and the manager has the same unanswerable excuse for the exhibition of anything that will enable him to pay his salaries on the Saturday.

In the "Camp at the Olympic," I had the advantage for the first time of the assistance of that admirable actor the late Mr. Robson, who personated in it the Spirit of Burlesque, and most pointedly gave my opinion of his mission. In reply to the observation, "I thought your aim was but to make us laugh," he answered—

"Those who think so, but understand me half,
Did not my thrice renowned Thomas Thumb,
That mighty mite, make mouthing Fustian mum?
Is Tilburina's madness void of matter?
Did great Bombastes strike no nonsense flatter?
When in his words he has not one to the wise,
When his fool's bolt *spares* folly as it flies;
When in his chaff there's not a grain to seize on,
When in his rhyme there's not a ray of reason;
His slang, but slang—no point beyond the pun,
Burlesque may walk—for he will cease to run."

The rage for mere absurdity which my extravaganzas so unintentionally and unhappily gave rise to, has lasted longer than I had anticipated, but there are unmistakeable signs, I think, of its subsidence. As I remarked elsewhere, the writers of what is called "the fast school" are killing themselves. They cannot live the pace—they must pull up, or break down, and the wisest will yet win by a head."* Mr. Gilbert is at present leading. He has come out of the ruck in gallant style, and is the first favourite with all the true lovers of the Drama.

For two more years I furnished the Haymarket with *Revues* at Easter, producing "Mr. Buckstone's Voyage round the Globe in Leicester Square," in 1854, and the "Haymarket Spring Meeting," in 1855, and writing the Christmas pieces for the Olympic for 1854, 1855, and 1856, viz., "The Yellow

* "Temple Bar Magazine" for November, 1861.

Dwarf," "The Discreet Princess," and "Young and Handsome." In all these pieces I had once more to rely upon acting rather than upon scene-painting. Mr. Buckstone, Mr. William Farren, Mr. Chippendale, and Mrs. Fitzwilliam gave every point to my dialogue in the Haymarket, and Mr. Robson being my Deus ex Machinâ at the Olympic left me nothing to desire in his admirable impersonations of the Dwarf, Prince Richcraft, and Zephyr, in my three last fairy extravaganzas. Robson had already made his mark in the travesties of "Macbeth," and the "Merchant of Venice," under the management of Mr. Farren at the same theatre; but on the opening night to which I have referred, he made a powerful impression on the brilliant and critical audience assembled to support Mr. Wigan's undertaking, by his performance of Desmarets, in Mr. Tom Taylor's drama of "Plot and Passion," evincing talents of a higher order than he had previously had an opportunity of doing, and established himself in the front rank of the profession as an actor possessing the rare gifts of genius as well as natural humour and general histrionic ability. His premature decease was a serious loss to the stage, which can ill afford to lose a great and original artist.

I have carried on my theatrical recollections to Christmas 1856, because after that date a lapse of three years occurred in my connexion with the drama, during which I was occupied with the duties of my new office, and employed my pen in archæological and other literary labour. I had been by no means idle. Previous to my appointment I had written and published an elementary essay on Heraldry, entitled "The Pursuivant of Arms," little dreaming at that moment that I should shortly have a legal claim to that title, a second edition of which was issued after I had become an officer of arms, and I am proud to say, converted some of the strongest opponents to my theory, which they frankly admitted justified the second title of my book, "Heraldry founded on Fact." I also translated two volumes of fairy tales by Madame D'Aulnoy, Perrault, and others, which were for the first time given in their integrity, with biographical and historical notes and dissertations, besides numerous contributions to the "Journal of the British Archæological Society," and papers for its annual congresses.

At the one held at Newark, in 1852, the late Duke of Newcastle was our President, and sumptuously entertained us at Clumber, as did also Colonel Wildman, at Newstead Abbey—rich with the recollections of Lord Byron—and the Earl of Scarborough, at that time Lord Lieutenant of the county, whose acquaintance I had made several years previously in London, and who came over to me at Newark, personally to invite the Association to a farewell entertainment at Rufford Abbey, at the close of the meeting. In the following year at Rochester, our President was my old friend Mr. Ralph Bernal, one of the shrewdest antiquaries and connoisseurs in England, the thirty-two days' sale of whose superb collection of China, articles of *virtù*, armour, and antiquities of every description, was one of the great events of the London season of 1855. In 1856 our Congress was held at Bridgewater (President, the Earl of Perth and Melfort), upon which occasion we made an excursion to Wells, where my examination of the west front of the Cathedral convinced me that Mr. Cockerell, who had published an elaborate account of the wonderful series of statues that adorn it, had fallen into some grievous errors respecting the personages represented. It was with considerable diffidence that I ventured to express my dissent to the opinions of that most accomplished and amiable gentleman; but many of the facts I was enabled to state were so incontrovertible, that I could not remain silent, and I have every reason to believe that my observations on the subject, read at a subsequent meeting, and published in the journal of the Association, carried conviction with them even to the mind of Mr. Cockerell himself, who requested to be introduced to me, shook hands with me most warmly, and assured me he had read my paper with the greatest interest, and felt that it "served him right" for quitting classical for mediæval antiquities. His lamented death occurred shortly afterwards, depriving the profession of one of its most esteemed members, and me of the pleasure of cultivating his acquaintance.

I append the following note from the late Lord Auckland, Bishop of Bath and Wells and in whose company I had examined the statuary.

ATHENÆUM, PALL MALL, S.W.
May, 15.

MY DEAR SIR,

I have just arrived in London, and have found there two copies of your very interesting paper on the statuary of the west front of Wells Cathedral, for which I beg to thank you very sincerely. I think you have completely demolished Mr. Cockerell's theory.

I remain,
My dear Sir,
Yours very truly,
AUCKLAND, BATH AND WELLS.

J. R. Planché, Esq.

CHAPTER XII.

In 1855 I had the pleasure of receiving the following kind note from Charles Dickens:—

Tavistock House,
Sunday, 7th January, 1855.

Dear Planché,

My children have a little story-book play under paternal direction once a year on a birthday occasion. They are going to do "Fortunio" to-morrow night, with which I have taken some liberties for their purpose. If you should happen to be disengaged, we should be delighted to see you, and you would meet some old stagers whom you know very well. We all know you to be on such familiar terms with the fairies that the smallest actor in the company is not afraid of you.

I am obliged to appoint a quarter past 8 (I mean that for an eight) as the latest hour of arrival, because the theatre is almost as inconveniently constructed as an English real one, and nobody can by any human means be got into it after the play is begun.

Very faithfully yours,
Charles Dickens.

J. R. Planché, Esq.

I was fortunately not engaged, and enjoyed the evening exceedingly. The little actors did credit to the "paternal direction;" and Dickens's histrionic ability is almost as generally well known as his admirable contributions to English literature. He was as fond of fairy lore as I was, and it was a great bond of union between us. He was extremely delighted on hearing one day, when we dined together at the house of a mutual friend, that I was about to publish a complete collection of the Countess d'Aulnoy's stories, and on my sending him an early copy, with a portrait of the Countess for frontispiece, acknowledged its receipt in the following note:—

TAVISTOCK HOUSE,
Third May, 1855.

DEAR PLANCHÉ,—

I am delighted with the book, and will try to write some little article in "Household Words" that shall do no violence to it.

There is a remarkable individuality in that curious portrait, and it is of a most satisfactory nature. She looks like a woman who could tell her stories *vivâ voce*, as well as write them.

Many thanks,
Very faithfully yours,
CHARLES DICKENS.

J. R. Planché, Esq.

Some years previously, Alfred Forester, to whom I

had mentioned my desire to produce some such work, sent me the characteristic offer of his services, of which here is a fac-simile, and subsequently forwarded to me four very clever designs illustrative of "The Fair One with the Golden Locks," "The Invisible Prince," and "Princess Rosette," which I regret the arrangements made by my publisher, Mr. Routledge, with other artists, did not allow me to avail myself of.

The success of the first volume of "Fairy Tales," which was confined to those of Madame d'Aulnoy, had induced Mr. Routledge to propose to me, in 1857, to compile a second, which should include the old nursery tales, as they were called, of Perault and other writers of similar fictions. Perault's stories had been sadly mutilated by English translators and reduced to "nursery tales" indeed. "Les Contes de ma Mère l'Oie," their original title, had been adopted in England, and "Mother Goose's Fairy Tales" had been in general circulation during my childhood; but I now wanted to examine the first edition in its original language. I had already searched the public libraries in Paris—the great national one in the Rue Richelieu, which has so often changed its designation that one can only identify it by its locality; the Bibliothèque de l'Université, now, I believe, unfortunately destroyed, and others in France, without success. It seemed ridiculous for an "homme de lettres," a "savant," an "antiquaire," to present himself to the authorities of such establishments and inquire for a copy of "Mother Goose's Fairy Tales!" However, on explanation of my object every facility was afforded me: but in vain. The *first* edition was not to be found. In the summer of this year I was invited by my old friend and companion on my voyage down the Danube, to accompany him and a connexion of his in a tour in Germany and Switzerland. We proceeded viâ Brussels and Spa to Trèves, and thence down the Moselle to Coblentz, Frankfurt, and Munich. In the library there I found, not "Les Contes de ma Mère l'Oie," but some numbers of "Le Mercure Galant," which afforded me some curious information. From thence we went by rail to Lindau, a much more picturesque route than we had previously travelled "en voiture" in 1827, crossed the Lake of Constance to Romanshorn, slept a night or two "on the margin of Zurich's fair waters," and halted for a few days at Lucerne. From thence through the Valley of Sarnem, which I had seen very faithfully depicted ages previously in Burford's Panorama in Leicester Square, and over the pass of the Brunig to Brientz; thence to Interlacken Thun, and home by Berne, Basle, Strasburg, and Paris. It would have been a very pleasant tour but for the state of health of my poor friend, who, however, seemed the better for his trip, and was when in good spirits one of the most agreeable of companions imaginable.

On my return to London, being still on "a wild (Mother) goose chase," I asked Mr. Frederick Byng if he thought there was any chance of obtaining the information I required from the Duke d'Aumale, whose library I knew was particularly rich in early editions of French works. He kindly undertook to inquire for me, and the result was the following courteous letter from his Royal Highness, to whom I had sent a copy of my book through the same channel:—

"25 Mars, 1858.

"Le Duc d'Aumale présente ses compliments à Monsieur Planché ainsi que ses sincères remerciments pour son aimable envoi. Il se serait acquitté plus tot de ce soin s'il n'avait voulu auparavant prendre connaissance du joli volume qui lui a été adressé. Malgré son incompétence il croit pouvoir féliciter Mr. Planché sur la grace et l'exactitude de la tradition, ainsi que sur les très bonnes et substantielles notices qui sont à la fin du livre.

"Mr. Planché y rapporte avec raison qu'un des types supposés de la Barbe Bleue est le Maréchal de Raiz qui fut brulé à Nantes en 1440. C'est l'opinion la plus répandue, je doute qu'elle soit fondée. J'ai retrouvé dans mes archives une copie ancienne du procès de ce Maréchal, qui était, je regrette de le dire, un très grand Seigneur et un très brave soldat. Il fut jugé et condamné pour une quantité de crimes effroyables, mais entièrement différents de ceux de la Barbe Bleue."

I value extremely the encomium it pleased his Royal Highness to pass upon my work; in the first place, because it is the opinion of a most competent critic; and, in the second, because there can be no doubt of its sincerity, as he might politely have acknowledged the receipt of the book without entering into any comments on its merits. His Royal Highness's information respecting the Maréchal de Raiz is extremely interesting and very important, inasmuch that it contradicts on official authority a report which had been circulated for centuries, and quoted without suspicion by French antiquaries.

Shortly after my appointment to the office of Pursuivant, I was returning from dining with a friend in the City, about eleven o'clock one evening, and got into a Brompton omnibus which overtook me in Fleet Street. There was only one person in it, seated quite at the farther end, and whom I could not see distinctly enough to recognise. He knew me, however, although he had evidently been dining out also, and had done more justice to the hospitality of his entertainer than I had to that of mine. He was a good-natured old tradesman, with whom I had dealt for many years, and who had always taken a kindly interest in me and my family. Stretching himself along the seat of the omnibus, he said. "Ah, sir, I shall live now to see you ride before the Lord Mayor." I thanked him for what I knew he meant to be a civility arising from some foggy idea he had formed of my new office, little dreaming that such an event would ever come to pass; but my old friend was a true prophet: for, on the 29th of April, 1856, it was my honourable but rather embarrassing duty to ride up to the carriage of his Lordship (the present Sir David Salomons, M.P.), almost on the very spot the prediction had been uttered, viz., the corner of Chancery Lane and Fleet Street, and deliver to him her Majesty's warrant for the proclamation of peace with Russia, in the City of London, and afterwards to ride oefore him, in company with my brother officers, to the Royal Exchange, where the proclamation was read by York Herald, and the proceedings terminated. It would have been quite un-English if such a ceremony had passed off without a blunder of some sort; and a most ludicrous one took place on this occasion. On arriving at Temple Bar I found the gates at which I was to knock three times and demand entrance had never been closed, and the Life Guards rode right through into the City before I could stop them. I was, consequently, obliged to send a trooper to call them back, and get the stupid people whose business it was to shut the gates in my face, that I might knock at them and have them opened again by the City Marshal, with the usual formalities in obedience to my instructions.

And why are such absurdities only visible in England? Simply in consequence of the tyranny of routine, or, as Charles Dickens satirically described official procedure, "the way not to do it." The jealousy of departments, the absence of some one with general authority competent to arrange and direct the whole affair, whatever it may be. At present, under such circumstances, certain orders are issued from the Lord Chamberlain's office, others from the Horse Guards, and communications are made at the last moment to bodies or individuals concerned, in obedience to precedent, in the observance of the ceremonial. Similar instructions are issued by the civic authorities, and both east and west of Temple Bar they are no doubt duly and punctiliously obeyed. But where is the Stage Manager? For this is a spectacle, remember, the success of which depends upon effect and *ensemble*.

On the occasion of which I am speaking, I received a notice at nine o'clock at night that I was to be at the College of Arms in uniform at ten the next morning. Of course I was there punctually, and we proceeded in a body from the College to St. James's Palace, where the proclamation of peace was to be read first by Garter King of Arms. No one was there to receive us—no room assigned for our assembling. The guard was relieving, and we had to battle with the mob at the entrance to the Colour Court, and await in the street the moment for our departure. Orders had been issued for an escort of Life Guards, and for a certain number of horses for us to ride. The escort was in Pall Mall and the horses in Cleveland Row; but there was neither orderly officer nor any other individual appointed to convey the information to the persons concerned. After standing in the mud surrounded by roughs much longer than was pleasant, at the request of Sir Charles Young I undertook a voyage of discovery, and ascertained the whereabouts of the horses provided for us and the escort appointed for the procession, which eventually was formed, Heaven knows how, and after Garter had read the proclamation on foot in the dirt instead of from a window of the Palace or some elevated position, we started on our journey eastward. "According to precedent," the beadles of the parishes in the City of Westminster were to follow immediately the squadron of Life Guards that headed the procession. They had been duly summoned; but it had never occurred to the persons who issued the order that since the last occasion on which their attendance had been required the majority of these officials had ceased to wear any distinguishing costume, and the consequence was that while some half-dozen made their appearance in blue coats with scarlet capes and gold-laced cocked hats, all the rest seemed to have been recruited from the tag-rag and bob-tail that had assembled to stare at them. The police west of Temple Bar did their duty admirably; but in the City all was "confusion worse confounded." Before we reached the Mansion House the whole procession was broken up and engulphed in the mob. Even the Life Guards could scarcely keep together, and gladly trotted off to London Bridge on their way back through the Borough, leaving us to shift for ourselves as best we might. Somehow or another we all managed to get safe into the Mansion House, where we had been invited to lunch by the Lord Mayor, the only part of the ceremony which was creditably performed.

The Press, of course, the next morning, naturally and deservedly commented upon the "sorry sight;" and "Punch," in a humorous poem, lampooned us to his heart's content. But what cared the Government? That which should have been a grand and imposing solemnity had, from want of consideration — blind adherence to precedent—and the absence of a duly authorised director, become a disgraceful and ludicrous farce; but nobody was responsible. No political capital could be made of it by either party. Peace had been proclaimed "according to precedent," and that was all they had to do with it. Precedent is a valuable guide in some instances, and saves a great deal of trouble in all: but "tempora mutantur," and it is necessary to consider whether or not there have been any changes in the course of years that would render a strict adherence to it advisable. That all the ridicule and much of the inconvenience and annoyance experienced by nearly everyone concerned in that procession might have been avoided by the exercise of a little discretion and the cordial co-operation of the various departments there cannot be a shadow of doubt; but in England such matters are looked upon with indifference by the powers that be, and it is worth nobody's while to take any measures for their improvement. God send it may be many, many years ere England shall be again involved in war, and as there can be no proclamation of peace till such a calamity has ended, let us hope that by that time red tape will be rotten, and precedent only consulted to know what to avoid.

In 1857 I was requested by Mr. Waring, in the name of the Committee of Management of the Exhibition of Art Treasures at Manchester, to arrange the Meyrick Collection of Armour, which had been kindly lent by its owner, Colonel Augustus Meyrick, as well as the numerous specimens borrowed from the Tower, Her Majesty's private and public apartments at Windsor, and the contributions of many noblemen and gentlemen who had been applied to and had liberally responded to the call. It was clearly intimated that my services were expected to be rendered gratuitously, and I had no hesitation in declaring my willingness to undertake the business on these terms, as I was anxious to try the effect of a strictly chronological arrangement, which even Sir Samuel himself had never completely effected. There was an express stipulation in the agreement with Colonel Meyrick that his collection should be kept distinctly separate. I had two bays allotted to me, facing each other, and therefore arranged the Meyrick armour on one side the nave, and that from the Tower, Windsor Castle, and private contributors in the bay immediately opposite. One advantage resulted from this necessity: it gave me the opportunity of repeating my lesson, and consequently impressing it more perfectly on the minds of the visitors. It was the first attempt to make such collections instructive, by familiarising the eye to the gradual progression of form and ornament, and by showing what could be accomplished despite all the obstacles arising from restrictive pledges, conflicting interests, limited space, and disadvantageous position, would, I trusted, have some influence on public opinion, both at home and abroad, and induce those who had the power to exert it in improving the character of those national collections which, instead of merely gratifying idle curiosity, should be made to afford most valuable information, artistic, historical, and biographical.

I shall mention one circumstance connected with this business, because it was not only interesting to me, but is illustrative of the state of knowledge existing on such subjects previous to Sir Samuel Meyrick's inquiries, and of the culpable carelessness of persons entrusted with the care of our national art-treasures.

One of the complete suits of armour kindly lent for exhibition on this occasion was sent by Sir Henry Dymoke, the hereditary champion of England, and had been presented to one of his ancestors on the coronation of George I., as the customary fee of the champion. From the fact of its being profusely ornamented with the letter E. under a crown, as well as, it is probable, from the dark colour of the suit, it was assigned without hesitation to Edward the Black Prince, and had always been esteemed so by the family to the day it arrived in Manchester. I was sorry to dissipate the agreeable illusion; but of course could not avoid doing so. The form of the breastplate and other portions of the armour was sufficient at a glance to indicate its correct date—late Elizabethan; but to set the matter at rest, upon taking off the placate or extra breastplate, on account of the great weight of the suit (which even without it was fully as much as might be trusted upon the wooden horse provided for it), there appeared on the breastplate beneath it the date 1585 (28th of Queen Elizabeth), which gave a real, and not a fictitious, value to the armour, and completely silenced the almost indignant objections to my opinion. What increased to me the interest of this discovery was that in the Grand Armoury at Windsor I had found a champfront and the portion of a saddle, the steel-plating of which was ornamented with precisely the same pattern, and that in the Meyrick Collection was a steel plate described by him as one "which protected the off side of the bur of a war saddle in the time of Queen Elizabeth, and presumed to have belonged to an officer of her guard." "*It was sold,*" he continues, "*as old iron with other pieces from the Tower of London,*" and having been bought by a dealer, was purchased by him for his collection. The other parts of the saddle he conjectured had probably disappeared in the same manner. It was, therefore, with great gratification I discovered at Windsor "the other parts" of the saddle which in Sir Samuel's time were not to be found, and which, not being at the Tower, had fortunately escaped being "sold as old iron," in company with the gauntlet of Henry Prince of Wales, and Heaven knows what other valuable relics; and on examining the suit sent by Sir Henry Dymoke, the identity of the remarkable pattern satisfied me that armour, champfront, and saddle-plates had been made by one hand for the same personage, whoever he might be, in the year 1585, and that if an officer of the Queen's Guard, as Sir Samuel Meyrick, who was not aware of the existence of the suit, had imagined, he must have been a very great officer indeed. Having, by Colonel Meyrick's permission, restored the plate in his possession to its original situation, the three scattered properties were reunited, after having been separated at least for more than a century, if not since the time of Elizabeth. Alas! that they should have been again divided.

I pass over the pardonable error of assigning the suit to Edward the Black Prince at the time when it was given as a fee to the champion in 1714; but the fact that such was the belief, renders the act more reprehensible. The gift out of the national collection of any armour supposed actually to have belonged to so celebrated an English prince was utterly indefensible. With the knowledge that the champion would rightfully claim the suit he wore as his fee, it should never have been selected for him; and what are we to say to a finely engraved steel-plate—a work of art of the 16th century—being "sold as old iron" by the persons in charge of the Tower armories? I shall have so much to say on this subject anon, that I will not dwell longer upon it in this chapter.

But speaking of armour, I must not omit to mention a most curious collection of which I had a passing glimpse in the Autumn of this same year, 1857, returning from Baden-Baden, viâ Heidelberg. It is at the Castle of Erbach, in the Odenwald, the residence of the Count of Erbach, and comprises besides many hundred ancient firearms and some complete suits of armour of the 16th and 17th centuries, an immense number of early weapons and ornaments of the Stone and Bronze periods, and several Roman shields and standards, found by an ancestor of the Count in some Roman remains on one of the neighbouring mountains, together with the military chest and other relics which had been evidently bricked up for safety by the soldiers who had occupied the post and contemplated returning to it. The wood and leather of the shields had perished, but the bronze framework of the forms seen on the Trajan Column and other Roman monuments was perfect, with the central ornaments of thunderbolts, &c. The standards, a whole row, were mostly intact, with their eagles, small round plates and other insignia, as well as I can remember, for I had scarcely an hour to see anything in. It is a collection which should be visited by every student in this branch of archæology.

CHAPTER XIII.

On the 25th of January, 1858, I had the honour of being officially present at the marriage of H.R.H. the Princess Royal with the Crown Prince of Prussia (now Prince Imperial of Germany), in the Chapel Royal, St. James's Palace; and in the month of May following was selected by Sir Charles Young to accompany him to Lisbon as one of the mission appointed to invest his Majesty Dom Pedro V., King of Portugal, with the insignia of the Order of the Garter. On Tuesday, May 11th, the platform of the Paddington Terminus of the Great Western Railway was crowded with fashion and beauty to witness the departure of the lovely Princess Stephanie of Hohenlohe, the affianced bride of Dom Pedro, for the country of which she was the Queen Elect. The Queen of England and H.R.H. the Prince Consort were present to take leave of her, and about 10 A.M. we started by the same special train for Plymouth, our party consisting of the Marquis of Bath and Sir Charles Young (the two Plenipotentiaries), Lord Burghersh (now Earl of Westmoreland), General Sir Harry Wakelyn Smith, Bart., G.C.B. ("the Hero of Aliwal"); Captain G. S. Swinny, his aide-de-camp; Percy Anderson, Esq., of the Foreign Office, Secretary to the Special Mission; William Courthope, Esq., Somerset Herald, Secretary to Garter; and myself.

We reached Plymouth about sunset, and embarked immediately, the Queen of Portugal on board the Portuguese Royal yacht, which was awaiting her, and we on board the *Diadem* 32-gun frigate, commanded by Captain Moorsom, inventor of the shell bearing his name, one of the squadron ordered to escort her Majesty to the Tagus; the others being the *Renown*, 80 guns, Captain Forbes, bearing the flag of Admiral Sir Henry Chadds; and two frigates, the *Curaçao* and the *Racoon*.

As Lisbon is not so well known to the generality of English tourists as Berlin or Vienna, or the Tagus as the Rhine and the Danube, I shall not trespass, I trust, on the patience of my reader if my account of this voyage is not so brief as those of my journeys in Germany and Switzerland, more particularly as it is connected with a public event to which subsequent circumstances have attached more than ordinary interest.

We remained at anchor in the Sound on Tuesday night with steam up, and at four o'clock the next morning, the royal yacht got under weigh, and, followed by the squadron, stood straight across Channel, and sighted the Isle of Ushant before breakfast. It was a lovely sunrise—the sky without a cloud, and a light, favourable breeze scarcely rippling the waters; and a very pretty sight was the yacht, with the Royal Standard of Portugal, leading the way, and followed by the four English vessels, "keeping station" two and two at equal distances from each other; but this agreeable prospect was not long to last. The wind freshened in the evening, and the *Diadem* justified her reputation for rolling. On the 13th we were

"In the Bay of Biscay, O!"

Bad weather came on. The Portuguese yacht was a fast ship, and the Admiral signalled from the *Renown* that we were to go ahead and keep pace with her. A dense fog, however, gathered about us, and we lost sight of the yacht, as well as of the rest of the squadron.

After two more days rolling and pitching in the Bay and off Cape Finisterre, the wind went down and the weather cleared up, but no sign of any of our ships; so we made all sail for Lisbon, sighted the Rock on Sunday morning (16th), and entered the Tagus at 5 P.M., saluting and saluted by Fort Belem. Our party slept on board that night, and landed on Monday morning about ten o'clock, the *Diadem* firing a salute and manning yards as the Mission left the ship. Apartments had been taken for us at the Hotel Durand, in the Largo de Quintella, by our Minister, Mr. (now Sir Henry) Howard, who came and lunched with us; but no tidings had been heard of the Queen, nor of the rest of the squadron. In the afternoon, however, news arrived that, in consequence of the bad weather, the royal yacht had put into Corunna; so no wonder that we lost sight of her, and in the course of the evening she entered the Tagus followed by the *Renown* and the *Racoon*, and some hours later by the *Curaçao*.

The next day we witnessed from the windows of the hotel of the Minister of Finance, in the Praça da Commercio, commonly called Black Horse Square, the landing of the Queen. The King came with his father, the ex-King Ferdinand, from the Palace at Belem, in great state; the antique carriages being themselves a sight, resembling in some degree the great gilt state-coaches of Her Majesty and of the

Lord Mayor, but with dome-shaped roofs, covered with crimson velvet; some drawn by eight horses, others by as many mules: all of course richly caparisoned. The King alighted on the quay, and entered the royal barge, manned by forty rowers in white jackets and scarlet caps of Italian form, reminding one of the Bucentaure at Venice. In about half an hour he returned with the Queen, and then proceeded to the Church of St. Just, to which we followed them in company with all the foreign Ministers, including the Pope's Nuncio, to whom we had been severally presented by Mr. Howard. Capital places had been reserved for us in the church, and we saw the whole of the ceremony of the marriage of their Majesties, and the coronation of the Queen, which occupied the greater part of the day, dining afterwards with Mr. Howard at his residence, at Buenos Ayres, on the banks of the Tagus. It was impossible for an Englishman to see Lisbon under greater advantages than it was my good fortune to do on this occasion. I had heard as much of the filth as of the beauty of the city, and had received the agreeable information on board the *Diadem* that the black plague was raging there at that moment. I saw nothing, however, either of dirt or disease. Lisbon was in holiday-garb—I may say in court-dress. The principal streets were all laid with fine gravel, unsightly buildings, masked by extremely well-painted scenery, and decorated with shields of arms of all the Kings of Portugal, and of the principal cities. Triumphal arches rose in every direction, and the balconies of all the houses were hung with rich velvets, costly tapestries, or gay draperies, according to the rank or wealth of the inhabitants. Every night the whole city was illuminated, and, standing as it does, like Constantinople, on seven hills, and most of them extremely steep, the effect from every point was singularly beautiful, particularly where a view of the Tagus could be commanded, as the British squadron, the Portuguese frigate, and other vessels were also illuminated, and from time to time burned blue lights and threw up rockets, in imitation of the fireworks at Fort St. George. To descend to domestic particulars, our beds were as clean and as good as they could have been at the best hotel in Paris, and the dinners not much inferior. Oranges freshly gathered, with the green leaves on their stalks, were a most agreeable novelty; but the fruit in general had not the flavour of our own, nor was the meat or poultry to be compared to those of England, nor, indeed, any part of Europe I have visited. A sort of red-legged partridge is bred there like barn-door fowls, and eaten all the year round apparently. They have not the slightest taste of game, and are by no means as good as a spring chicken.

On Thursday, the 20th of May, we were all presented to the King and Queen at a special audience in the palace at Belem, and attended the general reception afterwards, and that day week was named by his Majesty for the investiture. This arrangement gave us time to "see the lions"—there are not many at Lisbon—but Cintra, with its Moorish palace and Cork convent, was a great treat; and the church of Santa Maria, at Belem, founded by King Manoel, was extremely interesting for its curious architecture. The burial-ground of the British factory, with its tall black cypress trees, entwined by bright scarlet geraniums almost to their tops, well deserve a visit from every Englishman, not only for the singularly picturesque features of its scenery, but as the resting-place of Henry Fielding, our great English novelist, to whom a monument was erected there in 1830. There were no gay shops—no tasteful and tempting display of goods of any description, as in London or Paris—but "Gold Street" and "Silver Street" were appropriated to goldsmiths and silversmiths, and in a third street, of which I forget the name, had congregated all the workers and dealers in ivory. Other trades and professions were less gregarious. Toy-shops were few in number, and contained nothing but the commonest French and Dutch toys. One of the most striking objects in Lisbon is the bullock-cart, or waggon, a vehicle of the rudest and most primitive construction—each wheel of one solid piece of wood. It is drawn by a pair of fine large dun-coloured oxen, the handsomest creatures of their class I ever saw, and the whole affair seems to have come down to us unchanged since the time of the Visigoths. In any other country but Portugal there would be children's toys made in imitation of these remarkable national vehicles, and I was anxious to take some home with me for my grandchildren, but no such thing could I find. At length our valet-de-place managed to discover one in a dingy shop on the quay, but so ill-made, and conveying so little an idea of the original, that I declined giving the price they asked for it. Plums and other fruits, preserved by the nuns, sweetmeats (rebusados), and baskets made of the fibres of the aloe, were the only native productions I could find to invest in. The fans were Japanese, and the silver filagree ear-rings and necklaces manufactured for the most part in Madeira. In the matter of costume, also, I was greatly disappointed; a few muleteers and water-carriers alone reminding me that I was in the Peninsula, and I saw but one female in a mantilla. There was nothing of great antiquity or curiosity in the national armoury, and, with the exception of a sad memento of the terrible earthquake in 1755, in the ruined church of the Carmo, no object of remarkable interest to an archæologist.

There was a grand review on the 21st, at which the principal novelty to us was the artillery and ammunition waggons, drawn by mules; and on the 25th and 26th grand balls were given by the Conde de Farobo, at his beautiful villa of Laranjeiras, near Lisbon, and the British Minister, at Buenos Ayres. The former, at which the King, Queen, and all the Royal Family were present, and nearly 800 persons, was a magnificent affair. On the 27th the investiture took place at the palace of Belem, to which the Mission was conveyed in four royal carriages, that for the plenipotentiaries drawn by eight grey horses, and the other three by eight mules, attended by outriders and running footmen in state liveries, and an escort of lancers. After the ceremony, for the details of which I must refer the curious in such matters to the Gazette, we dined with their Majesties, covers being laid for forty-two, and subsequently took coffee with them in the drawing-room, making our final bows to them at ten o'clock. Early on Saturday, 29th, the squadron left the Tagus, and on June 2, after a speedy and pleasant run of five days, we landed at Portsmouth, all well, and without the slightest misadventure.

It was altogether a most enjoyable and interesting excursion. Lisbon was a place I was very unlikely to visit *mere motu*, and though I confess that I had heard so much of the Tagus that I was rather disappointed by the tameness of the scenery, still it is a noble river as regards breadth, and the view of Lisbon from it is undoubtedly imposing. The public gardens of San Pedro d'Alcantara are small, but pretty, and command a good view of the most picturesque portion of the city. We strolled up to them shortly after we landed, and Garter, Courthope, and I were sitting under the welcome shade of a noble tree—for it was blazing hot—when I was startled by some one near me exclaiming "Why, Planché!" I certainly had no idea of anyone knowing me in Lisbon, in which I had not been two hours, but the speaker proved to be an old acquaintance, at that time a member of Parliament, who, as he informed me, usually visited Portugal with his wife about this period, and was staying with the brother of the Duchess of Saldanha, a native of England. At the Finance Minister's, on the following day, I made the acquaintance also of Mr. Clare Ford, son of my old friend familiarly known as "Alhambra" Ford, from his residence in, and writings on, Spain, so that I speedily found myself "en pays de connaissance." At the opera, where a box was placed at our disposition, I was much amused by a performance of "Le Prophète," in the skating scene of which the corps de ballet, male and female, were continually falling in the most natural manner imaginable. They had been provided with the proper skates, which move upon small wheels, but, as they had never seen ice, they were utterly innocent of the art of skating, and literally "came down with *a run*" nearly every time they attempted it. The singing was mediocre, but the scenery very creditable. The effect of a red wintry sun, in the skating scene, was extremely good.

Another entertaining circumstance occurred at the Villa of Laranjeiras, on the occasion of the grand fête there on the 25th, which I have previously mentioned. The ball was preceded by amateur theatricals. There is a pretty private theatre attached to the villa, as large nearly as the Strand theatre, in London, but having only one row of seats in the box circle. The Countess was (let us hope *is*) a very agreeable actress, and the Count a good musician, playing the violoncello and other instruments; indeed, so fond of music, that, we were informed, he would not engage a male domestic who could not form, if required, a member of his orchestra, which, I can testify, was on this occasion a very creditable one. The piece selected for performance was a one-act French vaudeville, entitled "Le Crinolin," that much abused, but much beloved, article of a lady's toilette having recently become the vogue in Paris, and rapidly acquiring favour with the fair sex in all the capitals of Europe, Lisbon not excepted. A royal box was tastefully fitted up for their Majesties and suite on the left side of the house, as it generally is in England. The pit was assigned to gentlemen only, and the box tier, with its one row of seats, specially reserved for the ladies. To this portion of the theatre there was but one entrance, on the extreme right, by a small door, at which the Countess placed herself to receive her guests, gracefully indicating with her fan the seats they were expected to occupy. From the peculiarity of the construction, which rendered passing each other an impossibility, there could be no preference accorded to rank. It was "first come first served," and, consequently, the fair Lusitanians had to follow their leader in Indian file, whoever she might be. The earliest arrivals took their places in what might be called "open order," and, being all dressed for the ball, according to the last advices from Paris, the whole tier was speedily occupied entirely by some twenty or thirty ladies. As there were at least three or four times that number to come, the fan was in constant action, courteously entreating the occupants to "close up," a signal obeyed at first with a tolerably good grace, but, as the pressure increased, the most rueful glances were exchanged. The ample crinolines were visibly collapsing, but the inexorable fan still waved "move on," until the force of nature could no further go, and, though many were inevitably excluded, the whole circle was packed as close as the one-shilling gallery of Drury Lane on boxing-night. Of the vaudeville I need say nothing more than, being full of hits at the unfortunate article of attire which was crushed and suffering so severely during the performance, it seemed like adding insult to injury, a cowardly striking of some one that was down, and it was impossible for any man with the least gallantry openly to laugh at it. But though bad began, "worse remained behind." The performance ended, their Majesties and all the company repaired to the ball-room, with which the theatre communicated by a general staircase. It was really piteous to see the condition of the costly dresses of the ladies as they emerged from the place in which they had been "cabined, cribbed, confined," for upwards of an hour—to witness their despair as they vainly endeavoured to restore the crumpled skirts and dilapidated flowers to something like their pristine perfection. To describe the scene upon that staircase is impossible; but, happily, it is unnecessary, as where is the fair reader who cannot imagine it, and sympathise with the sufferers?

We had visited Laranjeiras a few days previously in the day-time, it being one of the show places of Lisbon, and there I saw, for the first time, the magnificent flowering plant called "Bougainvilliers," from the admiral of that name, I believe, who first brought it to Europe. It was little known in England at that time, but has since been successfully cultivated by several gentlemen in this country. One of the most novel sights to me in Portugal were the hedges of the corn-fields, which were composed of aloes and geraniums.

With Sir Harry Smith I contracted a great friendship, too soon, alas, terminated by his death. Captain Moorsom also did not long survive that pleasant trip to Portugal, much of the enjoyment of which, it is but justice to say, was due to the cordiality of all our companions.

CHAPTER XIV.

After the retirement of Mr. Alfred Wigan from the Olympic, in 1857, I had occupied myself but little with the drama. Messrs. Robson and Emden, who had succeeded them, offered me my own terms for a comic drama on a French subject I mentioned to them; but, after I had completed it, I discovered it had been already dramatised by Mr. Wigan, so that its production at the Olympic, under the circumstances then existing, could not be thought of. It was afterwards accepted by Mr. Webster, and performed at the Adelphi in July, 1859, under the title of "An Old Offender," Mr. Toole sustaining the principal character; and about the same time, Mr. Harris having taken the Princess's Theatre, applied to me for a piece to introduce his management, as I had done for Buckstone at the Haymarket, and Wigan at the Olympic. On this occasion, I made an attempt to introduce a new style of drama to the English stage, a comedy in verse, after the fashion of those acted at the fairs of Saint

Germain and Fontainebleau in France, and of which a collection was published, entitled "Le Théâtre de la Foire," partaking of the nature of extravaganza, but more poetical in their composition, and in the plots of which Arlequin, as a cowardly, greedy rascal, was usually introduced as the valet of the lover, not a dumb pantomimist, like the English harlequin, but speaking and singing with the rest of the characters. "Love and Fortune," as the piece was called, was produced at the opening of the Princess's Theatre, 24th September, 1859, the *title rôles*, as the French call them, being charmingly sustained by Miss Louisa Keeley, who made her *début* in London as Love, and Miss Carlotta Leclercq as Fortune. Tastefully put on the stage, and extremely well acted throughout, I believe this piece would have benefited the treasury of the theatre as much as it did my reputation with all those whose judgment I most highly value, had not Mr. Harris, against the advice of every one who was privileged to offer it, persisted in producing it as an afterpiece, instead of a "lever de rideau," for which it was so obviously intended. He drew up his curtain to a long melodrama, translated from "Le Roman d'un jeune homme pauvre" (the same piece was subsequently adapted by Dr. Westland Marston for Sothern at the Haymarket), the principal character in which, being very indifferently acted by a new importation from the provinces, tested the endurance of the audience till nearly eleven o'clock, so that when my trifle began the majority, dissatisfied and wearied out, had retired to their beds, and no higher compliment could have been paid to me than that any mortal creature who was not compelled should sit out "Love and Fortune." Its favourable reception at such an hour of the night was next to a miracle; but, of course, all the allusions to the new management were much less effective than they would have been earlier in the evening, and before a failure had soured the temper of the public.

As in the case of "The Birds of Aristophanes" also, I found that, notwithstanding all the precautions I had taken to prevent the press and the public mistaking my intentions, two or three of the former, and, no doubt, many more of the latter than I could possibly ascertain, expected from me one of those absurdities which had found such favour in their sight, and were determined to look upon "Love and Fortune" in that light, and no other.

Not only had I described it in the bill simply as "a dramatic tableau in *Watteau* colours," but I had appended to the title a quotation from the song of April in my version of "Cymon," which distinctly stated:—

> "It is not a Burlesque nor an Extravaganza,
> But a something or other,
> That pleased your grandmother,
> And we hope will please you in your turn."

But, no! It was all in vain. A burlesque or extravaganza they were determined to consider it, and to criticise it accordingly. One writer complained that there were not so many puns in it as usual: there not being one in the whole piece, I having specially avoided the introduction of anything which would give it the character of burlesque. The majority, however, understood and appreciated it, and in one notice it was observed that "the piece fell like an unknown jewel amongst the audience." There is an old saying, as true as it is coarse, descriptive of the preference usually accorded to the most unfortunate sheep in the flock, and I am well aware of the tendency of authors to cling most fondly to those of their works which have been least successful. I feel, as one of the tribe, that occasionally there may be some excuse for this partiality. The poet may have written "over the heads" of his readers. The dramatist may have been misinterpreted by his actors, and, in either case, though he must bear the blame, he is not likely to agree with his censors, but feels more tenderness for his disregarded darling. I freely confess that in this instance, as in the previous one of "The Birds," their comparative failure in point of attraction has not in the slightest degree affected my opinion that, both as regards motive and execution, they are not surpassed by any of my more popular productions, or shaken my confidence that they will yet one day justify that opinion.

In 1860, an opportunity was afforded me which has rarely, I think, been vouchsafed by Providence to a dramatic author. Five-and-thirty years after the production of Oberon at Covent Garden, I revised it for the purpose of its being translated into Italian and revived at Her Majesty's Theatre. Mr. E. T. Smith had added to his anxieties and responsibilities, as the lessee of Drury Lane and other places of public entertainment, the enormous burden of the old Opera House. Mr. Mapleson, at that time a member of his cabinet, called on me at the College of Arms with a liberal proposal from Mr. Smith to undertake the reproduction of Oberon in a foreign garb, and it was with sincere pleasure I gave my assent, more particularly as I was informed the music was to be under the supervision of Mr. Jules Benedict. Deeply as it was to be regretted that Weber had not lived to superintend the revival of his work in England at a time when the improvement of musical taste, and the increase of musical knowledge, would have enabled him, as well as me, to remodel our opera, and relieve it from that redundance of dialogue scenes and incidents indispensable at the period of its composition; the musical world will acknowledge that the task could not have been confided to a more competent substitute than his favourite pupil and affectionate friend. By such hands it was sure to be performed as reverently as efficiently.

The limited space behind the curtain in the old Opera House, where the stage was nearly all proscenium, prevented many of the mechanical effects so tastefully designed and accomplished by Messrs. Grieve and Bradwell at Covent Garden from being reproduced by Mr. Beverley at Her Majesty's Theatre; but all that painting could do, I need scarcely say, was done for it, and, unlimited power having been given me by Mr. Smith in the wardrobes, the piece was put upon the stage with as much splendour, and, in many points, with more correctness, as regarded the costumes and appointments, thanks to the kind information afforded me by Mr. Lane, the erudite Orientalist and translator of "The Arabian Nights' Entertainments." The cast, including Mongini, Madame Alboni, and Madame Titjiens, could scarcely have been surpassed, and, although the fear of tampering with the music of Weber restricted in some measure our alterations, the piece is no longer "a drama with songs," and holds a post of honour in the repertoire of Italian Opera.

To revert to other matters, at the congress of our association in 1858 at Salisbury, under the presidency of the Marquis of Aylesbury, I felt it my duty to demolish the popular tradition of the effigy of "the Boy Bishop," much to the disgust of a relative of the venerable Dean Hamilton, who declared "Mr. Planché might as well have stolen it!" The dean, however, in proposing thanks to me for my lecture, observed that, much as his townsmen might regret the dissipation of a popular belief, the truth was more precious than any error, however agreeable, and that a still deeper interest was attached to the effigy, which I had shown to be that of one of their bishops, whose heart only had been buried in their cathedral.

In 1859, our congress at Newbury was presided over by the Earl of Carnarvon, whose opening address was one of the most admirable orations I ever listened to, and elicited an equally admirable eulogy from the Bishop of Oxford.

At this congress I had the great pleasure of making the acquaintance of the Rev. Charles Kingsley, one of the greatest modern English authors in almost every branch of literature.

In the summer of 1858, being, with my son-in-law, Mr. Whelan, on a visit to Lord Londesborough, at Grimston Park, near Tadcaster, Yorkshire, I was present at a grand entertainment given by his lordship to his principal tenantry in that county. It was a day fête, the company assembling about noon. There was a sumptuous déjeûner, or early dinner, in the riding-house, and a large marquee erected for dancing in the park, on the confines of which is a field called Battle Acre, being the place, according to tradition, where the Lancastrians made their last ineffectual stand against the forces of the rival house of York in the decisive conflict of Towton Field. During the dancing, I strolled down into "the Acre," which is celebrated for a singular natural curiosity. A quantity of wild white roses annually spring up and blossom in a particular portion of it, and all attempts to destroy them by the farmers of the land had failed up to that period. The general opinion appeared to be that they had been originally planted by the victorious party in commemoration of the triumph of the White Rose, and probably on a spot where a pile of their slain had been buried. Lord Londesborough had used his endeavours to prevent their extirpation after he became possessed of the property, and at the time I speak of they still continued to make their annual appearance. The following verses, suggested by this interesting fact, were strung together on the spot, and a copy of them given to Lady Londesborough the next morning at breakfast. As they have never been printed, the singularity of the subject will render excusable their introduction here.

THE FLOWERS OF TOWTON FIELD.

A BALLAD OF BATTLE ACRE.

THERE is a patch of wild white roses that bloom on a battle-field,
Where the rival rose of Lancaster blush'd redder still to yield;
Four hundred years have o'er them shed their sunshine and their snow,
But in spite of plough and harrow, every summer there they blow;
Though rudely up to root them with hand profane you toil,
The faithful flowers still fondly cluster round the sacred soil;
Though tenderly transplanted to the nearest garden gay,
Nor cost, nor care, can tempt them there to live a single day!

I ponder'd o'er their blossoms, and anon my busy brain
With banner'd hosts and steel-clad knights repeopled all the plain.
I seem'd to hear the lusty cheer of the bowmen bold of York,
As they mark'd how well their cloth-yard shafts had done their bloody work;
And steeds with empty saddles came rushing wildly by,
And wounded warriors stagger'd past, or only turn'd to die,
And the little sparkling river was cumbered as of yore
With ghastly corse of man and horse, and ran down red with gore.

I started as I ponder'd, for loudly on mine ear
Rose indeed a shout like thunder, a true old English cheer;
And the sound of drum and trumpet came swelling up the vale,
And blazon'd banners proudly flung their glories to the gale;
But not, oh! not to battle did those banners beckon now—
A baron stood beneath them, but not with helmed brow,
And Yorkshire yeomen round him throng'd, but not with bow and lance,
And the trumpet only bade them to the banquet and the dance.

Again my brain was busy: from out those flow'rets fair,
A breath arose like incense—a voice of praise and prayer!
A silver voice that said, "Rejoice! and bless the God above,
Who hath given thee these days to see of peace, and joy, and love;

Oh, never more by English hands may English blood be shed,
Oh, never more be strife between the roses white and red.
The blessed words the shepherds heard may we remember still,
'Throughout the world be peace on earth, and towards man good-will.'"

In the autumn of 1859 died dear Leigh Hunt. After my leaving London in 1853, I saw but little of him; and the latest, indeed only—letters I find of his after that date are a brief note in acknowledgment of one of mine to him, on the occasion of his wife's death, in 1857, and the following, which, from internal evidence, I presume was in the year preceding:—

7, CORNWALL ROAD, HAMMERSMITH,
October 15.

KINDEST greeting for greeting, my dear Planché. I am very seldom indeed in your quarter; very seldom further out in my own than a walk's distance before dinner or tea; and it is only within a very late period, and these in rare instances, that the ill state of health, aggravated by years of sorrow, has allowed me to visit again my oldest friends in London. Nevertheless, the first time I am near your house I will assuredly take my chance of finding you at home, and I hope you will do as much for me here at Hammersmith under the like circumstances. I never see your name in the newspaper without rejoicing in your constant success, and I delighted in the new bit of colour, painted-window like, that was thrown about it by *heraldry*—a favourite theme of mine. Will the theatres ever let you go? and could you not come and talk about it some evening over a cup of tea, if you condescend to drink such a thing? I am almost as invariably at home as the tea-chest itself, and a note at any time the day before would have about three hundred and fifty-five chances or so to one to be able to find me. Tea any time from 7 to 10.

With kindest remembrances to your daughters,

Ever truly yours,

LEIGH HUNT.

Your letter only reached me on Friday.

The last is without any date or place of residence :—

KINDEST thanks to dear Planché for his words of condolence, and apologies for not sooner acknowledging them. But sorrow cannot at all times speak, even with the pen; and Planché knows this particular sorrow, and that melancholy fact.

His grateful friend,

LEIGH HUNT.

So much justice has been done to his memory by Lord Houghton and others of our mutual friends since his decease, that any words of mine would be superfluous.*

* By a most unfortunate oversight, my own copy of the "Lays and Legends of the Rhine" (the *three* parts, with the music), containing numberless notes in pencil by Leigh Hunt, was, with several other books I had left at Ash, sold with the library of my son-in-law, the Rev. Henry S. Mackarness, after his decease, 26th December, 1868, by a country auctioneer, utterly ignorant of the interest attached to it, and most probably for a few shillings; and as it was undescribed in the catalogue, even by title, but lumped with "Books various," I have been unable to trace into whose hands it has fallen. It was handsomely

On the 20th of December, 1860, died Alfred Bunn, aged 62. It may be said of him—

> "Nothing in his life
> Became him like the leaving of it."

He was a strange compound: by no means bad hearted, wonderfully good tempered in difficulties and disasters, and endured with the greatest fortitude the most violent attacks of a cruel complaint to which he was subject; but in health and prosperity he was imperious and occasionally unjust, and sadly addicted to that common fault of theatrical managers, the using up of his performers. What natural talent he possessed was uncultivated; his language and manners were coarse, and his taste deplorable. His management was sheer gambling of the most reckless description, in no one instance that I can remember terminating prosperously, whatever might have been the success of certain productions in the course of it. A brief engagement as acting manager for Messrs. Delafield and Webster, during their operatic speculation at Covent Garden, was, I believe, his latest connection with the Theatre. He made a trip to the United States, returned

bound in green morocco, with gilt edges; and if this description should by some fortunate accident lead to its discovery, its restoration to me by its present possessor would be an obligation I could never sufficiently acknowledge.

and gave lectures, wrote a book about the Stage, retired to Boulogne, where he embraced the Roman Catholic faith, and died in the odour of sanctity. Michael Balfe, who had composed several of his operas, visited his grave some time after, and told me he had pronounced over it the following brief and characteristic funeral oration, "Well, never mind, poor Alfred! 'We may be happy yet.'"* The popular composer has recently, in the prime of his life, departed also to that "undiscovered country," following too soon his tuneful contemporary, Vincent Wallace. He (Balfe) was at work on an opera of mine at the time of his death.

* The refrain of one of Bunn's ballads, of which Balfe had composed the music.

CHAPTER XV.

During the last decade, death had been specially busy amongst my friends and acquaintances, professional and private. Amongst the best known to the public were Mrs. Bartley and Mrs. Glover, in 1850; Richard Jones, the comedian, who had retired, and was a teacher of elocution; Dowton (the best *Sir Anthony Absolute* I ever saw), and good-natured Sam Beazley, in 1851; Luttrell, in 1852; Charles Kemble, in 1854; Rogers and Sir Henry Bishop, in 1855; Braham, Madame Vestris, and Charles Young, in 1856; Charles Macfarlane (my collaborateur in Knight's "Pictorial History of England" and other publications), George Bartley, Harley, and Mrs. Nisbett, (Lady Boothby) in 1858; and Lady Morgan and Charles Farley, in 1859.

Of the majority of these more or less celebrated persons I have already related such anecdotes or peculiarities as might be interesting to the reader. There is one, however, most celebrated, who died in 1852, who, by what some people would call "a fate," I have been unhappily prevented from claiming as either a personal friend or acquaintance, although I have every reason to believe that, but for a singular chain of events, he would have been both—Thomas Moore.

As early as 1827, I received from him the following letter, in acknowledgment of a copy of the "Lays and Legends of the Rhine," which I had sent to him.

SLOPERTON COTTAGE,
July 23, 1827.

DEAR SIR,

I beg you to accept my best thanks for the two beautiful volumes which I have just received. I had already known and admired the first, though I was not lucky enough to possess it, and I feel very grateful to you for adding such a valuable ornament to my musical library. Allow me to hope that on my next visit to town I may be fortunate enough to make your acquaintance, and believe me,

Your much obliged and faithful servant,

THOMAS MOORE.

Accordingly, next season, he called upon me at Brompton, but I was not at home, and, on my returning his call, I was equally unfortunate. This occurred more than once afterwards; and at Mr. Horace Twiss's, Lady Morgan's, and other mutual friends, we continually missed each other, sometimes only by a few minutes. On the first occasion of my dining in company with Mr. Rogers, at the Duchess-Countess of

Sutherland's, he asked Mr. Luttrell and me to meet Moore, who had promised to breakfast with him the next morning. I went, of course, and so did Luttrell; but there was no Tom Moore. A note arrived from him to say he was obliged to breakfast at Holland House. Again and again similar disappointments took place. One day I was chatting with Haynes Bayly in the balcony of the Athenæum, when he suddenly said, "Here comes Tom Moore." "Where?" I exclaimed eagerly, as I had never set eyes on him; but before he could point him out to me, he had passed under the balcony in which we were standing, and was no longer in sight. On expressing my vexation, Bayly said, "Oh, never mind, he's coming in here. Let us go downstairs, and I will introduce you." Downstairs we hastened, but there was no Tom Moore. On inquiry, the porter informed us that Mr. Moore had simply asked for his letters, and, being told there were none, had not entered the club, but gone down the steps into St. James's Park. During the last season of my engagement at the Haymarket—1847—returning home to dinner, I met Mr. Carter Hall, who asked me what I was going to do that evening. On my replying, "Nothing particular," he said, "Well, as you are disengaged, Tom Moore is coming to us, and we shall be happy if you will meet him." "I should be only too delighted, but I fear it's impossible." "What do you mean?" I told him briefly how invariably I had been disappointed, and that I really felt it was not to be. He laughed, and assured me that I should be fortunate this time, for that Moore was going to dine quietly and early with a friend who had promised faithfully to bring him at eight o'clock; but, he added, "Mind you are punctual, for Moore is far from well, and will not stay above an hour." I had just come from the theatre, and knew there was nothing, barring accidents, which could necessitate my presence that evening, so gladly accepted Mr. Hall's invitation. It was no party—only two or three friends and a quiet cup of tea. We should have Moore all to ourselves. How I rejoiced that I had met Mr. Hall! I hurried home, dressed, and had just finished dinner, when a servant came round from Farren's house in Brompton Square, with a note desiring to see me at the theatre as soon after eight as possible on most particular business. Farren was stage manager. Mr. Webster was out of town. I could not venture to neglect the summons, as I could form no guess of what the business might be. It was past seven o'clock, and Farren, who had to play in the first piece, was on the stage at that moment. He had not been at the theatre in the morning, so had not had an opportunity of speaking to me. There was no help for it; go up to town I must. But Moore was to be at "the Rosery" at eight precisely, and would not stay long. At least I should see and speak to him, if only for a minute. I was at Mr. Hall's at 10 minutes to eight. Eight o'clock struck, but no Moore; a quarter past eight, but no Moore. It was agony point. I left the house under a promise from Mr. Hall that, if Moore did come, he would detain him as long as possible. I had a vehicle in waiting, and told the coachman to drive as fast as he dared to the Haymarket, rushed up to Farren's room, who was undressing, and found that "the particular business" might have been communicated in the note he had sent me, and attended to at my leisure. I was out of the theatre again in five minutes, and back at the Rosery before nine, to hear that Moore had arrived immediately after I left, and had but that instant departed. As I felt, it was not to be! I am not aware that he ever visited London again. At any rate, I never had the happiness even to behold him.

The name of Charles Macfarlane would have been more widely known, had not the most important of his contributions to English literature been published, though not exactly anonymously, in works in which individual authorship was merged in the personality of the general editor. His share in the composition of

Knight's "Pictorial History of England," edited by George Craik, was by far the largest. It comprised the entire "Civil and Military History," and is, in my humble opinion, the most spirited, as well as most accurate, of any extant. The chapters recounting the great struggles between the rival houses of York and Lancaster, for graphic power and lucid exposition, are particularly remarkable. For the same publisher he compiled two pleasant little volumes of table talk, for which I wrote a brief history of stage costume. He was a most amusing companion, and a warm friend.

My theatrical foster-father, as he very justly called himself, John Pritt Harley, died "in harness"—almost upon the stage. He was seized by "the fell serjeant" while acting in the Princess's Theatre, and to the inquiries of those about him answered, in the words of Bottom the Weaver, "I have an exposition of sleep come upon me." Being asked who was his doctor, he replied, "I never had any;" and these are said to have been the last intelligible words he uttered. Not only was I indebted to him for my first introduction to the theatre, but for the zealous and effective support I received from him as an actor in so many of my dramas, commencing with "Amoroso," in 1818, and terminating with "Not a Bad Judge," in 1848.

With Mr. and Mrs. George Bartley I had only a professional acquaintance. The lady had been accepted by the public as a leading tragédienne, and her husband was a sensible, unaffected actor, without any pretension to genius, but thoroughly dependable to the extent of his ability. He was also a courteous, discreet gentleman, well calculated to fill the position he so long sustained, under various lessees, of stage manager. Of the intelligence of a British public his opinion was not flattering. "Sir," he would say to me, "you must first tell them you are going to do so and so; you must then tell them you are doing it, and then that you have done it; and then, by G—d" (with a slap on his thigh), "*perhaps* they will understand you!" British public, on your honour, as ladies and gentlemen, is this true? Without "indorsing the bill," I will only say that his advice was most valuable to young writers. Perspicuity is a primary qualification in the plot of a play, and its absence cannot be compensated for by either language or incident. Mr. and Mrs. Bartley visited the United States—I forget in what particular year—but shortly after they were fairly in blue water, one of the crew became mutinous, and received a very severe cut on the head from, I believe, the captain, in the presence of the passengers. Mrs. Bartley, who was beginning to suffer from the *mal de mer*, was much shocked and alarmed, became very ill, and retreated immediately to her cabin, from which she did not emerge again till they were almost in sight of port. The first day that she ventured on deck the man she had seen cut down was at the wheel. Approaching him with kindly interest, she inquired, "How is your head now?" and received for answer, "West and by north, ma'am!"

When Bartley first joined the Covent Garden company, Fawcett, an excellent actor, was stage-manager, and in possession, of course, of all the best parts. One day he sent for Bartley, and said, "George, I'm going to give you a chance. Hamlet is put up for next week, and you shall play the 'First Gravedigger.' I've plenty to do, and it is but fair to give you a turn." Bartley expressed his gratitude. Fawcett shook hands with him and walked away, muttering to himself, but loud enough for Bartley to hear him, "There's a wind at night comes up that cursed grave-trap enough to cut one's vitals out!"

Charles Farley, who attained the venerable age of eighty-seven, is described in a theatrical obituary as a "pantomime-arranger." This is doing him scant justice. He was not only a good melodramatic actor, but sustained very creditably a line of character parts in the plays of Shakespere and the best of our old English comedies—Roderigo, in "Othello," Cloten, in "Cymbeline," Osric, in "Hamlet," "Cacofogo, in "Rule a Wife and have a Wife," and many others; notably, although utterly ignorant of French, Canton, in "The Clandestine Marriage." So little did he know of the language of our lively neighbours, that he is reported to have waited day after day at the doors of one of the theatres in Paris in order to witness the first performance of a new grand spectacle, entitled, as he imagined, "Relache," mistaking the bills with that word only in large letters, which he saw posted up there, to indicate the production of some important novelty. During the visit of the allied sovereigns to Europe, Farley strolled one afternoon into the house of the eminent printsellers, Colnaghi & Co., Pall Mall East, to whom he, and all the theatrical profession indeed, were deeply indebted for the great and gratuitous assistance so liberally rendered to them by those gentlemen in matters of costume and scenery. "What a pity you were not here a little sooner, Mr. Farley," said Mr. Dominic Colnaghi to him, as he entered. "The Emperor Alexander was standing on this very spot not a quarter of an hour ago, looking at that portrait of Napoleon"—a very fine one then on view there. "Indeed!" said Farley eagerly; "and what observation did he make on it?" "He said, 'C'est très-ressemblant.'"

"Ah!" rejoined Farley, with a deep sigh and a mysterious shake of the head, "he might *well* say that!" My friend Dominic was too much of a gentleman to inquire what interpretation his interrogator had given to the important words which had escaped the lips of the Emperor of all the Russias.

Of Sydney Lady Morgan so much has been related by herself, as well as by others, that I shall only say "ditto," as I am bound to do, to all the acknowledgments of the kindness and encouragement received from her by every young aspirant to literary distinction with whom she became acquainted; and that I recollect with pleasure the many agreeable receptions I have been present at in William Street, Lowndes Square, and the still more agreeable conversations I have enjoyed with her *tête-à-tête* on occasional calls in the morning. At one of them she told me a story, which, as it is particularly illustrative of her tact, humour, and presence of mind, I shall venture to repeat, not being aware that it has been previously printed. She had invited a large party to dinner, and on the day specified was dressing to receive her guests, when a note was brought to her, containing a "reminder" from a lady of rank that she was expected to dine with her that same evening—an engagement she had utterly forgotten. The hour she had named for her own dinner was six; that of the one she was invited to, seven. Her mind was made up in an instant. She finished her toilet, received her company, sat down with them to dinner, and a few minutes before seven informed them of her dilemma, begged them to excuse her for an hour or two, and finish their dinner quietly; she would rejoin them as speedily as possible. Off she drove to her friend's, dined there, and returned home before nine, bringing away with her Tom Moore and several other desirable additions to her own party.

One of the most picturesque ruins I have ever seen in England is Bodiham Castle, near Battle, in Sussex, and it is a favourite spot for picnics with families in the neighbourhood and for fifteen or twenty miles round about. Being within that distance from Heronden Hall, my son-in-law's place at Tenterden, he frequently drove friends who were staying with him over to Bodiham for a lunch *al fresco*, returning by seven to dinner. In the summer of 1857 I was on a visit to him and my daughter, and a party was made up of the company in the house for one of these pleasant excursions. The weather was all that could be wished, and, after an enjoyable drive and a capital luncheon, we were taking a last stroll round the outer walls of the castle, when a most musical and joyous laugh rang in our ears. "That's Lady Boothby!" exclaimed my daughter, instinctively, and almost as she spoke, Lady Boothby came running out of one of the towers, pursued by two beautiful children, their straw hats garlanded with hop-blossoms, and followed by her mother, her brother, and her sister Anne, wife of the son of a Scotch lord of session, and mother of the children aforesaid. Lady Boothby was at that time residing at St. Leonard's, and had driven over with her family for the same pleasant purpose as ourselves. Of course they recognised me directly, and we all joined company, made the little folks happy with the remaining portion of the fine fruit we had brought with us, and laughed and chatted till the lengthening shadows warned us it was more than time we should start on our homeward journey. Mr. Whelan and I escorted Lady Boothby to her carriage, and there I shook hands with her for the last time! Within six months of that date she, her mother, sister, and brother—the whole of that joyous group, with the exception of the lovely children—were in their graves! Her mother and sister were first taken ill, and Lady Boothby succumbed to the anxiety and exertion of her affectionate personal attendance on them. Her brother, a rising young barrister, died almost suddenly; whether before or after his sister I do not recollect, but within the brief period I have named.* Such sad and sudden

* The poor girl from whom I received these melancholy details,

devastations in families are of too frequent occurrence to render this instance remarkable; but the recollection of that "merry meeting," to the renewal of which we looked thoughtlessly forward, is one which can never be effaced. My dear son-in-law, Mr. Whelan, and another beloved member of our family who was present on that occasion, have also been taken from us, and Bodiham Castle has ceased to be associated in my mind with any feelings except pain and regret.

Miss Cotterell, a niece of Lady Boothby, was some eight years subsequently seized with a fit at rehearsal on the stage of Her Majesty's Theatre, and expired in a few hours, in the 25th year of her age.

CHAPTER XVI.

In 1860 the "Savage Club," of which I was not a member, paid me the great compliment, considering who *were* members, to request I would write for them a prologue to their "joint-stock" burlesque on the subject of the "Forty Thieves," about to be performed by the authors themselves at the Lyceum, "for the benefit of the widows and families of two literary gentlemen recently deceased." Her Majesty and H.R.H. the Prince Consort graciously patronised the performance, and honoured it with their presence, accompanied by Prince Arthur and the Princess Alice; and the subjoined lines were, I am told (for I was out of town at the time), so well spoken by the late Mr. Leicester Buckingham, that they nearly obtained the unprecedented honour of an encore:—

PROLOGUE TO THE "FORTY THIEVES."

Two or three sentences, with your good leaves,
Ere you pass one upon the "Forty Thieves,"
Who, in a winding-up act, now propose
To bring this joint-stock business to a close.

The rumour runs—and each of us believes in it—
A joint-stock company with forty thieves in it,
Who may all act with more or less rascality,
Cannot lay claim to much originality;
And this deponent positively swears
That every one who has in ours ta'en shares,
Paid for them but in joke—and yet feels certain
He can't be called on—save before the curtain—
An after-clap he has no cause to dread;
Our liability is limited.
Too limited, I fear, you may reply,
Is our ability—without a lie.
No matter. In this desp'rate speculation
We did not seek the "bubble reputation,"
Nor our own nests to feather do we aim;
To succour others is our "little game;"
And, should we find we've played it well to-night,
We can but be transported—with delight.
Atrocious punsters! villanous jest breakers!
We laugh the dull old Dictionary maker's
Abuse to scorn. Admit the fact, and mock it.
The men who made these puns would pick your pocket,
And don't mind getting two months with hard labour
Like this again, to help a needy neighbour.
Boldly we say, friends, countrymen, and lovers!
Lend us your hands. Though pledged to Gallic glovers,
You'll grant, we're sure, as patriotism bids,
Some small protection to poor English kids.
By you, we trow, sirs, will the boys be breeched;
The ladies for the girls shall be beseeched.
Petticoat influence was always great,
And, judging by the petticoats of late,
We may presume, without being offensive,
Such influence was never more extensive:
Hear us, ye beauties, then, in box and stall,
Come with a hoop, and kindly, at our call,
From your vast superfluity let fall
Some drapery for those who've none at all.
Though, iron-bound, your garments may not yield,

Your hearts by fashion never can be steeled,
And you can aid us, without impropriety,
In the wide circles of your sweet society.
Don't frown, for we are serious, we protest,
There's many a true word may be spoke in jest;
We've double meanings, but no double dealings,
And though we play on words, we don't on feelings.
The charity which smoothes misfortune's pillow
We hope will cover every peccadillo,
And save the thieves who shall, in crambo verses,
Cry "Open Sesame" to cram-full purses.
When we can screen one shorn lamb from sharp weather,
Hang us, if we don't always hang together!

In June, 1861, I was again requested by the "Savage Club" to write a prologue for them to another joint-stock burlesque on the subject of "Valentine and Orson," which they were about to act at the Lyceum, for the benefit of the family of Mr. Ebenezer Landells, a well-known wood-engraver. Monsieur Chaillu's description of and theory respecting the Gorilla was at that time the subject of much interest and discussion, and "Punch" had dedicated a cartoon to it. My young friend Henry J. Byron, well made up from the woodcut, delivered the following lines with excellent effect, on Wednesday evening, 19th June:—

PROLOGUE TO "VALENTINE AND ORSON."

From a gay woodcut—no dull tract with trees on,
Behold me here! "The Lion of the Season."
Mr. Gorilla! I announce myself,
For the stage-door keeper, poor timid elf,

Soon as he saw me in the distance dim,
Bolted !—no doubt for fear I should bolt him.
His fear was groundless. Really, I am not,
The great Gorilla Monsieur Chaillu shot.
That monster, about whom there's so much jaw,
Must be the perfect one the world ne'er saw;
Nor am I e'en like those whose bones you see,
But *débonnaire*, and full of *bonhommie*.
In short, of Mr. Punch's own creation,
Proof of his power of investigation;
Cut out of wood myself, to aid I came
The orphans of a wood-cutter of fame.
Stern fate has left them few sticks and small stock,
We trust to save some chips of the old block!
A strange wild set of harum scarum Savages,
Of whom the town before have felt the ravages—
Have formed a club—with which they take great pains
For their poor friends to cudgel their own brains.
From this you might suppose, no brains they've got,
But you'd be wrong—for they've dashed out a lot
On paper—which is now from duty free,
In hopes to pay the Widow's tax on tea.
The times and their intents are savage, wild,
They've seized upon the story of a child—
Torn it piecemeal—mangled its mother's tongue,
Excruciating puns from out it wrung;
And are exulting in the hope soon after
To feast upon your groans and shrieks of laughter.
Well, what from Savages can you expect?
Yet glimmerings of sense you may detect,
There's method in their madness,—much barbarity
Is oft enacted in the name of Charity;
While, on the other hand, we sometimes find,
We "must be cruel only to be kind."
And now, perhaps, you may begin to see,
To speak the Prologue, why they fixed on me;
I'm thought a link, though some the fact dispute,
Between the "genus homo" and the Brute—

Something that was, ere pegtops made the man,
Or "Wild in woods the lordly savage ran."
Now granting that in war all weapons are fair,
Particularly in Gorilla warfare,
And without weighing of each fact the value,
Or standing on the matter *shilly-Chaillu*,
Whether I'm both at once, or one, or t'other,
Say, "Am not I a Savage and a brother?"
Do I not bear in this especial case,
A strong resemblance to the human race?
Then let me hope, with pardonable vanity,
To prove a link 'twixt our and your humanity.
In brief,—for sure I need no longer pause,—
In your good-will let me insert my claws;
Spare not, I pray, your purses or your palms,
The actors crave your hands—the fatherless your alms.

On the 12th of July following, my comedy, in five acts, entitled "My Lord and my Lady," principally founded on Alexander Dumas' "Un Mariage sous Louis XV.," but strengthened with an underplot suggested by a French vaudeville, the name of which has escaped me, was first performed at the Haymarket for Mr. Buckstone's benefit, having been written fourteen years previously for Mr. Webster during my engagement with him, expressly for Mrs. Nesbitt, Mrs. Glover, Mrs. Humby, and Mr. Hudson: but not produced at that time, in consequence of an unfortunate misunderstanding. Charles Mathews having returned from America with his second wife, the present Mrs. Mathews, that popular pair sustained the characters of Lord and Lady Fitzpatrick, intended for Mr. Hudson and Mrs. Nesbitt. Mrs. Wilkins, a handsome woman, but an indifferent actress, was a very poor substitute for Mrs. Glover; but Buckstone was delicious as Groundsel, and the comedy ran fifty nights.

The terrible destitution in Lancashire in this year (1862), caused by the closing of the mills in consequence of the civil war in America, which had put a sudden stop to the importation of cotton, excited great sympathy throughout the British dominions. Noble subscriptions were raised and benevolent efforts made in all parts of the kingdom to alleviate the distress of the unfortunate but wonderfully patient sufferers, who, instead of rioting or resorting to any acts of desperation inimical to the public peace, or destructive of private property, bore their privations with a courage and resignation truly admirable, numbers of them wandering over mountain and moor to gather medicinal herbs for sale, and by such slender and precarious means patiently endeavour to support their starving families. Amongst the many kind exertions made in aid of the Lancashire Relief Fund were those of the officers of the Royal Artillery, stationed at Woolwich, who gave three amateur theatrical performances, the proceeds of which were applied to that excellent purpose. One of the pieces selected was my extravaganza, "Theseus and Ariadne," and I received a request from the committee of management, through Lieutenant Lionel Gye (a son of Mr. Frederick Gye of the Italian Opera), to write a prologue for the occasion. I was too happy to be enabled to contribute in any way to the furtherance of so laudable a work, and sent them the following, which was printed, and sold in the temporary theatre :—

When threaten'd, England's honour or repose,
The British soldier well his duty knows;
To mount, to march, to fight, to bleed, to die,
But never weakly yield, nor basely fly.
We boast not this—all who deserve to bear
The name of soldier, so would do and dare;
But claim with honourable pride we may,
The courage to *endure* and to *obey*.
Need you the proof? 'Tis not in battles won,
The shatter'd colours, nor the captured gun;
Not in the charge, though Balaklava's vale
Of hopeless valour saw the sanguine trail!
Nor in the shock—though Inkerman's dark hill
Could tell of iron nerve and iron will!
'Tis in the frozen trench,—the fever'd camp,—
The famish'd fort,—the pestilential swamp,—
Where war is stripped of all its pomp and pride,
The metal of the manly heart is tried!
Who can forget? Sure none of British strain,
The ship that founder'd in the Indian main?*
Upon whose deck, steady as on parade,
Their last command the noble band obey'd;
And to the grave,—of all but their renown,—
Shoulder to shoulder, in their ranks went down.
If we, as soldiers, glory in such deed,

* The *Birkenhead*, lost off Cape of Good Hope, 1852.

Must we not honour those in bitter need,
Who, with like courage, face *their* fearful doom?
The humble heroes of the Mill and Loom!
No frenzied outbreak of despairing men
Scares the dull town,—disturbs the quiet glen;
No wail of suffering woman renders less
Their brave endurance of prolonged distress!
Of all that to privation lends a smart,—
Of hope deferr'd that maketh sick the heart!
No trumpet cheers them in their struggle hard,
No cross, no clasp, their valour will reward:
Their only prayer throughout this trial dread,
Again to labour for their daily bread.
Pale, patient, mute, around the factory door,
Which opens to the living stream no more;
In groups they stand, or wandering o'er the plain,
Cull herbs which yield no medicine for *their* pain!
Brave fellow-warriors! honour ye we do,
And muster here to-night to help you too!
Receive it as the soldier's tribute paid
To gallant conduct—not as alms—but aid.
Would we could more: but what we can we will.
Friends! for our cause forgive our want of skill.
It is a cause—if e'er one was—demands
The best support of English hearts and hands.

In November this year, my opera of "Love's Triumph," the music by Vincent Wallace, was produced at Covent Garden. I cannot pass without a word of reprobation the barbarous treatment to which this opera was subjected, in accordance to a common practice in England, but which would not be tolerated elsewhere. Being produced before Christmas, as soon as the holidays arrived it was sacrificed, as too many have been before it, to the pantomime. The length of the dull, monstrous, hybrid spectacle which has superseded the bright, lively, and laughable harlequinade of my earlier days, precluding the possibility of giving the opera before it, in its integrity, not only were several airs omitted, but duets and concerted pieces cruelly hacked and mutilated, without reference to the author or composer, to the injury of their reputation, and serious loss to the publisher of the music, who had paid a considerable sum for the copyright, and was thus deprived of the advantage he had counted upon from the nightly singing of those airs, which were omitted, not for want of merit, but for lack of time; and this, remember, by a management which solicited the support of the public for a national opera! Can it be wondered at that the musical world looks coldly upon speculations, which such conduct would evince, were entered into not for the love of the art, but solely for the advancement of private interests, both professional and pecuniary. In France the author and composer would have their remedy at law against any manager guilty of such injustice.

On the 10th of March, 1863, at the marriage of their Royal Highnesses the Prince and Princess of Wales, I had the honour to head the procession of the bride and bridegroom to the altar of St. George's Chapel, Windsor.

In the month of October following, the British Archæological Association held its annual congress at Leeds, under the presidency of Lord Houghton; Mr. Monckton Milnes, with whom I had been many years acquainted, having been recently raised to the peerage with that title. On this occasion I had the pleasure of enjoying his hospitality at Fryston, and also of visiting, in his company, Mr. and Mrs. Meynell-Ingram, at their most interesting mansion, Temple-Newsom, in which a room, wherein Henry Darnley, the unfortunate husband of Mary Queen of Scots, was born, retains the furniture of that period. A noble gallery, in which we lunched in company with Admiral Sir Henry Keppel and Sir Henry Rawlinson, who were staying in the house, contained many fine specimens of the ancient masters; and the avenue through the park, visible from the windows, is only equalled by the Long Walk at Windsor—a fact acknowledged by his Majesty King George IV., when he visited Temple-Newsom.

There had been considerable difference of opinion respecting the proper pronunciation of Lord Houghton's title, and on my return to town I committed to paper the following lines, which were afterwards printed by his Lordship's request, for private distribution. A garbled version full of blunders found its way into a Dublin newspaper and was attribued to Lord Palmerston!—

A LITERARY SQUABBLE.

THE Alphabet rejoiced to hear
That Monckton Milnes was made a Peer,
For in this present world of letters
But few, if any, are his betters:
So an address, by acclamation,
They voted, of congratulation,
And H, O, U, G, T and N,
Were chosen the address to pen,
Possessing, each an interest vital,
In the new Peer's baronial title.
'Twas done in language terse and telling,
Perfect in grammar and in spelling;
But when 'twas read aloud—O, mercy!
There sprang up such a controversy
About the true pronunciation
Of said baronial appellation.
The vowels O and U averred
They were entitled to be *heard*.
The Consonants denied their claim,
Insisting that they *mute* became.
Johnson and Walker were applied to,
Sheridan, Bailey, Webster, tried too:
But all in vain, for each picked out
A word that left the case in doubt.
O, looking round upon them all,
Cried, "if it be correct to call
T, H, R, O, U, G, H, "*throo*"
H, O, U, G, H, must be "*Hoo*,"
Therefore, there can be no dispute on
The question. We should say 'Lord *Hoo*ton.'"
U "brought," "bought," "fought," and "sought" to show
He should be doubled, and not O,

For sure if "ought" was "*awt*" then "nought" on
Earth could the title be but "*Haw*ton."
H, on the other hand, said he
In "cough" and "trough" stood next to G,
And like an F was thus looked soft on
Which made him think it should be "*Hof*ton."
But G corrected H, and drew
Attention other cases to;
"Tough," "rough," and "chough," more than "enough"
To prove O, U, G, H, spelt "*uff*,"
And growled out in a sort of gruff tone,
They must pronounce the title "*Huff*ton."
N said emphatically "No!"
There is D, O, U, G, H, "*Doh*,"
And *though* (look there again!) that stuff
At sea, for fun, they nick-named "*duff*"
He should propose they took a vote on
The question, "should it not be *Ho*ton?"
Besides, in French, 'twould have such force—
A lord, was of "*Haut ton*" of course.
Higher and higher contention rose,
From *words* they almost came to blows,
Till T, as yet who hadn't spoke,
And dearly loved a little joke,
Put in his word and said "Look there!
'Plough' in this *row* must have its *share*."
At this atrocious pun each page
Of Johnson whiter turned with rage,
Bailey looked desperately cut up,
And Sheridan completely shut up;
Webster, who is no idle talker,
Made a sign indicating "Walker!"
While Walker, who had been used badly,
Just shook his dirty dog's ears sadly.
But as we find in prose or rhyme,
A joke made happily in time,
However poor, will often tend
The hottest argument to end,

And smother anger in a laugh;
So T succeeded with his chaff,
(Containing as it did some wheat),
In calming this fierce verbal heat.
Authorities were all conflicting,
And T there was no contradicting.
P, L, O, U, G, H, was *plow*.
Even "enough" was called "enow;"
And no one who preferred "enough"
Would dream of saying "Speed the Pluff!"
So they considered it more wise
With T to make a compromise,
And leave no loop to hang a doubt on,
By giving three cheers for "Lord {Hough / *How*} ton!"

CHAPTER XVII.

In 1864 I completed and published a work which had occupied every moment I could spare to devote to it for the last three years. My son-in-law, the Rev. Henry Mackarness, Rector of St. Mary's-in-the-Marsh, had been presented by the Archbishop of Canterbury to the perpetual curacy of Ash-next-Sandwich, called in clerical circles in former days "the stepping-stone," as the archbishop was himself the vicar, and the incumbent for the time being usually received, after some few years' good service in the parish, the best piece of preferment in the gift of His Grace, of whom he had been, as it were, the deputy or lieutenant. My archæological hobby was spurred into a state of violent excitement and activity by my introduction to this—hitherto unvisited by me—"Corner of Kent." I had some dim notions of Roman Richborough and Pagan-Saxon Gilton, but of the mediæval antiquities of Ash, and its highly interesting parochial history, I had formed no conception from the meagre account in Hasted.

Shortly, therefore, after my first visit to the vicarage, I set to work to collect materials for the history of the parish, and from a simple guide or hand-book—my original intention—it grew into a goodly volume in royal octavo, profusely illustrated, as much to my surprise as to that of several Kentish antiquaries, one of whom wondered what I could "find to say about Ash!"

In April, 1865, two Missions were simultaneously despatched to bear the garter, one to the King of Denmark, and the other to the King of Portugal, Dom Louis, who had recently succeeded his brother, Dom Pedro V. I should have much preferred accompanying the former, as I had never seen Copenhagen; and the inspection of the museum of Danish antiquities there would have been a rare treat to me. Sir Charles Young, however, having elected to go to Denmark, requested me to take charge, as secretary, of the Garter Mission to Lisbon, appointing Walter Blount, Esq., Norroy King of Arms, his deputy, and Mr. George Adams, Rouge Dragon Pursuivant, as third officer. The first plenipotentiary on this occasion was the Earl of Sefton, his military attachés being Major-General Lord Henry Percy, C.B. and V.C., and Lieut.-Colonel Dudley Carleton, Coldstream Guards; Mr. Charles Stuart Aubrey Abbott, of the Foreign Office (now

Lord Tenterden), officiating as secretary to the special mission.

On Saturday, the 15th of April, the Earl of Sefton and Earl Cowper, the latter nobleman having been appointed first plenipotentiary to Denmark, gave a joint dinner to the members of both Missions at the St. James's Hotel, Piccadilly, including consequently with all those above named (excepting Lord Henry Percy, who was on a visit to the Prince of Wales at Sandringham), Viscount Hamilton, the Hon. Evelyn Ashley, the Hon. J. F. Stuart-Wortley, Lieut.-Colonel Tower, Coldstream Guards; Hon. E. Scott Gifford, of the Foreign Office, secretary to the special mission; Sir Charles Young, Garter; A. W. Woods, Esq., Lancaster Herald; and William Courthope, Esq., Somerset Herald, secretary to the Garter Mission.

Both Missions left on the Monday morning following 17th April, the Danish proceeding by Dover and Calais, and we by 11.30 train from Waterloo station to Portsmouth, accompanied by the Rev. Mr. Hopwood, uncle to Lord Sefton, and brother-in-law of the Earl of Derby, who was going to Lisbon, and the Hon. Frederick Leveson Gower, brother to Earl Granville, who left us at Godalming. We reached Portsmouth at 2 p.m., and found awaiting us on the platform Mr. Church, the Admiral's Flag-Lieutenant, who conducted us to the carriages sent to convey us to the new dock-landing, where we were received by Sir Michael Seymour, Port Admiral, and Admiral Sir Sydney Colpoys Dacres, in one of whose barges we were rowed to a small steamer, the *Fire Queen*, which took us out to Spithead. There we again entered the barge, which had followed us, and were rowed alongside H. M. S. the *Edgar*, 71 guns, Captain Hornby, the flag-ship of Admiral Dacres, in which we were to proceed to the Tagus. We were received on board by Captain Hornby and his officers, assembled on the quarter-deck, and the marines under arms. I had a special letter of introduction to Captain Hornby from his uncle, my dear old friend, the late Field Marshal Sir John Fox Burgoyne, G.C.B., and was most kindly welcomed by him. We sat down almost immediately to luncheon, and were then shown our cabins. The servants, with all the luggage, having arrived by another steamer, and everything being on board, we weighed anchor about 3.30 and stood out to sea, followed by the *Hector*, iron-clad, 24, Captain Preedy, rounding the Isle of Wight before dark, and were joined during the night by the *Black Prince*, 41, Captain Lord Frederick Kerr, the *Defence*, 16, Captain Phillimore, and the *Prince Consort*, 35, Captain Welles (all iron-clad), from Portland.

Tuesday, 18th, about noon, sighted the *Achilles*, four-masted iron-clad, 20, Captain Vansittart, ordered by telegram from the Admiralty to join the fleet ten miles south of the Eddystone at this hour. As she neared us she saluted the admiral's flag with fourteen guns, the *Edgar* returning the compliment with seven. The *Achilles* then, by signal, took her station between the *Black Prince* and the *Prince Consort;* the *Defence* having also by signal quitted that position and dropped astern of the *Hector*. The fleet then proceeded in two lines, the right being formed by the *Edgar*, the *Hector*, and the *Defence*, and the left by the *Black Prince*, the *Achilles*, and the *Prince Consort;* and this order was beautifully kept the whole way to the Rock of Lisbon.

During the night of the 19th we cleared Channel and began crossing the bay. The ship rolled considerably, but the weather was much better than when I was previously in that latitude; and on Friday, the 21st, we were out of the bay and off Vigo by 9 a.m., Oporto by noon, and steering direct for the Berlings (Berlengas), a remarkable group of rocks starting out of the sea, with a lighthouse on one of them. At midnight I was startled out of a sound sleep by what appeared to me an awful explosion; a second following immediately upon it, I ascertained that the iron-clads had commenced great gun practice by "flashing signals," the inventor of which (Captain Colomb) was on board the *Edgar*. Notice had been considerately given to the members of the Mission generally, but by some accident I had not heard of it, or I should have remained up to witness the sight. However, I saw it pretty well from my own cabin window, and a very fine one it was. The crews of the fleet were purposely kept in ignorance of what was to take place, the object being to see how quickly they could be ready for action, and the trial was most satisfactory. They were all blazing away in a marvellously short space of time, the *Black Prince*, I believe, being first by only a minute or two. Such a roar! More than 130 guns of the heaviest metal firing as fast as they could load for nearly an hour. What the Portuguese peasantry or fishermen thought of it on the coast, for we were pretty close in shore, it would be hard to say. If any thing could "astonish the natives"—which from my little experience of them I should say it was difficult to do—I think our tars succeeded on that occasion. It is not every landsman who has seen a sham fight at midnight between five men-of-war in the Atlantic.

Next morning by 7 we made Cape Rocco (the Rock of Lisbon), and lay-to off the mouth of the Tagus, it being too thick to see our landmarks for crossing the bar in safety. The weather began to clear at noon, and all the ships having furled sails and formed in one line, the *Edgar* leading, steamed past Fort St. Julian, and up the river, the *Edgar* saluting the Portuguese flag at Fort Belem with twenty-one guns, the Fort replying with an equal number, and the whole fleet dropped anchor in the port of Lisbon about 2 p.m.

Mr. Abbott went on shore immediately with Lieutenant Church, to call on Sir Arthur Magenis, the British Minister (for, alas! our former friend, Mr. Howard, and his amiable family were no longer at Lisbon) to report the arrival of Lord Sefton, while Colonel Dudley Carleton in another boat landed at the Custom House stairs, and proceeded to the Hotel Bragança (our quarters on this occasion) to see that everything was ready, and send down the carriages for the Mission. Several Portuguese naval officers in the meanwhile came on board to offer compliments and civilities, as did the captain of the United States frigate *Sacramento*, which was lying alongside of us, a mischievous looking craft, of which we had read much during the war. The captains of our own fleet also came to pay their respects to the admiral.

On the return of Colonel Carleton and Mr. Abbott, two boats were lowered and manned, and all our party took leave of the admiral, and were rowed ashore,

Norroy, Adams, and I in the first boat, and Lord Sefton, with his personal suite, in the other, the *Edgar* saluting him with eighteen guns, and all the fleet manning yards.

On the Monday following we were received in special audience by the King at the Ajuda Palace, which was not finished when I was at Lisbon before. His Majesty spoke to each of us very graciously in an extremely low voice, and told me he remembered me very well. On this occasion I renewed my acquaintance with the Marquis de Bemposta Subserra, the introducer of ambassadors; Mr. William Smith, the British Consul; and Admiral Sir George Sartorius, Conde de Penafirma in Portugal, now Admiral of the Fleet in England, and whom I had previously known in this country.

The next day brought us the melancholy information of the death of the Czarowitch at Nice, and the consequent postponement of the investiture to Thursday, May 4th. In the interim I again visited Cintra, in company with my brother officers, and at more leisure inspected the Moorish palace, where you are shown the council chamber and the seat in which Don Sebastian sat for the last time before the fatal battle of Alcacer Quibir, August 4th, 1578. As the seats are all fixtures in the wall, and inlaid with glazed tiles, the statement may be received with more confidence than many similar. The hall of magpies (*Sala das Pegas*), so called from the ceiling being painted with innumerable magpies, each holding a rose, and in his beak the motto "Por bem," "for good," is a curious sight;* but the hall of arms, called also the *Sala das Cervos*, or hall of stags, was much more interesting to us heralds, the roof being painted with the shields of arms of seventy-four of the noblest families in Portugal, each dependent from a stag's head. Returning from Cintra we stopped at a village where there was a cattle fair, and it being the 1st of May it was pretty to see on the roadside groups of children, each with their little May queen

* I have strong doubts of the origin of these paintings, which are said to commemorate a court scandal in the time of Dom João I., and his Queen Phillippa of Lancaster, sister of Henry IV. of England. I suspect in this, as in innumerable similar instances, we should find the story had been fabricated to account for the singularity of the design, which would prove to be the badge or device of the king or the queen, and suggested as usual by the resemblance in sound to some name or possession, or assumed on some special occasion at a tournament. A derivation not so *piquante*, I admit, but of greater importance to the historian. It seems to have escaped the notice of the promulgator of the story, that the motto of Dom João was "Il me plait *pour bien*," which is several times repeated on his tomb at Bathalla. The words "por bem" are therefore simply an abbreviation of the motto, similar to the "Esperance" of the Percies, the "autre n'aurai" of Philip the Good, Duke of Burgundy, and, as I believe, the "Ich dien" of Edward the Black Prince.

enthroned on a stone or a bank, and crowned with flowers.

A sadder visit was one we made to the church of San Vincente, the burial-place of the royal family of Braganza. The coffins are all of the ancient trunk or coffer shape, covered with velvet, fastened with lock and key, and ranged on a shelf in chronological order. What made it sad to me was the sight of the coffins containing the bodies of the fine young King Pedro V. and his beautiful queen Stephanie, whom, only a few years before, I had seen married and crowned, and left in health and happiness, with the fairest hopes of a long and prosperous reign.

On my former visit to Lisbon there had been but one bull fight, and that upon the very day that we were steaming out of the Tagus, homeward bound. It may, therefore, be readily imagined that I took the first opportunity of witnessing this national entertainment, more particularly as I was aware that in Portugal the sickening scenes exhibited in Spain are ingeniously avoided, the points of the bulls' horns being tipped with wooden balls, so that no goring of horse or man can possibly take place. We had secured a private box on "the shady side," over the public *Lugares da Sombra*—though Heaven knows there was not more sun, or so much, as a July one in London—and sat out the worrying, for it was little more, of about nine or ten bulls out of the thirteen or fourteen which were advertised to appear, and left the Campo Santa Anna with a feeling of weariness and disappointment. The only incident that occurred of an exciting or amusing character was the leaping of one bull clean over the inner barrier, and attempting to scale the second, which occasioned a precipitate stampede amongst the spectators seated in that part of the Circo de Toros. Some half-dozen Spaniards took part in the sport. They were gorgeously dressed after the well-known Figaro fashion, and pompously announced in the programme as matadores, or bull-fighters of great celebrity, but exhibited no skill or agility greater than their Lusitanian brethren; and as to the bulls, the majority appeared to me to be old stagers, going through their performance with as little exertion as possible. Unprovoked by the red cloaks of the *capinhas*, and enduring with such stoical fortitude the fixing into their necks of *farpas* and *banderilhas* (the decorated barbed darts with which the tormentors are plentifully provided) that Tom Hood's assertion, "Bullocks don't wear *ox-hide* of iron" seemed inapplicable to their bovine brethren of Portugal. The best acting was displayed by some of the capinhas who pretended to be hurt, and came limping round the circo, holding up their hats to receive the small copper coins flung to them by the compassionate spectators.

The nine days' mourning of course deprived us of much public amusement and many official entertainments. There were no balls or banquets or evening receptions by the Foreign Ambassadors, as in 1858; but Lord Sefton gave some very pleasant dinners to members of the Mission and officers of the Fleet, one of which was graced by the presence of Lady Marian Alford and Lady Alwyn Compton, who arrived from Madeira *en route* to England. We also dined one day with Admiral Dacres on board, with Lord Frederick Kerr, Admiral Warden, and other officers; but were not sorry when the appointed day—May 4th—arrived, for the investiture, when we proceeded as previously in four state carriages, the three first drawn by six and the last by eight horses (no mules this time), with running footmen in the Royal liveries on each side and an escort of Lancers to the Ajuda Palace, where about 2 P.M. the ceremony took place, in the presence of the Queen (daughter of Victor Emmanuel, King of Italy), the Court, the whole Corps Diplomatique, and six officers from each of the British ships in the Tagus. We returned to the hotel in the same state and lunched, and then drove in private carriages to be photographed, in compliance with the desire of H.R.H. the Prince of

Wales, expressed to Lord Henry Percy, and started again about half-past six to dine with the King at seven. The Queen was not well enough to be present, so there were no ladies on this occasion; but after dinner and taking coffee with the King, his father, King Ferdinand, and the Prince Augusto in the throne-room, we were invited to inspect Her Majesty's suite of apartments on a lower story, where we saw her and the infant Prince Charles, then about two years old. One of these rooms is entirely lined, ceiling and all, with beautiful Oriental alabaster, a present to her Majesty from the Khedive of Egypt. A fountain plays in the centre, and a quantity of golden cages containing singing and other birds depend from the roof. The next day we had a grand review, or rather parade, in the open space on the banks of the Tagus and facing the Palace of Belem; and on Saturday, the 6th of May, we were in our old berths on board the *Edgar*, and under weigh for England, I being the fortunate possessor of the identical bullock-waggon which I had contemptuously declined purchasing seven years previously, no other having been made, apparently, during the whole of that period or to be found throughout Lisbon. There it had remained, covered with dust, on the same high shelf, I had seen it in 1858, and, *faute de mieux*, I paid the ten shillings originally asked for it, almost grateful that the toyman did not raise his price for this unique specimen of Lisbon workmanship, for which as many pence would have been a sufficient remuneration. Such was the rate of progress in art and commerce in Portugal a few years ago. Whether the increase of railroads and other national improvements have quickened its pace latterly, this deponent sayeth not; but certainly at the time I speak there was little to tempt the most prodigal traveller to open his purse-strings, the shops in Gold Street and Silver Street exhibiting, as far as my recollection served me, the same articles hung up in the same windows, or if not, the *fac-similes* of those I had seen before in them.

The *Black Prince* had left us a few days previously for Ireland, and the *Defence* had received orders to remain in the Tagus to accompany the Russian Fleet, expected to arrive with the body of the Czarowitz. So we had with us only the *Hector*, the *Achilles*, and the *Prince Consort*. Sunday, 7th, was one of the most lovely days I ever remember; but Monday was miserable, with heavy rain, and extremely cold, the wind, too, was dead against us, and so continued for two more days, the *Hector* falling short of coal was allowed to make straight for England, but we being under sail, made hardly any way at all; at length the wind fell, the weather cleared, and putting on the screw, we began to make up for lost time. Chatting with Mr. Love, the Admiral's Secretary, in his office, we were startled by the terrible cry of "Man overboard!" We rushed out on deck, and found a poor fellow had fallen from the fore-rigging while the ship was going under sail and steam at nearly eight knots an hour. Fortunately he could swim; a life-buoy was thrown to him, which he caught; the engines were stopped, and the sails taken in; a boat lowered and manned with all speed. It was grand to see how the gallant fellows pulled! The boat seemed to fly over the waves. The man was by this time nearly half a mile astern of us; but they reached him in an incredibly short space of time, though it seemed an age, no doubt, to him, and in about twenty minutes he was on board again all right, having helped to pull the boat back—one of the best things he could do. It was a most exciting time, and had the man been lost, would have been most painfully impressed on my memory. I have now, thank God, only the recollection of the promptitude and energy of his brave messmates, which so speedily relieved the anxiety of all who witnessed the accident. On the 12th we were through the Bay and in the Channel, and parted company with the *Achilles* and *Prince Consort*, which left for the Isle of

Portland, and on Saturday, May 13th, sighted the Isle of Wight at sunrise, and dropped anchor at Spithead shortly after breakfast. All well.

The mail bag having come on board with the letters, the Admiral found amongst his, one that certainly had not been posted on shore, containing the following lines :—

God bless our gallant Admiral, where'er his course he steers !
May honour, health, and wealth, be his for many happy years,
May life be like his own good ship when under easy sail,
A fleet of friends around him, "keeping station," ne'er to fail.
"Church" for his Flag Lieutenant—for Secretary, "Love,"
A man has nought to fear below, and all to hope above !
So when his cruise is over, in that Haven may he be,
Where no sad "Lists of Punishments" they'll worry him to see.*

I am sure the good wishes of the writer were heartily echoed by every member of the Mission, for nothing could exceed the kindness and attention paid to us all by Sir Sydney Dacres and every one under his command. The pleasure of this voyage, like that of the former, was, I am thankful to say, unchequered by any misadventure, and procured me some valuable additions to the circle of my friends and acquaintances.

* He had told us that nothing vexed and pained him so much as being compelled to sign the lists of punishments sent to him, without having the power to remit or modify any sentence which appeared to him unnecessarily severe.

CHAPTER XVIII.

In August, 1865, our association met at Durham—president, His Grace the Duke of Cleveland, K.G.—and I was then enabled to say that I had inspected every cathedral in England, and nearly all in company of the most competent guides and expositors. Durham was the only one I had never seen previously, even at a distance. But, interesting as it undoubtedly is in its architectural features, it contained no particular object for me to study or descant upon. The deficiency was, however, amply made up by the effigies in the church at Chester-le-Street and the paintings in Lumley Castle. I made a few brief observations respecting them upon the spot, which were utterly misunderstood by the persons reporting them, and gave rise to some absurd letters and notices, not only in a local paper, but in a London journal, the least competent to deal with such a subject, my criticisms on the works themselves being ridiculously misrepresented as attacks upon the authenticity of the Lumley *Pedigree!* In fact, as far as the paintings were concerned, I had increased their real importance and value, which had been very much under-rated by Mr. Surtees, the county historian, though as an archæologist I was bound to point out the errors into which the public might be led by an implicit belief in the accuracy of the costume, civil or military, in which the various personages were represented, Saxons and Normans being armed and habited after the fashion of the fifteenth century.

On my return from the North I paid a short visit to Paris, where at the Porte Saint-Martin I saw that popular monstrosity "La Biche au Bois," the subject of which fourteen years previously I had dramatised for Madame Vestris, and produced at the Olympic under the title of "The Prince of Happy Land; or, the Fawn in the Forest." To me, the glittering gallimaufry in which all the ingenuity and beauty of the original fairy tale was lost and destroyed, was one of the dullest and most indecent exhibitions I ever witnessed. The charming story on which it professed to be founded was scarcely recognisable. The Kingdom of Fishes and other scenes foisted into the piece, *à tort et à travers*, from earlier spectacles, had nothing to do with the plot, and admirable as I admit was the ogling of the amorous *Dauphine*, and picturesque as was the appearance of the all but stark naked Princess of Ethiopia, it was melancholy to contrast the dreary, stupid spectacle with the bright, sparkling, epigrammatic Féerie Folie, "Riquet à la Houpe," which had fascinated me on the same boards in 1821, and originated the series of my fairy extravaganzas in England.* Why cannot the reckless concoctors of these undramatic conglomerations invent titles for them unassociated with the delightful tales, of which they disdain to follow the plots, and ruthlessly destroy the point and interest?—nay, worse, for the playful wit, the subtle satire, and moral lessons of the originals, substituting inane buffoonery and gross indecency. Is it too much to connect the low tone of taste and morals of a public that can patronise such frivolous and meretricious exhibitions with the decadence of national grandeur and the general disorganisation of society?

At the Vaudeville on this occasion I saw Mons.

* I was the more impressed with this feeling in consequence of being engaged just then in throwing into irregular verse the dear old story of "The Sleeping Beauty," to accompany a set of wood-cuts by the Messrs. Dalziel, from the designs of Mr. Richard Doyle; and having to avoid repeating any lines in my dramatic version, produced at Covent Garden in 1840, I was endeavouring to treat the subject more poetically (if I may be permitted the expression) than I had done in the Extravaganza. It was published by Messrs. Routledge the following Christmas under the title of an "Old Tale newly Told."

Sardou's powerful drama, "Les Deux Sœurs," which had caused an excitement of a far different description in literary circles as well as amongst playgoers generally, the object of the author being undisguisedly to demonstrate the evils arising from the consideration of marriage by the Roman Catholic Church as indissoluble. The play was superbly acted by all. Madame Fargueil, sustained with inimitable skill the character of the guilty sister, and the terrible duel across the table ending in the death of the seducer and the suicide of the husband was almost too shocking, I admit, for representation. Still, it was not vulgarly sensational. There was an object, a grand object, in the mind of the dramatist. Right or wrong, he felt he had a stern lesson to read, and he did not flinch in the doing it. There has been much controversy in this country respecting the plays of Mons. Sardou, and they have been a source of some perplexity to the Lord Chamberlain. That, looking at them from an English point of view, they contain scenes "*un peu fort*" there is no disputing; but they possess this immense superiority over the sensational dramas with which our stage has been for some time deluged, that they are intended to teach, and not simply to excite, and that they are models of ingenious construction and dramatic dialogue; more natural in character and purer in sentiment than those of Victor Hugo or Alexandre Dumas (father or son), which alone can be compared to them for brilliancy of language or novelty of stage-effect.

In September this year I was applied to by Mr. Buckstone to adapt for him Offenbach's opera bouffe, "Orphée aux Enfers," with a view to the first appearance at the Haymarket of Miss Louise Keeley, who he promised should be adequately supported by vocalists he would engage expressly for the piece, there not being one in the company who professed to sing operatic music. It was necessary also that Orpheus should play the violin, and there were other difficulties to be got over. The good intentions of Mr. Buckstone, however, only went the way of cartloads of similar excellent materials, to pave the regions we were about to lay the scene of in the Haymarket, and failed to induce any singers of celebrity to set their feet on them. I was so accustomed, however, to this sort of disappointment in an English theatre that it did not much disconcert me. I wrote the piece as well as I could, and got it acted as well as I could, William Farren, who had received a musical education, making a pleasant Jupiter; Mrs. Chippendale, a splendid jealous Juno; Miss Helen Howard representing Public Opinion in a style calculated to obtain its favourable verdict; and an old favourite and true artist, Mr. David Fisher, playing Orpheus with intelligence and "the fiddle like an angel." Miss Louise Keeley was a charming Eurydice, and sang like a little nightingale; so, with the addition of pretty scenery, pretty dresses, and some pretty faces, we pulled through pretty well. It was not Offenbach's opera: but the piece went merrily with the audience, and ran from Christmas to Easter. As far as I was concerned, the press was most laudatory, and welcomed my reappearance as a writer of extravaganza, after a lapse of nine years, with a cordiality that was extremely gratifying to me, considering the change that in the meanwhile had come over the spirit of that class of entertainment.

In June, 1866, I was promoted to the office of Somerset Herald, and during the greater part of the year principally engaged in editing "Clarke's Introduction to Heraldry," for Messrs. Bell and Daldy. It was one of the earliest and handiest little books published on the subject in a popular form, having existed upwards of eighty years, and gone through seventeen editions; but the real value of the science of Heraldry becoming daily more apparent in this age of progress and critical inquiry, it was necessary now that the work should undergo thorough revision: that exploded theories should be omitted, and erroneous opinions corrected, and the work rendered a more trustworthy handbook to an art as useful (*pace* Mr. Lowe) as it is ornamental.

I am not going to bore the reader with an essay on Heraldry, which had been pretty nearly abandoned as a silly and useless pursuit. The critical spirit of archæology has within the last half century done much to correct the prejudice, and the curious and important information to be derived from the study of armorial devices is rapidly becoming appreciated by even the general public. An Earl of Pembroke is reported to have said to a herald, "Why, you silly man, you don't even understand your own silly trade." It is too probable that a century ago the earl might have been right as regarded the man, and there can be at any rate but little doubt the too frequent appointment of incompetent persons to offices of so special a nature tended in a great measure to lower the public estimation of a science which can boast the names of Camden, Dugdale, Vincent, and Glover in the list of its professors.

In 1867, two simultaneous Garter Missions were decided upon—one to bear the Order to the Emperor of Russia, and the other to invest the Emperor of Austria. On this occasion I was kindly offered my choice as to which I would accompany. Of course my inclination was to the former, as I had seen Vienna and nearly all the principal cities in Germany, and might never have another chance of visiting St. Petersburgh and Moscow, particularly with such advantages as would have been afforded me by my official position under such circumstances. I should also have gone out thither as secretary to the Mission, as I did to Portugal on the last occasion. It was evident, however, that Sir Charles Young wished me to accompany him. Without being actually ill, he was visibly failing. We were very old friends, and he dwelt with marked emphasis on the observation that it was the last journey we should take together, as it proved to be. Lancaster Herald (now Sir Albert Woods), who succeeded him in the office of Garter, also seemed desirous that I should be of their party; and so I gave up my hopes of seeing the Neva and the Kremlin, and agreed to revisit the Danube and the Graben.

The Vienna Mission consisted of the Marquis of Bath (whom I previously accompanied to Portugal) and Sir Charles Young, the two plenipotentiaries; the Earl Brownlow, Viscount St. Asaph, the Right Hon. Sir Henry Storks, G.C.B.; Colonel the Hon. Percy Fielding, Coldstream Guards; Armar Lowry-Corry, Esq., of the Foreign Office, Secretary to the Special Mission; Albert W. Woods, Esq., Lancaster

Herald, Secretary to the Garter Mission, and me. On Saturday, the 20th of July, we left Charing Cross by the 8.30 p.m. train for Dover, crossed immediately to Calais, dined or supped, whichever you please to call it, and proceeded *viâ* Paris, travelling night and day (with the exception of a few hours' rest on Monday night at Munich), and reaching Vienna on the evening of the 23rd, where apartments had been provided for us by the Emperor at the hotel of the "Archduke Charles." While at dinner, Lord Bloomfield, our ambassador at the Court of Vienna, arrived with his secretary, and we were severally introduced to him.

On the 24th we were received in special audience by his Imperial and Royal Apostolic Majesty, at the Burg Palace, and dined in the evening with Lord Bloomfield, at the British Embassy, where for the first time I met a statesman of European celebrity, Baron (now Count) Beust, then at the head of the government, and at the present moment the representative of the Emperor of Austria in this country.

Matters proceeded more rapidly here than they did in Portugal. The investiture was fixed for the day following (Thursday, 25th), and shortly after noon we proceeded in four of the Emperor's state-carriages to the Burg Palace, where we were received at the Ambassadors' entrance by a guard of honour, and met in the first antechamber by the Landgrave Von Furstenburg, Grand Master of the Ceremonies, who conducted us into the second, where we were received by the Count de Crenneville, Grand Chamberlain, who ushered us into the Grand Council Room, where the Emperor, surrounded by his Court, stood in front of the throne, and the investiture took place with the usual formalities.

After the ceremony we returned to the hotel, and changed our uniforms for plain evening dress, to dine with the Emperor at 5 o'clock at Schönbrunn.

As we ascended the staircase we were met by one of the officers of the household, who gave to each of us a card with a broad silver edging, on which was indicated the places assigned to the bearer at the Imperial table, mine being inscribed—

Mr. J. Robinson Planché.
Est prié de se mettre à table à gauche de
Ministre le Baron John.

Baron John being the new Minister for War, who had superseded his unfortunate predecessor on the conclusion of peace with Prussia. As Baron John spoke nothing but German, my conversation with his Excellency was exceedingly limited, but most fortunately for me, I had the pleasure of having on the other side of me Count Taaffe, one of his Majesty's chamberlains, and most intimate friends from boyhood, who spoke French fluently, and a more agreeable person it would be difficult to find in any country. I never had a pleasanter dinner in my life, or, as may be imagined, a much better one; and it was impossible for me to avoid recalling the day when, in 1827, I had passed through that very room little imagining that I should ever be a guest at that table, and drink "Imperial tokay," in company with its august master. Truly, "it was an honour that I dreamed not of." After dinner, as at Lisbon, we followed his Majesty into an adjoining apartment, where coffee was served, and on the Emperor's retiring, His Serene Highness Prince Hohenlohe led us through the palace out upon a terrace from which a flight of steps at each end led down into the gardens, where cigars were furnished to all those who smoked, which I need scarcely say was nearly everybody.

Here I expected our entertainment would conclude, but another and most especial compliment was still to be paid to the Mission. Some eight or ten Imperial carriages of a form resembling those now so fashionable in London, called Victorias, containing each only two persons, drew up under the terrace, and we were invited to take our seats in them with Lord Bloomfield and some of his attachés. My companion was Mr. Bonar, the principal Secretary to the Embassy, and now our Minister at Berne; and we were then driven at a foot pace all through the Palace gardens up to "The Gloriette," and round to the menagerie, where some alighted to see the animals, and eventually back to the Palace, where our own carriages were in waiting. Mr. Bonar informed me that this was one of the highest compliments the Emperor paid to his visitors—that no other carriages were ever permitted to drive through the gardens—(His emphatic words were—"Gods cannot drive here!")—that a promenade of this description had not taken place for some years, and that as soon as it was terminated an army of gardeners would be set to work to efface every track of the carriage-wheels.

It was twilight when we left Schönbrunn. Sir C. Young and some of our party returned to Vienna, but the majority of us drove to a Volksgarten in the vicinity of the Palace, called "Die Neüe Welt" (The New World), where a grand gala was taking place, and all the guten leute of the capital enjoying themselves: dancing to Strauss's own excellent band, led by the maestro himself, or listening to three or four others in various parts of the gardens, which were prettily laid out and tastefully illuminated. We stayed for about an hour, and then drove leisurely back to the city, reaching our hotel before eleven.

The two following days we were occupied in returning the calls of the officers of the Imperial household, the Ministers, and the Corps Diplomatique, and preparing for our departure. With the exception of the banquet at Schönbrunn and the dinner at the British Embassy, there were no entertainments at Court, no receptions or balls at the hotels of the foreign ambassadors. The beautiful Empress was at Ischl, so we were deprived of the presence of ladies at the Palace.

Austria was in mourning, nationally and socially. The crushing disaster of Sadowa—the infamous murder of the Emperor Maximilian—were events of too recent occurrence to permit of any official festivities beyond those absolutely demanded by courtesy on such an occasion; and let me here remark that the public testimony of England's respect and friendship at such a moment, afforded by the procession in state of the Garter Mission through the crowded streets of the capital, bearing the ensigns of the noblest Order in the world from the Queen of Great Britain to an ancient and faithful ally, doubly stricken by political misfortune and family affliction, was evidently deeply felt and appreciated by the whole population. Every hat was raised as the plenipotentiaries passed, and there was no mistaking the expression of satisfaction on the faces of the honest Viennese at witnessing not simply a mere show, but a solemn proof of the generous sympathy of a gracious sovereign and a great nation.

The Order of the Garter is the only one conveyed by its officers in state to the foreign sovereign on whom her Majesty is pleased to confer this signal and coveted distinction.

This fact has frequently induced some rigid economists, who begrudge the fair expense of these Missions, to inquire why the ensigns should not be sent in a box by a Queen's messenger to our Minister at the foreign court, and be presented by his Excellency to the sovereign in private audience, as similar decorations are transmitted by other European potentates. With due deference, I would urge that very fact as a reason for the continuance of a custom which not only raises the high estimation entertained in England of the Order itself, and consequently increases the value of the honour conferred, but in the most public and solemn manner manifests the good feeling of this country towards the people whose monarch is the chosen recipient. The political importance alone of the instance I have described was, I am convinced, worth double and treble the cost of it to this country. There is such a thing as being penny wise and pound foolish, and, as far as my experience goes, I am not aware of any place in which, in matters of state or art, there is so much proof of it as in England.

While at Vienna I naturally snatched an opportunity of refreshing my recollection of the celebrated Ambras collection of ancient armour in the Belvidere Palace. It appeared to me much smaller than when I saw it in 1827. What there is is exceedingly fine, but it is arranged, as formerly, only for effect, and without any attempt to render it instructive by chronological order.

Our party separated at Vienna, and Sir Charles Young, Woods, and I returned home *viâ* Munich, Strasbourg, and Paris, getting "en passant" a hasty peep at the Exposition, and I, by myself, at "La Grande Duchesse de Gerolstein."

CHAPTER XIX.

In consequence of the formation of the new street from the Thames Embankment to the Mansion House (now Queen Victoria Street), a small portion of the south side of the Herald's College was taken down, and a new front to it erected. On commencing this work, in 1868, the figures of the lion and unicorn sejant, which had surmounted two square brick pillars in the court-yard, were removed and placed upon the ground. The accidental position given to them, and in which they remained, close to the side wall of the building during a considerable period, appeared to be so ludicrously suggestive of an altercation between the parties, that I made a sketch of them, and sent it to "The Builder," with an imaginary conversation, which, as it has not been printed elsewhere, I take the liberty to introduce here, with the wood-cut, which has been kindly lent to me by the editor.

UNSUPPORTED SUPPORTERS.

THE Lion and the Unicorn,
  Who deign'd till very lately,
The Heralds' College to adorn,
  On pillars tall and stately,

Unceremoniously, one day,
  Were hoisted from their stations,
And on the pavement left to stay,
  Pending the alterations.

The Lion sadly wanted *or*,
  The Unicorn lack'd *argent*;
Clearly they'd ne'er been thus before
  "*Depicted in the margent.*"*

* The customary reference in a patent of arms to the painting of those granted by it.

It therefore seem'd of the offence
  A serious aggravation
That folks with arms of less pretence
  Obtained full compensation,

While they, supporters of the Crown,
  For centuries, unaided,
Who had graced standards of renown,
  Were to vile *flags* degraded.

The Unicorn, in language strong,
  The Lion laid the blame on:
"Without a growl to bear this wrong
  A blot will be your fame on.

"If of us quadrupeds you were
  The king, or e'en the regent,
You would be *rampant*, not beg there,
  Like a tame poodle—*sejant!*

"As *dexter* 'tis your right to make
  Them equal justice minister;
If I should up the matter take,
  They'd call the motive *sinister*.

"The British Lion, you! My brain
  Whirls round, it so provokes me!
For half-a-crown I'd break my chain,—
  My collar almost chokes me!

"'*Dieu et mon Droit*,' no longer may
  You boast as your proud motto;
'*Adieu, mon droit*,' you'd better say,
  And join Parkins & Gotto." *

So saying, like a vicious colt,
  To cut the matter shorter,
He made a sort of demi-volt,
  And rump'd his co-supporter.

* One of the many firms professing to find arms, and who are most successful in doing so—for those who have none.

The Lion winced at the last sneer,
But only gave a whistle,
And said, "My ancient friend, I fear
You've trod upon your thistle.

"The motto you to England brought—
Excuse me, comrade, if I sigh
To find you set it now at nought—
Was 'BEATI PACIFICI.'

"Prithee don't let the Heralds see
Us, thus '*addorsed*,' good brother,
When we in every sense should be
'*Respecting one another*.'

"In youth I'm willing to admit
More '*combattant*' was I, sir;
But then I'd much more pluck than wit,—
I'm older now and wiser.

"I can complacently repose
Beneath my well-won laurels;
And mean no more to poke my nose
In everybody's quarrels.

"Nor does it suit my present views
To roar for every trifle:
I've got—and can, if need be, *use*—
But won't *strain* my new rifle.

"You seem to have forgotten quite
The world's in constant movement;
And neither King's nor Lion's might
Can long repel improvement.

"London of a new street had need,
And heralds by profession
Were bound to lead, and not impede,
A grand public procession.

"The posts we held were on the go,
And fallen soon had seen us,

We had nothing to support, you know—
Not one poor coat between us.

"But re-installed in the new court,
And gay with paint and gilding,
We shall our dignity support
With that of the whole building.

"Facing a street so broad and fine—
When to our seats we've vaulted—
My crown will cut a greater shine,
Your horn will be exalted.

"So blazon not a long dull roll
Of bickerings and bereavements,
Display the power of self-control—
The greatest of *atchievements*."

'Twas all in vain: the Unicorn
Was deaf to explanation,
And, with a toss up of his horn,
Declined more conversation.

I regret to add that the dear old lion's hopes were disappointed. There were architectural and *material* obstacles to the reinstatement of these ancient worthies. The posts they occupied have been abolished. A younger lion and unicorn have been appointed to new situations, having successfully scrambled through a competitive examination; and a bare subsistence in some obscure locality is all that can be allowed to their venerable predecessors on their compulsory resignation. The case, I believe, is not singular.

The congress of our society, held that year at

Cirencester, under the presidency of Earl Bathurst, will be memorable for the violent controversy it gave rise to respecting the magnificent, perhaps unequalled, series of painted glass windows in the church at Fairford, not only the design, but the execution of which our lamented associate, Mr. Henry Holt, contended should be ascribed to Albrecht Dürer, in accordance with a local tradition which, in the course of three centuries, had, like so many similar accounts handed down to us, preserved a modicum of truth amidst a mass of contradictory and unfounded assertion. In proof of his opinion, which was as strenuously disputed by the Rev. Mr. Joyce (son-in-law of the rector, Lord Dynevor) and several antiquarians and artists of eminence, Mr. Holt referred to the wood-cuts in the "Nuremberg Chronicle" and other early works of that description which he also attributed to the same great master, and his remarks on this subject were so startlingly opposed to all the received ideas concerning not only the life and works of Dürer, but the origin of printing, wood-engraving, block-books, and playing-cards, that the controversy threatened to involve the whole world of letters, and draw into its vortex many eager combatants who had calmly contemplated the contest while it was confined to painting on glass.

The question, as far as it concerned playing-cards,

touching the subject of costume, woke up me, for I have the greatest respect for the old adage, "ne sutor, &c.," and therefore, though much impressed by the arguments and facts adduced by Mr. Holt, had refrained from discussing points of art which I had but a superficial knowledge of with men who had made them their study. But on dress and armour I had a few words to say, and I said them. They have no business here, and therefore those whom it may concern are respectfully referred to my papers on the subject in "The Builder" and the journal of our society.* I have only to observe that the question, which affects the whole history of printing, and much of that of painting, is by no means settled, and that the sudden and deeply regretted death of my intelligent and enthusiastic friend Mr. Holt has deprived the public of a mass of most interesting information respecting Albrecht Dürer which he had collected at Nuremberg during numerous visits made for that express purpose, and was arranging for publication by Mr. Murray, of Albemarle Street. Since that sad event, the controversy has died away; but I am inclined to believe the results will be of more

* "On Early Wood-engraving in Connection with Playing-cards." *The Builder* for Nov. 19, 1870.

"Notes upon New Theories." Journal of the *B. A. A.* for March, 1871.

importance some day to literature and art than may be generally imagined at present.

A kind invitation from Lady Molesworth to pass a few weeks this autumn at Pencarrow afforded me an opportunity of visiting some interesting portions of Cornwall, the only county in England I had not previously visited: the rock-throned ruins of Tintagel Castle, traditionally assigned to the legendary King Arthur; the river Camel, deriving its name Cam-alan, which signifies "the crooked river," from its continuous windings, on the romantic banks of which the great founder of the Round Table is said to have been slain, and several ancient British and Roman remains of great interest. In the lovely grounds of Pencarrow itself is a Roman fort, or entrenched camp, the lines of which are remarkably perfect. During my stay here I sketched out some little dramatic trifles, which I published afterwards as "Pieces of Pleasantry for Private Performance," and, on my leaving, I was flattered by being requested to write some verses in the visitors' book, which contains autographs, drawings, and original compositions of a host of eminent persons who have enjoyed the tasteful and cordial hospitalities of that most pleasant mansion. The following were my "reflections"—

ON LEAVING PENCARROW.

CUNNING Camel! I've a notion,
Wherefore thou art ever winding,
As if to the thirsty ocean
Thou had'st failed a channel finding.
Most mysteriously meand'ring—
Stead of flying like an arrow,
Straight a-head—thou keepest wandering
Round and round about Pencarrow!

'Midst its groves and moorlands doubling,
Like a hunted hare—zig-zagging;
Rapidly o'er rocks now bubbling,
Lazily in pools now lagging.
In the deepest bottoms hiding,
Struggling through the gorges narrow,
Leaping, dashing, creeping, gliding,
Anywhere, save from Pencarrow!

Who can wonder, "Crooked River,"
Once that thou hast found thy way in,
Thou shouldst use thy best endeavour,
Such a paradise to stay in?
Surely none, who like me quitting,
Envy e'en yon tiny sparrow,
On the window-sill there sitting,
Not forced to fly from sweet Pencarrow!

Farewell! farewell! thou stream romantic,
Reluctantly the law fulfilling;
Which bids thee to the wide Atlantic,
Conduct thy waves howe'er unwilling.
Adieu, Tintagel! Hantigantic!
Danish Fort and British Barrow,
Crab's-pool, Pentire, and nearly frantic,
I finish with—Adieu, Pencarrow!

At the close of this year, the authorities at the South Kensington Museum having obtained from Lieutenant-Colonel Augustus Meyrick, to whom Sir Samuel Rush Meyrick had bequeathed his property, the loan of his invaluable collection of armour, antiquities, and objects of art, at Goodrich Court, I was requested, in accordance with an express stipulation in the agreement, to arrange the armour at Kensington as I had previously done at Manchester, and also at Goodrich Court on the return of it from that exhibition.

The gallery selected for its display was admirably adapted for the purpose, having a fine range of large windows on the south side of the Horticultural Gardens,* and of just sufficient length to enable me to carry out in the most complete manner the chronological arrangement which had hitherto been only partially effected. I had there space, and what was of even more importance, light, to my heart's content, and those best acquainted with the collection declared that they had never before had an idea of its extent, beauty, and value. With the intelligent assistance of

* One of those wherein the National Portraits had been exhibited in 1866. A most interesting collection, on which I wrote a series of articles in the *Builder*, showing the value of heraldry and costume in testing the authenticity of ancient paintings.

Mr. C. A. Pierce, at that time on the staff of the Museum, I think I succeeded in proving that picturesque effect might be obtained without sacrificing the instructive character of the exhibition by a confusion of armour and weapons of all centuries, as in all the armouries at home or abroad that I have ever inspected.

The gallery was opened to the public on Saturday the 26th of December, 1868, and for three years formed one of the popular sights of London. At the conclusion of my Introduction to the official Catalogue, compiled by Mr. C. C. Black, Supplementary Assistant-Keeper, I observed: "Here terminates the collection of European arms and armour, which for historical interest, and (what is of even more importance to the institution to which it is at present confided) for *educational purposes*, I believe to be unrivalled in England or on the Continent. The grand object of its founder was INSTRUCTION, and his old friend and grateful pupil rejoices in the fortunate occurrence which has enabled him to assist in its further development." It may be imagined, therefore, with what deep regret I am at this moment witnessing the break-up and dispersion of that collection, the like of which it is no exaggeration to affirm, no sum of money could at present, if ever, enable an individual to form again. Not only the armour, but the whole of the art-treasures exhibited in conjunction with them, including the numerous rare and exquisite carvings in ivory bequeathed to Sir Samuel Meyrick, by our mutual friend, Mr. Francis Douce, amongst which are two boxes in the shape of roses, containing the original miniatures of Henry VIII. and Ann of Cleves, painted by Holbein, expressly to be interchanged between "the high contracting parties," were offered to the Government for the sum of £50,000, at which they had been valued by competent persons; but not even a bidding was made for them. These irreplaceable antiquities are fast leaving England, one Parisian dealer alone having bought to the extent of £12,000, and it is but too probable that the whole will be lost to us for ever. Such an opportunity to render more perfect the national armoury in the Tower, to enrich the ethnological department in the British Museum, and add to the art-treasures at South Kensington, as well as of recouping a considerable part of the purchase-money by the sale of all that was not specially required for the above purposes, will never, it may be safely predicted, occur again.

Looking at it from a pecuniary point of view, the mistake of the Science and Art Department of the Government has been a fortunate one for Colonel Meyrick; but the loss it has occasioned to science and art in England is, unhappily, irreparable.

The heavy calamity which befel my youngest daughter at the close of the year compelled me to relinquish that life of literary leisure I had for some time enjoyed, and the indulgence in archæological pursuits, which were very fascinating, but by no means remunerative. It was necessary for me to "put money in my purse," and I began to turn my thoughts again towards "the Theatre," the anxieties and vexations of which I had gradually become more and more reluctant to encounter. I had passed the scriptural age of man, and my children's children had sat upon my knees; but too many of them now unfortunately required more substantial accommodation. There is a very popular song which I heard my friend Mr. German Reed sing with great effect a few years ago, entitled "The Poor Man's Philosophy," wherein said poor man assures a certain "John Brown" that he can keep a wife and "a troop" of children, and enjoy his "otium cum dignitate," on a hundred per annum, having still a guinea he can spend, and various other little gratifications he can afford to indulge in. I confess I couldn't see it, and said to myself, "Let me talk with this philosopher;"

and these were my reflections on his ideas of domestic economy:—

JOHN BROWN'S ANSWER.

I've listened to your song—and, unless I'm very wrong,
There is much in it of what we now call "bosh"—Tom Smith.
It is easy so to sing; but to *do's* another thing,
And I fear that your philosophy won't wash—Tom Smith.
Of course that's not your name—but 'twill answer all the same,
For the person I'm presumed to argue with—Tom Smith.
And offended you can't be, as you've done the same by me,
For I'm no more John Brown than you're Tom Smith—Tom Smith.

What you love and what you hate—you're at liberty to state,
I've nothing upon earth with that to do—Tom Smith.
"*De gustibus non est*," I've no doubt you know the rest,
And besides—I've much the same dislikes as you—Tom Smith.
It's on matters of finance, in which there's no romance,
I would break with you a lance, if you please—Tom Smith.
I'm myself a family man, and I don't believe you can,
Contrive to live with yours on bread and cheese—Tom Smith.

You've "a hundred pounds a year"—well, let's even say it's clear,
Of Income-tax, that's not two pounds a week—Tom Smith.
But the cottage is "*your own*," so the rent must in be thrown,
Which I grant will help your income out to eke—Tom Smith.
Per contra, you've a wife, as dear to you as life,
I hope she is I'm sure for both your sakes—Tom Smith.
But the more you hold her dear, the more must be your fear,
If anything your little income shakes—Tom Smith.

Of children you've a troop—an interesting group,
But to tell how many form it you forgot—Tom Smith.
Say five or six in all, which for "a troop" is small,
Of bread and butter they must eat a lot—Tom Smith.

Of their clothes you may be spare—but they cannot go *quite* bare,
And on whooping-cough and measles you must count—Tom Smith.
And if only one be ill, I'm afraid the doctor's bill,
Might at Christmas prove a serious amount—Tom Smith.

'Tis philosophy no doubt trifles not to fret about,
And "sufficient for the day" is a fine text—Tom Smith.
But at your garden gate, do you never scratch your pate,
When you think what's in the cupboard for the *next*—Tom Smith?
The pot you know must boil, 'twould be better sure to toil,
And add by honest labour to your store—Tom Smith;
Than moon away your time, in philosophic rhyme,
Or sitting 'neath your shady sycamore—Tom Smith.

You bid me, as I pass, come and drain with you a glass,
But it cannot be of wine, or beer, or grog—Tom Smith.
It's more like "Adam's ale," I'm afraid, than "Bass's pale,"
And to drink, I water shun, like a mad dog—Tom Smith.
If a "guinea you've to spend," I advise you as your friend,
To put it in the Savings' Bank forthwith—Tom Smith.
You will want it before long, and sing another song,
Unless, as I suspect, you are a myth—Tom Smith!

With these convictions, therefore, and despite my recollection of the earlier description of that more happy man who was

"Passing rich with forty pounds a year,"

I set to work to see how I could improve my very precarious income, and entered into an engagement with Mrs. John Wood, who had taken the St. James's Theatre, and professed to me her intention to revive English comedy of the highest order, and to eschew anything in the shape of modern burlesque, sensational drama, &c., &c., &c. My position was that which I had held under Madame Vestris—superintendent of the decorative department, with "a seat in the Cabinet." The speedy abandonment of Mrs. Wood's "first principles," and the consequent collapse of the whole affair, is of too recent a date for me to say more than that I retired from the theatre as soon as I found I could be of no more assistance to it, having fortunately reserved my right to do so.

CHAPTER XX.

The general observations of the press on the arrangement of the Meyrick collection at South Kensington led to the partial accomplishment of an object I had for fourteen years been incessantly labouring to attain, viz., the improvement of the national Armoury in the Tower of London in accordance with the progress of knowledge, and a thorough reformation of the absurd system of its management and exhibition.

As early as 1855 a kind friend had transmitted my views, and the facts in support of them, to Lord Panmure, at that time the Secretary for War; and I have his letter before me, in which he says—

> "Mr. Planché certainly appears to be the very man for the place he aspires to; but I have heard nothing on the subject, and will hasten to make inquiries, because I consider our armour treasures at the Tower much too valuable to trust to common hands."

Nothing resulted, however, from these inquiries, and, during the reign of his successor, my own personal friend, the late Duke of Newcastle, the important business of the War Office, in consequence of the war with Russia, rendered it useless for me to move in the business; but in 1859 I was introduced to the Right Hon. Sydney Herbert, who expressed great interest in the question, and requested me to draw up a statement for his consideration. As that statement contains the *gravamen* of my arguments and suggestions, and has been made a public record, I print it here:—

SIR,

In obedience to your direction I have the honour to submit to you a statement, as brief as I can make it, of the late and present condition of the Tower Armoury, accompanied by such suggestions as you have kindly requested me to offer for its improvement and conservation.

In the year 1825, Dr. Samuel Rush Meyrick received the Royal commands to re-arrange the Horse and Spanish Armouries, as they were then called; but instead of that learned antiquary being permitted to exercise his taste and knowledge to the extent he desired, he was hampered by instructions which greatly detracted from the value of his services, and compelled him to compromise with a system which should have been utterly destroyed. He was allowed to place the principal equestrian figures in chronological order, and to do away with the gross absurdity of exhibiting a suit of the reign of Elizabeth as one that belonged to William the Conqueror; but, at the same time that he demolished "the line of kings," he was ordered to appropriate every suit to some great personage of the period to which it belonged, distinguishing the few that could actually be identified by stars upon the flags above them. This childish "make-believe" arrangement exists to this day, and so little care is taken to preserve the modicum of truth contained in it, that on my recent visit the card that indicated the suit which undoubtedly belonged to Robert Dudley, Earl of Leicester, was hanging at the nose of a horse placed five or six below the one it should have been attached to. Dr. Meyrick having been knighted for his gratuitous services, and the fact of his having re-arranged the collection honourably recorded in gilt letters upon a board placed in a conspicuous position in the Grand Armoury, the care and increase of it were confided to the chief storekeeper for the time being, whose qualifications for his important and responsible position did not include of necessity any knowledge of ancient armour, and he was consequently left to the tender mercies of dishonest dealers, or the discretion of casual advisers. The consequence has been, that although some valuable additions have been occasionally made, many palpable forgeries and clumsy casts have been purchased at large prices, whilst rare and genuine articles have been lightly rejected, and allowed to leave the country, or to pass into the hands of enlightened and liberal English collectors. I refrain from lengthening this paper by instancing facts, but am fully prepared to do so if desired. I can show that valuable articles which have been sold or abstracted from the Armoury, have been actually offered to the authorities, and rejected unrecognised by them; while the presence at this moment of the rankest forgeries, *some carefully preserved under glass*, is sufficiently notorious to antiquaries to substantiate my assertion, and spare me the pain of resorting to what might appear invidious personality. It is quite enough for my present object that, *there they are*. On whose authority—by whose advice—they were purchased, and, *after public exposure in the newspapers, still exhibited,*—is now a matter of secondary importance. No fault can be imputed to the purchasers beyond an error of judgment; the onus lies upon those who confided to them so peculiar and precious a charge, without ascertaining or caring whether or not they possessed the necessary qualifications. The present state of the Tower Armoury I have no hesitation in describing as disgraceful to a country in which archæological science is so rapidly progressing. Independently of the exhibition of the forgeries alluded to, the most egregious blunders have been perpetrated. In the setting up of genuine suits, helmets, gauntlets, and other pieces are mismatched and incorrectly appropriated. With the exception of the central line of equestrian figures, there is scarcely an attempt at anything like chronological arrangement; and on several of these, helmets are placed some fifty or sixty years earlier in date than the rest of the armour. The indiscriminate crowding of the glass cases with pieces of all periods and descriptions renders it next to impossible for the student to acquire information, or the visitor to be impressed with the real value and interest of the collection.

I have, lastly, to offer my humble opinion as to the steps which should be taken for the correction of these errors and the improvement of the collection. It will, I think, be conceded that both these objects are desirable, even in a pecuniary point of view.

The Armoury is shown to the public at sixpence per head, and between two and three thousand pounds have been annually received for admission. According to a printed return now before me, I find that in 1839-40, the number of visitors amounted to 84,872, and the sum received to £2,121. In 1840-41 the number of visitors was 95,231, and produced

£2,380. These receipts are surely capable of being increased by imparting continually fresh interest to the exhibition—by encouraging a taste for, and by disseminating a knowledge of, this branch of archæology. The Tower Armoury is *the only collection of objects of art or antiquity at the head of which there is neither an artist nor an antiquary!* I, therefore, consider the appointment of a competent and permanent curator as a matter of paramount importance. The mere re-arrangement, unaccompanied by continual supervision, would be useless, as experience has proved.

In reply to your observation, Sir, respecting "another purchasing power," I took the liberty to remark, that the case of the Tower differed widely from that of the British Museum, to which the admission is gratuitous, and for the support of which a grant of money is annually voted by Parliament.

The Tower Armoury is self-supporting. The money received for its exhibition renders it unnecessary to go to the House of Commons for assistance. The purchasing power already exists; it is the misapplication of it that calls for remedy. More than enough is taken annually for the payment of the requisite officers and attendants and the purchase of antiquities. The surplus is now transmitted to the Paymaster-General, I believe. I respectfully submit that every penny received from the public for admission to the Armoury should be expended in its improvement and preservation. In calling your attention to these circumstances, Sir, I feel I am performing a duty to the public generally, as well as to that literary and antiquarian portion of it of which I have been for upwards of forty years a humble but hard-working member.

That it would be most gratifying to me to be selected to fill such an office as I have indicated I frankly admit; but, with less hope of being believed, I as unhesitatingly declare that I would cheerfully resign any such pretension could I see the great object for which I am labouring likely to be carried out by a more competent person.

J. R. PLANCHÉ, Rouge Croix.

This statement was accompanied by the following letter :—

July 26, 1859.

SIR,

I herewith transmit to you the statement you desired me to drawn up.

For your private information, I beg to mention what, amongst other treasures, the Tower has lost by the present system.

The complete suit in which Sir Philip Sidney was killed at the Battle of Zutphen, the embossed figures on which were of solid gold. This national and magnificent relict was at Strawberry Hill, and is now at St. Petersburg.

A heaume of the time of King John, now at Warwick Castle.

The gauntlets of a fine suit, made for King Henry VIII., now in the Tower, *imperfect* from their absence. They had found their way out of the Tower, and on being brought back to it were ignored and refused by the authorities, and are now at Grimston.

A most singular ancient helmet, probably as early as the time of Stephen, if not actually the helmet of that monarch, or of his son, now in the Musée d'Artillerie, at Paris.

Two other helmets, one temp. Henry III., the other of the fifteenth century, with part of the crest remaining.

At the time these curious relics were rejected, a helmet, newly made at Vienna for theatrical purposes, was purchased at the price of £50, and is now in one of the glass cases at the Tower.

The only armour at Alton Towers that could possibly have belonged to the great Talbot was suffered by some gentleman sent down by the Tower to pass into the hands of dealers.

The back plate, a most elegant specimen, sold for £10, and is now in the collection of Lord Londesborough, at Grimston.

A chapel de fer of the twelfth century (unique), now at Geneva.

I, of course, only mention here what has occurred to my own knowledge. . . . . . .

I have the honour to be,

Sir,

Your most obedient, humble Servant,

J. R. PLANCHÉ.

To the Rt. Hon.
SIDNEY HERBERT, &c., &c.

Not hearing anything from Mr. Herbert on the subject, in the course of the following year I addressed to him a second letter:—

8, BENNETT STREET,
1st September, 1860.

SIR,

Upwards of a twelvemonth having elapsed since I had the honour of transmitting to you the statement you were kind enough to request me to send to you respecting the Armoury in the Tower of London, I trust you will pardon me if I again venture to call your attention to the subject.

* * * * * *

The late discussions in Parliament respecting the British

and South Kensington Museums might, I thought, have brought the state of the collection at the Tower under consideration, as there was at one time a suggestion in the public prints to remove the most valuable and instructive portions of the armour to one of those establishments.

In my letter accompanying the statement, I mentioned the many valuable articles which have been lost to the nation by the ignorance and neglect of the authorities.

I have to add to that list a superbly embossed casque of the sixteenth century, found in the Tiber, and probably a relic of the siege of Rome by the Constable de Bourbon. It has been bought for the Musée d'Artillerie, Paris.

A fine sword of the time of Edward III., worth at least £30, allowed to pass into the hands of a private gentleman for £10, at the recent sale of modern Hungarian weapons, amongst which it had by accident been included, while, as I am given to understand, several pounds were expended in the purchase of insignificant and ordinary articles.

I fear, Sir, that the very fact of the exhibition being a self-supporting one—a fact which ought to plead "trumpet-tongued" in its favour—is the cause of its neglect. Had the Government to apply to the House for a grant of money to keep up the national Armoury in the Tower, the abuses which are now patent would be speedily remedied.

I have the honour to be, &c., &c.,

To the Rt. Hon.
SIDNEY HERBERT, &c., &c.

This communication produced in a few days a letter from Mr. Maynard, Mr. Herbert's private secretary, simply expressive of Mr. Herbert's "regrets that at this moment he does not think it would be possible to create an additional officer at the Tower." My hopes being disappointed by Mr. Herbert, on whose love for the arts I had really calculated, I sought for other support; and an introduction to Lord de Ros, the Lieutenant of the Tower, and the appointment of my dear friend Sir John Burgoyne as Constable, induced me to entertain fresh expectations of success. Neither, however well inclined, had the power to assist me. From Lord de Ros, with whom I went through the Armoury, I received in 1868 the following letter :—

TOWER OF LONDON,
June 9th, 1868.

DEAR SIR,

I am extremely obliged to you for telling me the errors and mistakes in the Armoury; but, as I think I before explained to you, this is a matter taken entirely out of the hands of the Constable and his officers, and entirely handed over to the Store Department. Nothing would be easier than to show the mismanagement of those in charge; *but how should a storekeeper, however intelligent and zealous, be gifted with that antiquarian experience which should guide the arrangements of an ancient armoury?* I regret to say that I see no hope of improvement, unless a commission were appointed to go over the whole Armoury, set right the mistakes, and lay down some rules for the future.

Very faithfully yours,

DE ROS.

The lines which I have had printed in italics contain

the whole gist of the subject, and the fact has been urged by me again and again to the authorities unavailingly. But to proceed: in 1869, as I have stated, I was asked at an evening party, by a gentleman in a high position in the War Office, whether I was inclined to undertake the re-arrangement of the armour in the Tower, and give the Government the benefit of any suggestions I could make for its improvement and conservation. Of course I readily consented, and in a few days received an official letter to that effect from the Controller-in-Chief, the Right Honble. Sir Henry Storks, G.C.B., with whom also I had the pleasure of being personally acquainted; and the result was my being empowered to re-arrange the ancient armour upon the same plan that I had originated at South Kensington, and also to report upon its present condition and prospective maintenance.

Interesting as it might be to the antiquary, I feel it would be wearying to the general reader were I to enter into the details of my labours at the Tower, and I shall therefore limit my remarks to such points as affect the public, whether as desirous of profiting by the information to be obtained from the study of these relics of the feudal ages, or simply considering them as curiosities not to be neglected amongst the sights of London. One of my first steps was to go through the Armoury with Colonel Ewart, R.E., commanding the London district, and point out to him the want of space, light, and ventilation in the rooms appropriated to the exhibition in the Tower itself, and call his attention to the fact that the building which contained the Grand or Horse Armoury (as it is indifferently called) was simply an *annex*, through the roof and skylights of which the rain penetrated to the extent of forming pools of water in the gangways, and dripped upon the armour and weapons to their serious detriment, as the utmost vigilance of the attendants (only two in number) could not secure the steel from rust. What was still more alarming, a dirty hole at the west end, doing duty for an office, was a wooden shed with a coal-cellar in it, which any mischievous or careless person could set on fire in an instant, and cause another conflagration much more deplorable than the one which destroyed the small Armoury some years ago. After this preliminary inspection, and report of it to the authorities, I set to work, and in two months (without excluding the public for a single hour) completed my strictly chronological arrangement of the armour, as far as the extremely disadvantageous nature of the building permitted. At the conclusion of my second and final report to the Controller-in-Chief I again endeavoured to impress upon him the necessity of appointing a competent and permanent curator, who for obvious reasons should be independent of the chief storekeeper for the time being, who, according to the present system could order or prevent any alteration at his pleasure, the keeper of the Armoury being his subordinate, not having even the power of remonstrance. A more crying evil is, that, by the strict military organization of all services within what is complacently called "the fortress," the warders, who act as the showmen of the collection, have higher military rank than the gentleman who is responsible for the care of it, and treat with the greatest indifference and contempt any interference of his in their proceedings, which, from my personal experience and the complaints of visitors, I can state to have been occasionally as mischievous as they have been from time immemorial absurd.*

* A "Guide to the Tower of London and its Curiosities," published in the reign of George the Third, mentions a breast-plate desperately damaged by shot, which was shown as having been worn by a man, part of whose body, including some of the intestines, was carried away by a cannon ball, notwithstanding which, being put under the care of a skilful surgeon, the man recovered and lived ten years afterwards. "This story the old warder constantly told to all strangers, till his R.H. Prince Frederick, father of the present King, being told the accustomed tale, said, with a smile, 'And what, friend, is there so extraordinary in all this? I remember myself to have read in a book, of a soldier who had his head cleft in two so dexterously by the stroke of a scimitar, that one half of it fell on one shoulder, and the other half of

Whether the alterations I have been permitted to make are improvements, I leave the public to decide; I mean that portion of it—rapidly, I believe, increasing—which prefers truth to falsehood. That much remains to be done I am perfectly conscious; but, as I have stated in print elsewhere, "it will not be done till it is enforced by a voice much more powerful than mine, in the interests of that public who now, though 'they pay their money,' are not allowed to 'take their choice,' which would undoubtedly be to do as they do at the British and South Kensington Museums—contemplate and study as long as they please such objects as most amuse, interest, or instruct them, instead of being hurried in droves 'upstairs, downstairs, and in my lady's (Elizabeth's) chamber,' by imperative yeomen, nearly each of whom has his own favourite old story to tell, and his own particular old joke to crack, not always unaccompanied by injury to

it on the opposite shoulder, and yet, on his comrade's clapping the two sides nicely together again, and binding them close with his handkerchief, the man did well, drank his pot of ale at night, and scarcely recollected that he had ever been hurt.'" The writer goes on to say, that the old warder was "so dashed," that he never had the courage to tell his story again; but though he might not, it was handed down by his successors, by several of whom I have heard it repeated in my boyhood fifty years after the death of Frederick Prince of Wales. The old battered breast-plate is still in the collection, and has not been "sold as old iron," being thoroughly unworthy of preservation.

the valuable object by which he practically demonstrates it.

"I still hope that a mistaken economy and official routine will not long continue to influence those whose duty it is not only to preserve, but to improve this important and instructive collection—at present, I repeat, the only national one, chronologically arranged, or that is entirely self-supporting—and that the visitors who freely pay their sixpences to the amount of between two and three thousand pounds per annum will be permitted to employ a 'leisure hour' by studying at their ease and uninterruptedly the history of England in armour."*

Some of my readers may consider that I have dwelt too long upon this subject, though it really is not half exhausted; but, quite apart from any personal feeling, I submit it as a subject affecting the public at large. A priceless collection of national antiquities are still daily exposed to deterioration and destruction in a dark, ill-constructed, most inconvenient building, which is neither weather nor fire proof, while there is a long range of rooms on the east side of the White Tower itself, now occupied by carpenters' shops, which could be converted easily and inexpensively into as fine and light a gallery as that at South Kensington, and which,

* "The Leisure Hour" for January 1871 p. 59.

in addition to its advantages for exhibition, would afford the important one of allowing the public to pass without impediment through one Armoury into the other, instead of returning by the way they came, and hustling and pushing through the throng of new comers who are ascending the stairs conducting to the oriental collection and Queen Elizabeth's chamber. To those who take no interest in the matter I offer my apology for detaining them, and trust they will compassionately excuse the tediousness of an old gentleman suffering from a chronic complaint—armour on the brain.

CHAPTER XXI.

My recollections of the years 1869 and 1870, however deeply interesting to myself and family, have no claim to public attention, as far as my own "sayings and doings" are concerned; but many friends and professional acquaintances whose names were "familiar in our mouths as household words," are to be added to the "mortuary roll" I last recorded. Maria, Countess of Harrington (the beautiful Miss Foote), Sir George Smart, and Clarkson Stanfield in 1867; Charles Kean and Samuel Lover in 1868; Keeley and Drinkwater Meadows in 1869; and Balfe in 1870. Of these, Lover and Meadows were, from private connexion and "local habitation," the two with whom I was most intimate. Lover, till within a year of his death, was a constant guest at the tables of two of my most valued friends, and was wont to pay me the high and fully appreciated compliment of singing his new songs to me before making them public. Mr. Carter Hall, in his "Book of Memories," remarks that "The next delight to hearing Moore discourse the sweet music of his country, was to hear Sam Lover murmur 'The Angel's Whisper,' 'The Fairy Boy,' 'The Four-leaved Shamrock,' or abandoning pathos for humour, burst into one of those rollicking yet delicate songs that never called a blush, except of innocent pleasure, to a woman's cheek." That "delight" it was my constant good fortune to be the first to enjoy. Like his countryman Power, (if Power was his countryman, which is disputed,) he possessed great versatility of talent. He was a miniature painter of considerable ability, a successful novelist and dramatist, an agreeable and humorous vocalist in society, as a national lyric writer and composer second only in some respects to Moore, and surpassing him in delineation of Irish character. He tried his hand also, but not very successfully, as a public lecturer and entertainer, both in this country and the United States. Here is our invitation to his first essay in England:—

Patrick's Day!
24, Charles Street, Berners Street.

DEAR MISS PLANCHÉ,—

Lovers are strange people, you know—they always do what you don't want them. I have not sent you *the* song;

but I take leave to send you tickets to hear some others. Will you coax *Pa* to bring you to my *début* on Wednesday.

Yours, very truly,

SAMUEL LOVER.

Finally, he tried the stage—tempted, it is probable, by the great success of Power in Irish characters; but I believe his first appearance was his last, a most vexatious but supremely ridiculous accident entirely destroyed his confidence, and damaged him fatally in the opinion of his audience. It was in a provincial theatre—I forget where—and I believe in his own drama of "Rory O'More." He had to make his entrance through a cottage-door in the centre of the stage, which had a small bar of wood across it, representing the threshold. Over this he unluckily tripped and fell flat on his face, to the great amusement of the gallery. Recovering himself from his confusion, and cheered by the general applause with which a good-natured audience generously endeavoured to drown the recollection of his misadventure, he proceeded with the part; but, of course, with less spirit than he might have done under more favourable circumstances, and at the conclusion of the scene, having to make his exit through the same door, as malicious fate would have it, caught his foot again in the same bar, and was precipitated out of the cottage exactly as he had been into it. This was too much for the audience; the whole house was convulsed with laughter, and I am not quite sure that poor Lover summoned up courage to face it again. At all events, he speedily abandoned histrionics, and I never knew him to allude in the slightest manner to his disheartening *coup d'essai* in them, nor, of course, was it ever mentioned by me or any of the few who heard of it.

Meadows I had known, of course, from my first introduction to Covent Garden Theatre; but after my removal to Michael's-Grove Lodge in 1846, he became my opposite neighbour, and his kindness, and that of his wife, a daughter of Admiral Pridham, to me and my family at that distressing period, cemented our friendship, and must ever be gratefully recollected. Meadows was essentially a Shakesperian actor, brought up in the best schools, and, moreover, an excellent subject in a theatre. In private his whim and humour were as original as they were amusing. Here is a brief sample of his correspondence:—

6, *The Grange*—Wednesday.

MR. MEADOWS presents his compliments to Mr. Planché, who will much oblige Mr. Meadows by sending the order which Mr. Planché promised Mr. Meadows for Thursday. Mr. Meadows at the same time begs to thank Mr. Planché for the many orders Mr. Planché has given Mr. Meadows since Mr. Meadows had the pleasure of becoming the neighbour of Mr. Planché, prior to which, although Mr. Meadows was acquainted with Mr. Planché, there was, as it were, no acquaintance of a visiting nature between Mr. Planché and Mr. Meadows; but since Mr. Meadows arrived at the Grange, Mr. Planché has repeatedly opened his door to Mr. Meadows, for which Mr. Planché is considered as very kind, and also for Mr. Meadows' door having had the pleasure of opening to admit Mr. Planché; and should Mr. Planché feel as Mr. Meadows does, then Mr. Meadows and Mr. Planché must feel alike, although Mr. Planché and Mr. Meadows may not look so.

From Balfe, who died in October, 1870, I heard some anecdotes of Rossini, who had preceded him to the grave only twelve months, dying in November, 1869. I am not aware they have appeared in print, and therefore venture to repeat them as told to me.

At a musical *soirée* in Paris, a lady possessing a magnificent soprano voice and remarkable facility of execution, sang the great Maestro's well-known Aria "Una Voce," with great effect, but overladen with *fioriturí* of the most elaborate description. Rossini, at its conclusion, advanced to the piano and complimented the lady most highly upon her vocal powers, terminating his encomiums with the cruel inquiry: "Mais de qui est la musique?"

On another occasion, at a concert, a very indifferent

tenor, who sang repeatedly out of tune, was indiscreet enough to express his regret to Rossini that he should have heard him for the first time in that room, as, he complained, "Le plafond est si sourd." Rossini raised his eyes to the abused ceiling, and simply ejaculated: "Heureux plafond!"

Balfe also told me of an ingenious critical notice of a *débutant* at a lyrical theatre in Paris, who had solicited the support of a very influential journalist, notorious for receiving large *douceurs* from aspirants to public favour. The young man, by the advice of his friends, had waited on this important personage, and frankly declared that he was utterly unable at that moment to offer him anything worthy of his acceptance; but that if through his favourable report he succeeded in obtaining an engagement, he should consider himself bound by honour and gratitude to make him the most ample and substantial acknowledgment in his power. The great man dismissed him with a gracious bow, and the applicant, on the morning after his appearance, read the following notice of it in the journal he had most fear of: "C'est un jeune homme qui promet beaucoup; nous verrons s'il tiendra ses promesses." Whether or not the promising young man proved a satisfactory performer, I am unable to say.

I am now rapidly approaching the end of these volumes, and am reminded of several anecdotes which I have been in the habit of repeating, but have hitherto omitted in my Recollections as unconnected with the narrative or the personages named in it. Some of them, however, I venture to think, are sufficiently worthy to be recorded, though, of course, I cannot pledge myself to their exactitude; but "si non e vero," &c.

The following was related to me by a gentleman who assured me he heard it from the late Duke of Athol himself:—

One day at Blair Athol, his Grace, having entertained a large party at dinner, produced in the evening many curious and interesting family relics for their inspection, amongst them a small watch, which had belonged to Charles Stuart, and been given by him to one of the Duke's ancestors. When the company were upon the point of departing, the watch was suddenly missed, and was searched for in vain upon the table and about the apartments. The Duke was exceedingly vexed, and declared that of all the articles he had exhibited, the lost watch was the one that he most valued. The guests naturally became exceedingly uncomfortable, and eyed each other suspiciously. No person was present, however, who could possibly be suspected, and courtesy forbade any stronger step than the marked expression of the noble host's extreme annoyance and distress. Each departed to his home in an exceedingly unenviable state of mind, and the mysterious disappearance of the royal relic was a subject of discussion for several months in society. A year afterwards, the Duke being again at Blair Athol, was dressing for dinner, and in the breast-pocket of a coat which his valet had handed to him, felt something, which proved to be the missing watch. "Why, ——!" exclaimed his Grace, addressing his man by his name, "here's the watch we hunted everywhere in vain for!" "Yes, sir," replied the man, gravely. "I saw your Grace put it in your pocket." "You saw me put it in my pocket, and never mentioned it! Why didn't you speak at once, and prevent all that trouble and unpleasant feeling?" "I didna' ken what might ha'e been your Grace's intentions," was the reply of the faithful and discreet Highlander, who saw everything, but said nothing, unless he were directly interrogated.

I was not fortunate enough during a pleasant tour in Scotland and Ireland, which I made in 1867 after my return from Vienna, to meet with any adventure, or to become witness of any sample of native humour or wit, Gaelic or Milesian, which, considering that it included the Lake of Killarney and consequent familiar acquaintance with boatmen, carmen, and all the class of persons who have the reputation for national facetiousness, appeared to me rather surprising. The best Irish stories I ever heard have been told me in England. Here are some which were vouched for as authentic by the narrators.

My old fellow-traveller in Germany, himself an Irishman, being on the box of an Irish mail-coach on a very cold day, and observing the driver enveloping his neck in the voluminous folds of an ample "comforter," remarked, "You seem to be taking very good care of yourself, my friend."—"Och, to be shure I am, sir," answered the driver; "what's all the world to a man when his wife's a widdy?"

An acquaintance of mine who frequently visited Ireland, and generally stopped and dined at the same hotel in Dublin, on his arrival one day perceived a paper wafered on the looking-glass in the coffee-room, with the following written notice:—"Strangers are particularly requested not to give any money to the waiters, as attendance is charged for in the bill." The man who had waited on him at dinner, seeing him reading this notice, said, "Oh, Misther ——! shure that doesn't concarn you, any way. Your honour was niver made a stranger of in this house."

A nobleman I met at dinner some time ago told us he had been shooting at a friend's place on the west coast of Ireland, and that the gamekeeper had indulged in the most exaggerated accounts of the quantity of every description of game upon his master's estate. Nothing that ever ran or flew that his lordship inquired about but was asserted by the man could be found there by hundreds and thousands. Having for amusement's sake exhausted the catalogue of "fur and feather," probable or improbable, and received the most positive assurance of the existence of every beast or bird in abundance, he asked, "Are there any paradoxes?" This was rather a poser; but, after a moment's hesitation, the keeper answered, undauntedly, "Bedad, then, your lordship may find two or three of *them* sometimes on the sand when the tide's out."

"The mercy of God follow you!" exclaimed a beggarwoman in Dublin to a passing stranger; "Give a poor soul a halfpenny."—"I haven't got one." "Oh, the mercy of God follow——"—"Go away, woman!" "And (changing her tone and shaking her fist at him) *nivir overtake you!*"

On the 21st of March, 1871, I had again the honour to be present officially at a Royal Marriage in St. George's Chapel, Windsor, the occasion being the union of H.R.H. the Princess Louise with the Marquis of Lorne, and in the following month commenced the series of "Recollections" which appeared in "London Society," and formed the nucleus of these volumes. On the 26th of December was produced my latest contribution to the stage, "King Christmas: a Fancy-full Morality," at Mr. German Reed's Gallery of Illustration, the gratifying reception of which by both the Press and the public is of too recent a date to require more than my grateful acknowledgment. I may, however, be permitted to add, that my greatest pleasure was to perceive that the style of the dialogue and character of the songs had an attraction for the younger portion of the audience; and they found it was possible to derive some amusement from a piece written in passable English, having a rational object, and intelligently acted, with tasteful and appropriate scenery and dresses; but devoid of all the meretricious allurements which have latterly been supposed indispensable to the success of a holiday entertainment.

The performances of the admirable actors of the Théâtre Français in London during the past year came most opportunely to strengthen the growing desire of a large and important portion of the London public for a better order of things theatrical in our own country. Although a subscriber to the complimentary breakfast given to these perfect artists at the Crystal

Palace, I was unfortunately prevented by my duties at the College of Arms from being present at it. The speeches of Lord Granville and Mr. Wigan were strongly in favour of a movement which had its origin in a lecture delivered by Dr. Doran at a meeting of the Society for the Encouragement of the Fine Arts, Mr. George Godwin in the chair, who, in returning thanks to the lecturer, expressed his regret that in this great metropolis there should not be "one theatre uncontrolled by the predominant taste of the public." These happily chosen words so completely expressed the want of the literary world, and the only mode by which it could be gratified, that I wrote to the *Builder*, Mr. Godwin being the editor of that journal, the following letter on the subject, which appeared in its issue of 29th of April :—

"FOR AND AGAINST SHAKSPEARE."

SIR,—Under this title, I read in the *Observer* of last Sunday, "Dr. Doran, F.S.A., addressed a full meeting of the Society for the Encouragement of the Fine Arts, on Thursday evening last, at their Rooms in Conduit Street, Mr. George Godwin, F.R.S., presiding," and the very brief notice of the proceedings is terminated by the information, that "the chairman, in his closing remarks, urged the want of a National Theatre, not wholly controlled by the predominant taste of the public." Feeling so intensely as I do on this subject, I hunted the papers over for a leading article, or some strong editorial endorsement of this important opinion; but neither in the *Observer*, nor any other journal that I have seen, has there been any, the faintest echo of a chord which should, I humbly think, have reverberated through the public press, which so constantly professes its admiration of the genius of Shakspeare, and so frequently indulges in too truthful lamentations over the decline of the English drama.

Upon this hint I speak. If that admiration be genuine, if that lamentation be sincere,—and it would be an offence to doubt it,—considering the intellect, education, and general ability enlisted in the service of the "fourth estate," I adjure it in the names of England and Shakspeare—names indissolubly connected, and almost equally sacred in the eyes of all who are proud of their country and its literature—to exert its power and influence in the cause of that glorious drama which, though it can never be destroyed, is at present "a sealed book" to the rising generation. I was out of town, and not aware of the meeting: I am therefore ignorant of the precise words which may have been used by the chairman; but if not reported *verbatim*, their sense was, doubtless, to the same effect, viz., "the want of a National Theatre, *not wholly controlled by the predominant taste of the public*."

That is actually the want of a much larger portion of the public than I believe is generally suspected,—the want of thousands, I may say, in London alone, who rarely, if ever, enter a theatre, and of more thousands who do so to pass away an idle hour, to accompany a country cousin or a foreign visitor, or to gratify their children during the holidays. Let us grant that the predominant taste of the public is for "sensational drama" and burlesque,—and the truth of the axiom "that those who live to please must please to live,"—are those who have no taste for such entertainments to be shut out from the theatre altogether, because every stage in the metropolis is devoted to performances which they do not care to witness? It would ill become me to express an opinion on the class of compositions which evidently possesses considerable attraction for the general public; and I unhesitatingly avow that I enjoy a really good sensational drama, admirably acted, as I have often seen it, as much as any one. My natural inability to appreciate the merits of the prevailing style of burlesque does not induce me to propose that its admirers should be deprived of that which amuses them. All I, in common with that large portion of the play-going public I have mentioned, urgently desire, is the *assured* existence of a theatre in which the masterpieces of our unrivalled dramatic authors should be constantly and worthily represented, where—

> "Thoughts that breathe, and words that burn,"

should be uttered by actors who can feel and express them to an audience "fit," however "few," without the fear that their salaries will not be forthcoming on the following Saturday, and that the manager, disheartened by the appearance of empty benches, will change the bill, discharge a company he has *jobbed* at a week's notice, and endeavour to outrival his competitors by pandering to the predominant taste of the public.

That the lessee of a theatre heavily rented, with a heap of other liabilities on his shoulders which he cannot shuffle off, in addition to the salaries, which must be duly paid every Saturday, should, in the presence of nightly loss, disembarrass himself of such weekly pressure as he can, without actual dishonesty, escape, however distressing it may be to others, must be expected, while human nature is human nature; but at the present moment, when there are more theatres in London than ever before were known, and others in course of erection,—all privileged to perform any description of dramatic entertainment, and nearly all devoted to such as they consider in accordance with "the predominant taste" aforesaid,—is it not a just cause of complaint?—is it not, in fact, a national disgrace, that there should not be one in the vast metropolis, where those who can still enjoy the most sublime poetry, the most brilliant wit, and "the pure well of *English* undefiled," may resort for an evening's rational and intellectual amusement afforded by a creditable representation of the masterpieces of our unrivalled British dramatists?

Is it not a still greater opprobrium to us as a nation, possessing such art-treasures, and professing to be proud of them, that persons of high rank and men of large fortune can be found to support establishments the performances and performers at which it is not for me to criticise, and that not one English nobleman, not one English merchant prince, steps forward to lend a hand to raise the drama from the dust and oblivion into which it has gradually fallen, until it is actually unknown to the rising generation, who become naturally inoculated with the predominant taste of the public?

Hearken to the outcry for education!—compulsory education! Parliament is stormed. The existence of Government is threatened, so urgent is the demand, so vociferous are its supporters. Acts are passed, boards are formed, schools are multiplied; but no senator, no minister, appears to have reflected that a theatre devoted to the highest order of dramatic composition, conducted as such a theatre should be, is one of the finest schools for the cultivation of manners and morals, for the diffusion of useful as well as entertaining knowledge, for the teaching of *English*, for attuning the ear to eloquence and insensibly inculcating a taste for all that is grand in art and ennobling in nature, which happily might, so encouraged, become the predominant one of the British public. I could talk "upon this theme until mine eyelids would no longer wag;" but length of argument would only weary without convincing those who cannot at once see the case in the same light that I do, and it would be superfluous as regards the numbers who do. A *subvention*, as in other countries, it is idle to hope for from any English Government; but from public spirit, roused by the public press, there is nothing that need be despaired of; and if the feeble voice of one who has ardently loved, and honestly endeavoured to promote what he considered the true interests of the stage to the extent of his humble ability for fifty years, should be fortunately listened to by those who have the power to effect the object, so earnestly advocated by the chairman of last Thursday's meeting, and, as I learn from persons present, so enthusiastically responded to by his hearers, there may be yet a chance for the resuscitation of our national drama, and the permanent existence in London of a truly English theatre.

J. R. PLANCHÉ.

After some months, during which this letter remained unnoticed by the rest of the press, the subject was taken up by Mr. Tom Taylor, who wrote a series of articles in the *Echo* evening newspaper, containing some very strong but truthful observations on the present state of the stage, the causes that had led to it, and the chances of its regeneration. Meetings were also called by him, which were attended by many professional and lay well-wishers of the national drama, at which the steps to be taken for its encouragement and protection were fully discussed. It being then late in the season, it was proposed that plans should be sent in by those who had distinct views on the subject for the establishment of a Classical National Theatre, and that early this year they should be taken into consideration, and the one approved of by the majority acted upon as earnestly and industriously as possible. Nothing, however, has yet been done; but there are unmistakable signs of the awakening of a better spirit, and I have not abandoned the hope that the metropolis will ere long be enabled to boast a theatre in which the rising generation will enjoy, not spasmodically, but regularly, the best plays acted with intelligence, and placed on the stage reverentially and artistically. How is it, I ask again, that Government has never appeared to comprehend that such a theatre would afford the greatest assistance to the cause of education, which it professes to have so deeply at heart.

On the 27th of February in this year it was my interesting duty to attend Her Majesty in St. Paul's Cathedral on that memorable occasion when, surrounded by her illustrious family and loyal subjects, she offered publicly her thanks to Almighty God for the great mercy He had shown to herself and the whole nation by the restoration to health of "the rose and expectancy of this fair State," H.R.H. the Prince of Wales.

On that day I completed the seventy-sixth year of my age, and, devoutly mingling mine with the general thanks of England for the blessing Providence had conferred upon its Queen and people, added my humble acknowledgments of the many bestowed upon me throughout a long life of rarely interrupted health passed in the labour I love, amongst the beings I love, and at the approaching close of which I can with pardonable pride proclaim I have never lost a friend.

I have outlived any resentments I may have felt at the conduct of others, and quietly endeavoured to live down prejudices which have been unjustly entertained against me. I am still, thank God, able to work, and am working as hard as I have ever done during the last fifty years. The Queen has been most graciously pleased, at the instance of the Right Hon. the First Lord of the Treasury, to grant me a pension of £100 per annum from the Civil List; and till my right hand shall forget its cunning, it will endeavour to justify the flattering "consideration" expressed in the grant by labouring in the cause of art, especially in that of the one by which I was first fascinated, and which has been aptly described by the poet as—

> "The youngest sister of the arts
> Where all their graces meet,"

videlicet,

THE DRAMA.

THE END.

BRADBURY, EVANS, AND CO., PRINTERS, WHITEFRIARS.

TINSLEY BROTHERS' LIST OF NEW BOOKS.

A New and Important Book of Travels.

Unexplored Syria. By Capt. BURTON, F.R.G.S., and Mr. C. F. TYRWHITT DRAKE, F.R.G.S., &c. With a New Map of Syria, Illustrations, Inscriptions, the 'Hamah Stones,' &c. 2 vols. 8vo.

The Life and Times of Algernon Sydney: Patriot, 1617–1683. By ALEX. CHARLES EWALD, F.S.A., Senior Clerk of her Majesty's Public Records, Author of 'The Crown and its Advisers,' 'Last Century of Universal History,' &c.

The Life and Times of Margaret of Anjou. By Mrs. HOOKHAM. 2 vols. 8vo. 30*s*.

"Let Mrs. Hookham's history be as largely circulated as possible, and earnestly read in every home. The labour of investigation must have been immense; but Mrs. Hookham will have her reward for all the time she has spent in using it, inasmuch as she has provided what at least may be accepted as the most authentic and exhaustive relation of the events of the fifteenth century in England that has ever been written."—*Bell's Weekly Messenger.*

"The collection of the materials has evidently been a laborious task; the composition is careful and conscientious throughout, and it contains a great deal that is valuable and highly interesting."—*Pall Mall Gazette.*

The Court of Anna Carafa: an Historical Narrative. By MRS. ST. JOHN. In 1 vol. 8vo. 12*s*.

"Mrs. Horace St. John writes with a fluent and a practical pen, and tells a marvellous history, which exceeds in interest any sensational novel ever written." —*Publishers' Circular.*

The Two Sieges. By HENRY VIZETELLY, author of "The Story of the Diamond Necklace," &c. With numerous Illustrations. 2 vols. 8vo.

Judicial Dramas: Romances of French Criminal Law. By HENRY SPICER. In 1 vol. 8vo. 15*s*.

Recollections. By J. R. PLANCHÉ. 2 vols.

The Retention of India. In 1 vol. crown 8vo.

The Life and Adventures of Alexander Dumas. By PERCY FITZGERALD, author of "The Lives of the Kembles," &c. 2 vols. 8vo.

Now ready, the Second Series of

Incidents in my Life. By D. D. Home. In 1 vol. crown 8vo. 10*s*. 6*d*.

Prohibitory Legislation in the United States. By JUSTIN McCARTHY. 1 vol., 2*s*. 6*d*.

The Idol in Horeb. Evidence that the Golden Image at Mount Sinai was a Cone and not a Calf. With Three Appendices. By CHARLES T. BEKE, Ph.D. 1 vol., 5*s*.

WORKS BY CAPTAIN BURTON, F.R.G.S. &c.

A New Book of Travels.

Zanzibar. By CAPTAIN R. F. BURTON, author of "A Mission to Geléle," "Explorations of the Highlands of the Brazil," "Abeokuta," "My Wanderings in West Africa," &c. 30*s*.

Explorations of the Highlands of the Brazil; with a full account of the Gold and Diamond Mines; also, Canoeing down Fifteen Hundred Miles of the great River, Sao Francisco, from Sabarà to the Sea. In 2 vols. 8vo, with Map and Illustrations, 30*s*.

A Mission to Geléle. Being a Three Months' Residence at the Court of Dahomé. In which are described the Manners and Customs of the Country, including the Human Sacrifice, &c. 2 vols., with Illustrations, 25*s*.

Abeokuta; and an Exploration of the Cameroons Mountains. 2 vols. post 8vo, with Portrait of the Author, Map, and Illustrations. 25*s*.

Wit and Wisdom from West Africa; or a Book of Proverbial Philosophy, Idioms, Enigmas, and Laconisms. Compiled by RICHARD F. BURTON, author of "A Mission to Dahomé," "A Pilgrimage to El-Medinah and Meccah," &c. 12*s*. 6*d*.

My Wanderings in West Africa; from Liverpool to Fernando Po. 2 vols. cr. 8vo, 21*s*.

Letters from the Battle-fields of Paraguay. With Map and Illustrations, 18*s*.

The Nile Basin. With Map, &c. post 8vo, 7*s*. 6*d*.

WORKS BY GEORGE AUGUSTUS SALA.

Under the Sun. In 1 vol. 8vo.

My Diary in America in the Midst of War. In 2 vols. 8vo, 30*s*.

Notes and Sketches of the Paris Exhibition. 8vo, 15*s*.

From Waterloo to the Peninsula. 2 vols. 8vo, 24*s*.

Rome and Venice, with other Wanderings in Italy, in 1866-7. 8vo, 16*s*.

Dutch Pictures. With some Sketches in the Flemish Manner. 5*s*.

After Breakfast. A Sequel to "Breakfast in Bed." 2 vols. 21*s*.

Accepted Addresses. 1 vol. cr. 8vo, 5*s*.

History of France under the Bourbons, 1589-1830. By CHARLES DUKE YONGE, Regius Professor, Queen's College, Belfast. In 4 vols. 8vo. Vols. I. and II. contain the Reigns of Henry IV., Louis XIII. and XIV.; Vols. III. and IV. contain the Reigns of Louis XV. and XVI. 3*l.*

The Regency of Anne of Austria, Queen of France, Mother of Louis XIV. From Published and Unpublished Sources. With Portrait. By Miss FREER. 2 vols. 8vo, 30*s.*

The Married Life of Anne of Austria, Queen of France, Mother of Louis XIV.; and the History of Don Sebastian, King of Portugal. Historical Studies. From numerous Unpublished Sources. By MARTHA WALKER FREER. 2 vols. 8vo, 30*s.*

The History of Monaco. By H. PEMBERTON. 12*s.*

The Great Country: Impressions of America. By GEORGE ROSE, M.A. (ARTHUR SKETCHLEY). 8vo, 15*s.*

Biographies and Portraits of some Celebrated People. By ALPHONSE DE LAMARTINE. 2 vols. 25*s.*

Memoirs of the Life and Reign of George III. With Original Letters of the King and Other Unpublished MSS. By J. HENEAGE JESSE, author of "The Court of England under the Stuarts," &c. 3 vols. 8vo. £2 2*s.* Second Edition.

The Public Life of Lord Macaulay. By FREDERICK ARNOLD, B.A. of Christ Church, Oxford. Post 8vo, 7*s.* 6*d.*

Memoirs of Sir George Sinclair, Bart., of Ulbster. By JAMES GRANT, author of "The Great Metropolis," "The Religious Tendencies of the Times," &c. 8vo. With Portrait. 16*s.*

Memories of My Time; being Personal Reminiscences of Eminent Men. By GEORGE HODDER. 8vo. 16*s.*

Lives of the Kembles. By PERCY FITZGERALD, author of the "Life of David Garrick," &c. 2 vols. 8vo. 30*s.*

The Life of David Garrick. From Original Family Papers, and numerous Published and Unpublished Sources. By PERCY FITZGERALD, M.A. 2 vols. 8vo, with Portraits. 36*s.*

The Life of Edmund Kean. From various Published and Original Sources. By F. W. HAWKINS. In 2 vols. 8vo, 30*s.*

Our Living Poets: an Essay in Criticism. By H. BUXTON FORMAN. 1 vol., 12*s.*

Johnny Robinson: The Story of the Childhood and Schooldays of an "Intelligent Artisan." By the Author of "Some Habits and Customs of the Working Classes." 2 vols. 21*s.*

Ten Years in Sarawak. By CHARLES BROOKE, the "Tuanmudah" of Sarawak. With an Introduction by H. H. the Rajah Sir JAMES BROOKE; and numerous Illustrations. 2 vols. 25*s.*

Peasant Life in Sweden. By L. LLOYD, author of "The Game Birds of Sweden," "Scandinavian Adventures," &c. 8vo. With Illustrations. 18*s.*

Hog Hunting in the East, and other Sports. By Captain J. NEWALL, author of "The Eastern Hunters." With numerous Illustrations. 8vo, 21*s.*

Shooting and Fishing in the Rivers, Prairies, and Backwoods of North America. By B. H. REVOIL. 2 vols. 21*s.*

The Eastern Hunters. By Captain JAMES NEWALL. 8vo, with numerous Illustrations. 16*s.*

Fish Hatching; and the Artificial Culture of Fish. By FRANK BUCKLAND. With 5 Illustrations. 5*s.*

The Open Air; or Sketches out of Town. By JOSEPH VEREY. 1 vol.

Con Amore; or, Critical Chapters. By JUSTIN McCARTHY, author of "The Waterdale Neighbours." Post 8vo. 12*s.*

The Cruise of the Humming Bird, being a Yacht Cruise around the West Coast of Ireland. By MARK HUTTON. In 1 vol. 14*s.*

Murmurings in the May and Summer of Manhood: O'Ruark's Bride, or the Blood-spark in the Emerald; and Man's Mission a Pilgrimage to Glory's Goal. By EDMUND FALCONER. 1 vol., 5*s.*

Poems. By EDMUND FALCONER. 1 vol., 5*s.*

Dante's Divina Commedia. Translated into English in the Metre and Triple Rhyme of the Original. By Mrs. RAMSAY. 3 vols. 18*s.*

The Gaming Table, its Votaries and Victims, in all Countries and Times, especially in England and France. By ANDREW STEINMETZ, Barrister-at-Law. 2 vols. 8vo. 31*s.*

Principles of Comedy and Dramatic Effect. By PERCY FITZGERALD, author of "The Life of Garrick," &c. 8vo. 12*s.*

A Winter Tour in Spain. By the Author of "Altogether Wrong." 8vo, illustrated, 15*s.*

Life Beneath the Waves; and a Description of the Brighton Aquarium, with numerous Illustrations. 1 vol., 2*s.* 6*d.*

The Rose of Jericho; from the French; called by the German "Weinachts-Rose," or "Christmas Rose. Edited by the Hon. Mrs. NORTON, Author of "Old Sir Douglas," &c. 2*s.* 6*d.*

TINSLEY BROTHERS'
CHEAP EDITIONS OF POPULAR NOVELS.

By Mrs. HENRY WOOD, author of "East Lynne," &c.

The Red Court Farm. 6*s*.
A Life's Secret. 6*s*.
George Canterbury's Will. 6*s*.
Anne Hereford. 6*s*.
Elster's Folly. 6*s*.
St. Martin's Eve. 6*s*.
Mildred Arkell. 6*s*.
Trevlyn Hold. 6*s*.

By the Author of "Guy Livingstone."

Sword and Gown. 5*s*.
Barren Honour. 6*s*.
Brakespeare. 6*s*.
Anteros. 6*s*.
Maurice Dering. 6*s*.
Guy Livingstone. 5*s*.
Sans Merci. 6*s*.
Border and Bastille. 6*s*.

Also, now ready, uniform with the above,

Old Margaret. By HENRY KINGSLEY, author of "Geoffry Hamlyn," "Hetty," &c.

The Harveys. By HENRY KINGSLEY, author of "Mademoiselle Mathilde," "Old Margaret," &c. 6*s*.

A Life's Assize. By Mrs. J. H. RIDDELL, author of "Too Much Alone," "City and Suburb," "George Geith," &c. 6*s*.

A Righted Wrong. By EDMUND YATES. 6*s*.

Stretton. By HENRY KINGSLEY, author of "Geoffry Hamlyn," &c. 6*s*.

The Rock Ahead. By EDMUND YATES. 6*s*.

The Adventures of Dr. Brady. By W. H. RUSSELL, LL.D. 6*s*.

Black Sheep. By EDMUND YATES, author of "The Rock Ahead," &c. 6*s*.

Kissing the Rod. By EDMUND YATES. 6*s*.

Not Wisely, but Too Well. By the Author of "Cometh up as a Flower." 6*s*.

Miss Forrester. By the Author of "Archie Lovell," &c. 6*s*.

Recommended to Mercy. By the Author of "Sink or Swim?" 6*s*.

Lizzie Lorton of Greyrigg. By Mrs. LYNN LINTON, author of "Sowing the Wind," &c. 6*s*.

The Seven Sons of Mammon. By G. A. SALA, author of "After Breakfast," &c. 6*s*.

The Cambridge Freshman: the Adventures of Mr. Golightly. By MARTIN LEGRAND. 1 vol., handsomely Illustrated. 6*s*.

TINSLEY BROTHERS' NEW NOVELS.

The Golden Lion of Granpere. By ANTHONY TROLLOPE, author of "Ralph the Heir," "Can You Forgive Her?" &c.

Ready-Money Mortiboy: a Matter of Fact Story. 3 vols.

Under which King. By B. W. JOHNSTON, M.P. 1 vol.

Coming Home to Roost. By GERALD GRANT. 3 vols.

Under the Greenwood Tree. By the Author of "Desperate Remedies," &c. 2 vols.

Under the Red Dragon. By JAMES GRANT, author of "The Romance of War," "Only an Ensign," &c.

Hornby Mills; and other Stories. By HENRY KINGSLEY, author of "Ravenshoe," "Mademoiselle Mathilde," "Geoffry Hamlyn," &c. In 2 vols.

Saved by a Woman. By the Author of "No Appeal." In 3 vols.

Not Easily Jealous: a New Novel. In 3 vols.

Arthur Wilson: a Story. In 3 vols.

Rough but True. By ST. CLARE. In 1 vol.

Christopher Dudley. By MARY BRIDGMAN, author 'Robert Lynne,' &c. In 3 vols.

Love and Treason. By W. FREELAND. 3 vols.

The Soul and Money: a New Novel. In 1 vol.

Loyal: a New Novel. In 3 vols.

Fatal Sacrifice: a New Novel.

Sorties from "Gib." in quest of Sensation and Sentiment. By E. DYNE FENTON, late Captain 86th Regiment. 1 vol., post 8vo.

Just ready, uniform with 'Sorties from "Gib,"'

Midnight Webs. By G. M. FENN, author of "The Sapphire Cross," &c. In 1 vol. fancy cloth binding, price 10*s*. 6*d*.

TINSLEY BROTHERS, 18 CATHERINE STREET, STRAND.

The Harveys. By HENRY KINGSLEY, author of "Old Margaret," "Hetty," "Geoffry Hamlyn," &c. 2 vols.

Henry Ancrum: a Tale of the last War in New Zealand. 2 vols.

She was Young, and He was Old. By the Author of "Lover and Husband." 3 vols.

A Ready-made Family: or the Life and Adventures of Julian Leep's Cherub. A Story. 3 vols.

Cecil's Tryst. By the Author of "Lost Sir Massingberd," &c. 3 vols.

Denison's Wife. By Mrs. ALEXANDER FRASER, author of "Not while She lives," "Faithless; or the Loves of the Period," &c. 2 vols.

Two Plunges for a Pearl. By MORTIMER COLLINS, author of "The Vivian Romance," &c. 3 vols.

Barbara Heathcote's Trial. By the Author of "Nellie's Memories," &c. 3 vols.

Wide of the Mark. By the Author of "Recommended to Mercy," "Taken upon Trust," &c. 3 vols.

Title and Estate. By F. LANCASTER. 3 vols.

Hollowhill Farm. By JOHN EDWARDSON. 3 vols.

The Sapphire Cross: a Tale of Two Generations. By G. M. FENN, author of "Bent, not Broken," &c. 3 vols.

Edith. By C. A. LEE. 2 vols.

Lady Judith. By JUSTIN McCARTHY, author of "My Enemy's Daughter," "The Waterdale Neighbours," &c. 3 vols.

Only an Ensign. By JAMES GRANT, author of "The Romance of War," "Lady Wedderburn's Wish," &c. 3 vols.

Old as the Hills. By DOUGLAS MOREY FORD. 3 vols.

Not Wooed, but Won. By the Author of "Lost Sir Massingberd," "Found Dead," &c. 3 vols.

My Heroine. 1 vol.

The Prussian Spy. By V. VALMONT. 2 vols.

Sundered Lives. By WYBERT REEVE, author of the Comedies of "Won at Last," "Not so Bad after all," &c. 3 vols.

The Nomads of the North: a Tale of Lapland. By J. LOVEL HADWEN. 1 vol.

Family Pride. By the Author of "Olive Varcoe," "Simple as a Dove," &c. 3 vols.

Fair Passions; or the Setting of the Pearls. By the Hon. Mrs. PIGOTT CARLETON. 3 vols.

Harry Disney: an Autobiography. Edited by ATHOLL DE WALDEN. 3 vols.

Desperate Remedies. 3 vols.

The Foster Sisters. By EDMOND BRENAN LOUGHNAN. 3 vols.

Only a Commoner. By HENRY MORFORD. 3 vols.

Madame la Marquise. By the Author of "Dacia Singleton," "What Money Can't Do," &c. 3 vols.

Clara Delamaine. By A. W. CUNNINGHAM. 3 vols.

Sentenced by Fate. By Miss EDGCOMBE. 3 vols.

Fairly Won. By Miss H. S. ENGSTRÖM. 3 vols.

Joshua Marvel. By B. L. FARJEON, author of "Grif." 3 vols.

Blanche Seymour. 3 vols.

By Birth a Lady. By G. M. FENN, author of "Mad," "Webs in the Way," &c. 3 vols.

A Life's Assize. By Mrs. J. H. RIDDELL, author of "George Geith," "City and Suburb," "Too much Alone," &c. 3 vols.

Gerald Hastings. By the Author of "No Appeal," &c. 3 vols.

TINSLEY BROTHERS, 18 CATHERINE STREET, STRAND.

Monarch of Mincing-Lane. By WILLIAM BLACK, author of "In Silk Attire," "Kilmeny," &c. 3 vols.

The Golden Bait. By H. HOLL, author of "The King's Mail," &c. In 3 vols.

Like Father, like Son. By the Author of "Lost Sir Massingberd," &c. 3 vols.

Beyond these Voices. By the EARL OF DESART, author of "Only a Woman's Love," &c. 3 vols.

The Queen's Sailors. A Nautical Novel. By EDWARD GREEY. 3 vols.

Bought with a Price. By the Author of "Golden Pippin," &c. 1 vol.

The Florentines: a Story of Home-life in Italy. By the COUNTESS MARIE MONTEMERLI, author of "Four Months in a Garibaldian Hospital," &c. 3 vols.

The Inquisitor. By WILLIAM GILBERT, author of "Doctor Austin's Guests," &c. 3 vols.

Falsely True. By Mrs. CASHEL HOEY, author of "A House of Cards," &c. In 3 vols.

After Baxtow's Death. By MORLEY FARROW, author of "No Easy Task," &c. 3 vols.

Hearts and Diamonds. By ELIZABETH P. RAMSAY, 3 vols.

The Bane of a Life. By THOMAS WRIGHT (the Journeyman Engineer), author of "Some Habits and Customs of the Working Classes," &c. 3 vols.

Robert Lynne. By MARY BRIDGMAN. 2 vols.

Baptised with a Curse. By EDITH S. DREWRY. 3 vols.

Brought to Book. By HENRY SPICER, Esq. 2 vols.

Fenacre Grange. By LANGFORD CECIL. 3 vols.

Schooled with Briars: a Story of To-day. 1 vol.

A Righted Wrong. By EDMUND YATES, author of "Black Sheep," &c. 3 vols.

Gwendoline's Harvest. By the Author of "Lost Sir Massingberd," "Found Dead," &c. 2 vols.

A Fool's Paradise. By THOMAS ARCHER, author of "Strange Work," &c. 3 vols.

George Canterbury's Will. By Mrs. HENRY WOOD, author of "East Lynne," &c. 3 vols.

Gold and Tinsel. By the Author of "Ups and Downs of an Old Maid's Life." 3 vols.

Sidney Bellew. A Sporting Story. By FRANCIS FRANCIS. 2 vols.

Grif; a Story of Australian Life. By B. LEOPOLD FARJEON. 2 vols.

Not while She Lives. By the Author of "Faithless; or the Loves of the Period." 2 vols.

A Double Secret and Golden Pippin. By JOHN POMEROY. 3 vols.

Wee Wifie. By ROSA NOUCHETTE CAREY, author of "Nellie's Memories." 3 vols.

Oberon Spell. By EDEN ST. LEONARDS. 3 vols.

Daisie's Dream. By the Author of "Recommended to Mercy," &c. 3 vols.

Heathfield Hall; or Prefatory Life. A Youthful Reminiscence. By HANS SCHREIBER, author of "Nicknames at the Playingfield College," &c. 10*s.* 6*d.*

Phœbe's Mother. By LOUISA ANN MEREDITH, author of "My Bush Friends in Tasmania." 2 vols.

Strong Hands and Steadfast Hearts. By the Countess von BOTHMER. 3 vols.

The Lily and the Rose. By G. H. HARWOOD. 3 vols.

Love Stories of the English Watering-Places. 3 vols.

My Enemy's Daughter. By JUSTIN McCARTHY, author of "The Waterdale Neighbours," "Paul Massie," &c. 3 vols.

A County Family. By the Author of "Lost Sir Massingberd," &c. 3 vols.

Only a Woman's Love. By the EARL OF DESART. 2 vols.

Up and Down the World. By the Author of "Never—for Ever." 3 vols.

Lost Footsteps. By JOSEPH VEREY. 3 vols.

The Gage of Honour. By Captain J. T. NEWALL. 3 vols.

Twice Refused. By CHARLES E. STIRLING. 2 vols.

Fatal Zero. By the Author of "Polly," &c. 2 vols.

Stretton. By HENRY KINGSLEY, author of "Geoffry Hamlyn," &c. 3 vols.

False Colours. By ANNIE THOMAS (Mrs. PENDER CUDLIP), author of "Denis Donne." 3 vols.

In Silk Attire. By WILLIAM BLACK, author of "Love or Marriage?" 3 vols. Second Edition.

All but Lost. By G. A. HENTY, author of "The March to Magdala." 3 vols.

A London Romance. By CHARLES H. ROSS. 3 vols.

Home from India. By JOHN POMEROY. 2 vols.

John Twiller: a Romance of the Heart. By D. STARKEY, LL.D. 1 vol.

The Doctor of Beauweir. By WILLIAM GILBERT, author of "Shirley Hall Asylum," "Dr. Austin's Guests," &c. &c. 2 vols.

Mad: a Story of Dust and Ashes. By GEORGE MANVILLE FENN, author of "Bent, not Broken." 3 vols.

Buried Alone. By a New Writer. 1 vol.

Nellie's Memories: a Domestic Story. By ROSA NOUCHETTE CAREY. 3 vols.

Clarissa. By SAMUEL RICHARDSON. Edited by E. S. DALLAS, author of "The Gay Science," &c. 3 vols.

Love or Marriage? By WILLIAM BLACK. 3 vols.

John Haller's Niece. By the Author of "Never—for Ever." 3 vols.

Neighbours and Friends. By the Hon. Mrs. HENRY WEYLAND CHETWYND, author of "Three Hundred a Year." 3 vols.

Martyrs to Fashion. By JOSEPH VEREY. 3 vols.

A House of Cards. By MRS. CASHEL HOEY. 3 vols.

Out of the Meshes. 3 vols.

Wild as a Hawk. By Mrs. MACQUOID, author of "Hester Kirton," &c. 3 vols.

Diana Gay. By PERCY FITZGERALD. 3 vols.

Giant Despair. By MORLEY FARROW. 3 vols.

Francesca's Love. By Mrs. EDWARD PULLEYNE. 3 vols.

Polly: a Village Portrait. 2 vols.

Old Margaret. By HENRY KINGSLEY, author of "Ravenshoe," "Geoffry Hamlyn," &c. 2 vols.

Bide Time and Tide. By J. T. NEWALL, author of "The Gage of Honour," "The Eastern Hunters," &c. 3 vols.

The Scandinavian Ring. By JOHN POMEROY. 3 vols.

Tregarthen Hall. By JAMES GARLAND. 3 vols.

Tender Tyrants. By JOSEPH VEREY. In 3 vols.

Grainger's Thorn. By THOS. WRIGHT (the "Journeyman Engineer"), author of "The Bane of a Life," "Some Habits and Customs of the Working Classes," &c. 3 vols.

Church and Wife: a Question of Celibacy. By ROBERT ST. JOHN CORBET, author of "The Canon's Daughters." 3 vols.

CPSIA information can be obtained
at www.ICGtesting.com
Printed in the USA
LVHW031256060423
743358LV00019B/71

9 783382 133634